UNFINISHED

AMY SNYDER

FIERY SEAS PUBLISHING

Visit our website at www.fieryseaspublishing.com
This book is a work of fiction. Names, characters, places, and incidents either are products of the author's imagination or are used fictitiously. Any resemblance to actual persons, living or dead, events, or locales is entirely coincidental.
Unfinished

Cover Art by Juan Padrón
Editing by Vicki McGough
Interior Design by Merwin Loquias (mlgraphikdesigns@gmail.com)
ISBN: 978-1-946143-31-0
Library of Congress Control Number: 2017948770

Printed in the United States of America
First Edition:
10 9 8 7 6 5 4 3 2 1

DEDICATION

For Tim, my home.
Thank you for building my lucky writing desk.

And for Gillian and Dillon,
who make my world better every day.

Unfinished

Amy Snyder

CHAPTER 1

AS I STEPPED OUT OF the passenger side of the car, shielding my eyes from the sun, I couldn't help but wonder how on earth I got here. I mean, I knew how I physically got here, dropping off our twins at college. Alex drove me here, of course. He always drove. Everywhere we went, he drove. It wasn't that I couldn't drive, because I could. I was an exceptionally good driver actually. But at some point in our marriage, we got into this pattern where he drove everywhere we went, and I was always the passenger.

Anyway, here we were taking our babies off to college, to the very same college where Alex and I met, and I suddenly came to the harsh realization that I had accomplished absolutely nothing since I'd left this campus twenty-two years ago. Hadn't I been busy for the past twenty years? Sure. I'd definitely been doing something all these years. But if you asked me, I couldn't tell you exactly what it was that I'd been so busy doing. I mean, I remember doing lots of things. I was volunteering in class and hosting Girl Scout meetings. I was fundraising for the PTA and painting sets and sewing costumes. I was baking for bake sales and cooking healthy meals for my family and doing laundry and driving kids all over the state. But that couldn't have possibly taken up the last eighteen years of my life. There had to be more that I had done.

Watching all the bright-eyed 18-year-olds moving into their dorms, starting their adult lives, depressed me. Wasn't it just yesterday that I was a bright-eyed teenager with visions of a stellar future as a best-selling author? At 18, my whole life was ahead of me. Now at 45, I felt the best years of my life were behind me and I didn't like that feeling very much. Where did my life go?

"Hey, Bella, can you take this?" Alex's voice interrupted my ongoing inner monologue as he handed me one of Holden's smaller suitcases.

"Sure," I answered with a sigh.

"Are you ok?" he asked, trying to catch my eye, and I smiled. Always so intuitive. Though, I guess after being married twenty years and being together our entire adult lives, I read pretty much like an open book to him.

I breathed in deeply and contemplated spilling my guts all over him right there. Telling him how I felt pathetic and unaccomplished, standing there right where we started. How it seemed now like I had been glued to that very spot for the past twenty years. That the entire world had been working, creating, contributing, but I had done nothing since college. I wanted to tell him these things, but instead I answered, "I'm fine. It's just weird to be back here." My drama was sometimes a little too much for Alex, who was definitely the right-brained one in our marriage. I found it was sometimes best to temper my words.

He smiled. "The first time I saw you, you were sitting right over there." He put down the duffle bag he was carrying to put his arm around me, pointing at the steps of the dorm in front of us.

"I remember." I answered. I had been waiting for my roommate to go to dinner with me. Back then I would rather have starved than eat alone, which might explain why I was so thin in college. "The first time you put your arm around me we were walking to class right over there." I pointed toward the large building next door. Nostalgia was such a beautiful thing. It was amazing how quickly I was taken right back to those early days. How everyone told us we would never last. How fun it was to prove them wrong, year after year.

I looked up at Alex, so much taller than me, yet he never made me feel small. I never felt like we were mismatched. His just slightly too-long hair curled in the autumn breeze. We smiled at each other and I momentarily forgot about all my failures. Though, I did wonder how Alex managed to look so damn good after all these years, where I felt weathered and worn. My once baby-fine and shiny blonde hair was now brittle and straw-like from years of punishing color treatments. Shouldn't Alex's hairline be receding at least a little bit by now?

Alex leaned in to kiss me, but Holden interrupted. "Would you two give it a rest?" he whined as he dragged himself out of the car.

"Seriously, guys," Vivian followed suit with an eye roll. I had to laugh. For two kids who couldn't have been more different, they were certainly awfully the same sometimes.

Alex and I smiled together, united in the joy of embarrassing them. "Just think, buddy." Alex patted Holden on the back. "You could meet your wife here."

"Don't hold your breath," Holden muttered and walked off as if he didn't know us at all. Vivian just shrugged and shook her head, grabbing a bag and following Holden into the dorm. I watched them walking away from me and my heart sank, though I took solace in the fact that at least they had each other here. They had always been so close growing up, though their teenage years certainly took a toll on their relationship. But when it came time for them to make their college lists, their favorite schools were the same. Though, they swear they didn't know each other's top choice.

"Aren't you going to miss them?" Alex joked. It was true that the teenage years had not been easy on us as parents. It seemed like one day, my sweet little boy was silly and affectionate and making all kinds of crazy noise, and the next, he was sullen and quiet and only spoke in one-word sentences. Holden was still a good kid who got into very little trouble, but I still missed that silly, crazy (and affectionate) boy every day. I wasn't sure if I was going to miss the teenage silence, and my perceived rejection, of Holden being home but ignoring us. He was in sharp contrast to Vivian, who navigated her teenage years with tears and door slamming instead of silent removal. But where Alex was kidding about missing the kids, I was borderline psychotic about them leaving. Borderline.

We helped Holden first, carrying his bags up the stairs to the place that would now be his home. "Do you want any help unpacking?" I asked, knowing that he wanted us to disappear as quickly as possible. I had been hoping that we could spend some time walking around the campus or at the very least take them out to lunch, but both Holden and Vivian had been adamant that we were to drop them and leave. Like it was no big deal. Like we did this every week. Like I sent my kids away every day.

"Mom…" he said with an eye roll.

"Just thought I'd ask," I sighed.

Alex gave a slight nod to the door and I steeled myself for our goodbye.

"Take care, buddy," Alex clapped Holden on the back. Holden turned to him and shook his hand and Alex was able to pull him in for a quick Bro-hug. Such a manly goodbye.

"Mom," he turned to me and I was surprised to hear his voice crack. Maybe he would miss me after all.

"Goodbye, Holden, honey. See you soon." I wasn't planning on hugging him, trying to give him his space and all, so I was overjoyed when he wrapped his arms around me – his long, giant arms. He was so tall, like Alex, and broad-shouldered and manly. When did he get so tall? I couldn't help but remember the morning he left for Kindergarten and his head barely came up to my belly button. Now, my head barely came up to his chest. "Call us," I said as I pushed away. I needed to get out of there soon before I lost it.

"I'll text you," he laughed. And that was it.

Vivian's goodbye was even quicker, one floor below Holden's in the same dorm. She was pushing us toward the door before Alex had even let go of her last bag. I hoped it was because she was too afraid to cry in front of the girls whom she hoped would be her new friends. I tried to stall as I was waiting for a moment to happen. Some special mother-daughter moment that we would remember forever as the moment I finally let go, but it didn't happen. "Love you, guys," she chirped as she ushered us to the door. And she meant it. But I still wanted more. I needed more.

"Let's go." Alex put his arm around me and guided me out the door. Alex was always the one to tell me when it was time to go.

We walked down the hall, his arm around me, just like we had all those years ago. Alex didn't talk to me. He knew full well that if he did, I would burst into tears. So, he waited, just holding me tightly, practically holding me up as we walked down the hall. None of the other parents looked like they were going to collapse, by the way, just me. I couldn't understand it.

We were leaving our children? Alone? Why wasn't everyone freaking out?

Once Alex and I got outside and I could feel the fresh air on my face, I could breathe. My racing heart slowed.

"You ok, now?" Alex asked me with smirk.

"I think so." I took a deep breath. "Let's just get the hell out of here."

He nodded and opened the car door for me, ever the gentleman, he was. "You don't want to go visit some of our old haunts? We could go check out the third-floor ladies room in the library?" he winked at me, alluding to an old make-out spot of ours. I know, gross. But it was college.

I definitely wasn't in the mood. How could I be when all I could feel was the ground falling out from beneath my feet? But I appreciated him for trying. "Not today, babe. Maybe next time, ok?"

"OK, fine," he sighed. "I'll just take you home."

We headed toward the car, but I spun back for one last look at the campus where my dreams of being a writer actually seemed possible. My heart started thumping hard again. I told myself it was just because I was saying goodbye to the twins, but both my heart and my head knew it was more than that. It wasn't about losing my children. It was something about being there, in that place where my adult life began, that spun my brain like I was falling off a cliff.

I always thought I'd be a writer. Even as a little kid, when the other kids were playing wiffle ball in the park, I was more likely to be sitting in the grass pretending to be watching, when really, I was making up stories in my head about all the kids playing, or when I was feeling especially inspired, I was writing in a marble notebook. As a kid, all the time I spent writing made me feel weird and different. Looking at my life now, I never would have guessed I would've turned out so ordinary.

I simply expected that a writer was what I would grow up to be. Whenever I was writing it just felt like that was what I should be doing and, though I knew it was a long shot that I'd ever be any kind of a success at it, I always tried to hold onto the dream that one day I would be a real, live writer. But somehow, somewhere along the way, I got off that track.

I didn't know how I got so far off course in what seemed like the blink of an eye. After college, I took a job that I didn't care about so I would have time to write "on the side." I hated that job. I moved on to being a receptionist because there I could actually write at work, pausing only to answer the phones and greet people at the door. But the environment didn't lend itself to creativity. At least, that's what I told myself at the time. So, I quit. Again. I bounced from job to job for years, turning down promotions that would've interfered with my writing, sabotaging several real careers I could've had until I became a mother. I promptly quit my job to stay home and raise our children all the while making empty promises to myself about getting my writing on track in my "free time."

And that pretty much brings us to today. Nothing to show for the past twenty years, with the lovely exception of a sweet, wonderful provider of a husband and two remarkable college-aged kids.

Isn't that enough? Sure. It's always been enough. Too much. It made me complacent. I settled into a lovely little life. A life that I've loved, mind you. I certainly don't mean to minimize my family and all they mean to me. But now, as I mentally prepared myself to go home with Alex alone, no children to keep me busy, I found myself wanting more. I wanted something to show for it all. Something more than the dozens of smiling family photos that lined our walls. I wanted success. I wanted to be special. I wanted to impress someone with something I've done. I wanted something that was mine.

It's not like I haven't been writing for the past twenty years, because I have. I've barely stopped writing since I was ten, under the covers of my bed with a flashlight writing away when I should've been sleeping, training myself for a future where I neither needed nor desired more than five hours sleep. I did stop writing novels for the five years while we fought through the baby to kindergarten years in a sleepless haze. Though, even then, I wrote, keeping what I called 'Mommy journals.' I just got away from writing novels for awhile. Quite honestly, the creative juices were all used up just getting through the days back then. As soon as Holden and Vivian were off to Kindergarten though, I was right back at the novels. That is, if I wasn't too busy volunteering as class mother or acting as PTA president or whatever other obligation that kept me away from writing. I did what I could to devote every available moment to writing. There just weren't enough hours in the day for everything I needed to do and I certainly didn't have enough energy to do everything I wanted to do.

Self-reflection aside, here's my real problem: in all my years of writing, I haven't exactly finished a novel. Not one. I must have started at least fifteen different books over the years, though I couldn't name them all. I poured my blood, sweat, and tears into some of them, (and some of them never made it past the first few pages) but not one of them had an ending. Fifteen unfinished novels. No conclusions. No grand finales. No closure. I had come close a couple of times, but when it came down to Act III, I could never seem to finish. I could never come up with an ending that seemed worthy of everything my characters had been through. I'd lose interest or some other priority would come up and by the time I got back to it, I didn't even care who these characters were or what they were doing. Of course, if my characters weren't interesting enough to even keep the writer interested, what chance did I have at ever having anyone else want to read about them?

Still, I wrote. I just couldn't help it. My brain would just start rambling and I would just start writing. I would type away without structure or storyline and just write, letting the characters go where they would. This was my favorite part of writing. When the screen was blank, my head was filled with ideas, and my purse was filled with scraps of stories or lines of dialogue written down on the backs of receipts and cocktail napkins and coupons or whatever other paper I could find when an idea struck me. I loved getting started, when it didn't need to be refined and perfect, it just was what it was. It always came so easily when I first got started. It was only when I got close to the end, the elusive resolution, that the words stopped pouring out of me.

This was it, I told myself every time I started on my latest brilliant idea. This was the story that was going to make all my dreams come true. I had worked tirelessly on my latest, *The Woodpecker*. Starring Emily, the mother who lost her son to a vengeful ex-husband; and Daniel, the son who returned to her from London after fifteen long years. Poor Emily with her abusive husband, and her inability to leave him, and her stepchildren who just couldn't bring themselves to love her. And poor Daniel who just wanted his Mum.

This was my masterpiece, I told myself. This was the best thing I'd ever written. All my other books were just preparing me to write this one. If only I knew how to end it. Which of course, I didn't. So, there it sat on my dining room table.

More often than not, when I was writing, I would get sidetracked by one holiday or another (after all, my army of nutcrackers didn't march themselves out of the basement every Christmas) or some home improvement project (of course, the basement bathroom needed to be painted again) and my latest story would end up, unfinished, on a shelf in the closet next to all the other stories that were going to make all my dreams come true. I had a separate box for every story. Each box contained the partially finished manuscript, some sort of an outline, usually with no ending, and every note of inspiration that I jotted down along the way. I would carefully label each box and line them up on the shelf of the closet, like that was where they belonged. I tried not to let the enormity of my failures overwhelm me each and every time I put a box, filled with my dreams, back on the shelf.

This time it was the twins leaving for college that sidetracked me. All the packing and preparation. It seemed to take months, though looking back, I had no idea what had taken us so long to prepare. Anyway, *The Woodpecker* currently sat on my dining room table in my empty house, collecting dust. It'd been so long since I'd looked at it, I couldn't even remember where I was.

****

The ride home was mostly silent. I was buried under all the thoughts in my head and couldn't seem to tear myself away from the passing scenery out the window. How was it possible I was the mother of two college-aged children? It was easy for me not to have a career, a life of my own, when I was busy being "Mom of the Year." And now they were both gone, both off starting their own lives. As I looked out the window, we flew past the changing trees in a blur. That's how I felt. The past twenty years were a blur. A blur marked with so many happy snapshots that it made me feel that the best years of my life were behind me. They were behind me and they went too fast.

Alex ignored me most of the trip home. I knew I should be commiserating with him, but somehow, I couldn't get out of my own head. Fortunately, Alex was a man of few words and knew that if I wanted to talk to him, I'd talk to him.

"We need gas," he said quietly to forewarn me of our upcoming stop.

I nodded silently. He reached over and took my hand as he pulled into the rest stop. "You still have me, you know." He said, stroking my cheek with his free hand.

"I know. And I'm glad." Alex looked so deeply into my eyes that it made me nervous. It was like he was looking at my soul. I didn't want him to see that. My soul was a mess right now.

He moved his hand to the back of my neck, pulled me close and kissed me ever so softly on the lips. Just enough of a kiss that it left me wanting more. "What is with you today?" I asked him.

"I don't know," he smirked. He was very smirky today. "Maybe I'm just looking forward to having you alone in the house." I giggled like a schoolgirl and bit my bottom lip. I couldn't help it. Like I said, Alex still looked like he hadn't aged a day.

"I need a Coke," I said, pulling away from him reluctantly. My life-long addiction to Coca-Cola began in college when everyone else developed a taste for coffee. I don't care how much cream and sugar you put in it. Coffee tasted like battery acid to me. No, I haven't actually tasted battery acid, but I'm pretty sure it's what coffee tastes like. Coke was the only caffeine I had to get me through those college all-nighters. I know it's bad for me, and I've tried a million times to quit, but I just never seem to be able to give it up for good. "I'll be right back." I climbed out of the car, my knees just a little bit weak. I wasn't sure if that was arthritis setting in or if Alex was making my knees feel like rubber. Probably a little bit of both.

While inside the rest stop, I found myself a ladies' room, managing to completely avoid looking in the mirror. I didn't want to depress myself further by seeing how old I looked. I was sure I looked terrible – old and worn. My eyes were probably puffy from crying which meant my forty-five-year-old face was splotchy and my nose was red. My hair was probably wrecked from messing with it all morning, trying to get that one piece in the front to stay behind my ear, which it never would.

Back in the store, I pulled a Coke from the refrigerator. The store was empty except for me, the clerk and a guy at the coffee machine in the back, who appeared to be wearing a full tuxedo at 11:30 in the morning. I couldn't help but stare at him for several reasons. First, he was wearing a full tuxedo at 11:30 in the morning, though his tie was undone. His unshaven face clearly stating he had been out all night. What he was doing at a rest stop in the middle of upstate New York, I couldn't tell you. Second, he was gorgeous, movie-star gorgeous. Definitely a *what-the-hell-is-a-guy-like-you-doing-in-a-place-like-this* kind of moment. And third, he looked exactly like Cody. Or the image I had in my head of what Cody would look like if he were actually a real person.

Cody was a fictional character from one of my many unfinished books. He was my least favorite character I'd written, ever. Shallow, self-centered, and narcissistic. He was a bad boy. Not a bad boy with a heart of gold. Just a bad boy. He had no regard for anyone but himself. And he was known to stay out all night and wear a tuxedo from time-to-time. I never quite got around to giving him any of those redeeming qualities he needed to be a worthwhile character. I was also never quite sure from what part of my imagination Cody came from or why I started writing about him in the first place.

This gorgeous creature at the coffee machine caught me staring at him, and raised his coffee and his eyebrows to me as a toast. I raised my Coke back at him in some weird moment of rest-stop solidarity and went to the counter to pay. Tuxedo guy followed me.

"Hey, how ya doing?" he said from behind me in line.

I didn't answer because it seemed like a rhetorical question and because he suddenly gave me the creeps. That, and I was reasonably embarrassed to have been caught staring at him. I just smiled over my shoulder instead, threw my money on the counter and left.

"Take care," Tuxedo Guy called after me.

"Thanks, you too." I called without looking back and headed back to our car.

Alex was done pumping gas and was sitting in the car waiting for me. It occurred to me that ours was the only car at the station.

"Did you see that guy?" I asked Alex as he started the car.

"What guy?"

"The guy in the tux." I looked at the store to see if he had come out yet. I couldn't see inside the tinted windows.

"In a tux?"

"Yeah, I saw him inside, but – "

"There's no one else here, Bella. There are no other cars."

"I know that. That's why am asking you if you saw him." I insisted, frustrated as always with Alex's logical conclusions.

"I didn't see him." Alex pulled back onto the highway.

"Weird."

CHAPTER 2

WE RETURNED HOME ABOUT TWO hours later and everything was quiet. Too quiet. It reminded me of when we first moved to the suburbs from the city when the kids were babies. The silence was deafening. I remembered desperately missing the sounds of the city – the horns honking, the people yelling or just talking too loud. They were the sounds that annoyed me to no end when I lived there, but once they were gone, I couldn't stand the silence. It was too still. I missed the sounds of people, and passion and vitality. Now, with the children gone, I missed the sounds of music and video games, the sounds of doors opening and closing. The sounds of life.

After a quiet Sunday that consisted mostly of me either staring out the window or doing chores that didn't need doing just to keep myself from crying, Monday came and I had to go back to work. I hated working. It messed with my psyche. I especially hated my current job. So much so that I had to ask myself every day what the hell I was doing there. I would remind myself that my part-time schedule gave me a little cash and a lot of time for writing…writing that I wasn't currently doing.

Anyway, I dragged myself out of bed in the morning just as Alex was leaving. "You going to be ok today?" He put his arms around my waist.

"Please stop asking me that." I rolled my eyes and pulled away from his grasp.

"You've barely said ten words since we dropped the kids off, Bella. I'm supposed to be the quiet one, remember?"

It was true. I was at a total loss for words. I just didn't feel like talking, which was extremely unusual for me. Usually, I bombarded Alex with my non-stop, inconsequential chatter, blathering about one thing or another. A solid third of which he didn't listen to anyway. But the house seemed so quiet, so empty since we got back, that talking seemed so disruptive, like making noise in the library. "I'm sorry," I told Alex. And I meant it. I was sorry that I was retreating so far into myself that I was leaving my poor husband alone. "Dinner tonight?" I took his hand.

"How about I take you out to dinner?" He pulled my hand to his lips and I had to admit that getting out of the house seemed like a good idea. I nodded. "Good." He kissed my forehead. "See you later, Belly."

I sighed as I watched him leave. I always loved it when he called me Belly. Just having that one little word between us, made me feel forever special and attached to him. You'd think any reference to my sagging midsection would offend me. But I liked it. I don't know why. Maybe because it implied some sort of closeness that right now I desperately needed.

My given name was Mirabelle. I was named after my mother's favorite restaurant. My parents always called me Mira, which I hated. It sounded far too much like mirror. "Mirror, Mira, on the wall," the kids used to chant at me in some sort of teasing that seemed torturous when I was in third grade, but in hindsight was really no big deal.

It was Alex who first called me Bella in college, and thankfully, it stuck. I haven't been Mirror Mira since, which was good as self-reflection was never one of my favorite tasks.

****

After a morning of procrastinating, surfing the Internet, and picking up the house, which wasn't messy because there were no kids home to mess it up, I managed to get myself to work. I walked in the front door with an ugly feeling in the pit of my stomach, like I had just eaten something rancid. Not only did I hate every single second I was there, but every moment there was a reminder of my failure to do something important with my life.

I was a Lunchroom Monitor in one of the elementary schools in town. It was a simple job. Keep the kids safe and under control. But somehow, I never felt like soft-spoken me was the right person for the "under-control" portion. It was me versus one hundred kids every day. And every day the kids won. Every single damn day those kids got the best of me. I was outnumbered and outmatched. It wore on me until I forgot how cute little kids could be. In the lunchroom, you didn't see the well-behaved kids. I'm sure they were in there somewhere. But I was far too busy with the troublemakers to see any of the nice kids. It was just the nature of the beast.

Take Kyle for example, who couldn't seem to follow the very simple rule of staying in his seat, to save his life. When I would tell him to sit, he would do one of two things. Either ignore me completely and go about doing whatever he was doing that got him out of his seat to begin with. Or he would actually listen to me, but then make disparaging comments to his friends about me. I know I shouldn't give a crap what some first-grade derelict thought about me. But somehow it still hurt.

The only redeeming thing about my job was the few hours each week I got to spend working in a classroom. Those few short hours, helping a kid that needed help instead of screaming at them in some vain attempt to control them, were the only thing that kept me from quitting. Well, that and that Alex said we needed the money. Personally, I found it hard to believe that my pathetic excuse for an income was of any consequence, but the budget was Alex's department. Anyway, every year, I hoped for more classroom time and less lunchroom time. And every year I got just a little bit more. Just enough to keep me coming back. But never enough to make me happy or fulfilled in any way. Never enough to balance the torture of the lunchroom.

Jeremy was a kindergartener who was very much in his own little world. He wasn't very good at following directions, sitting still, paying attention or socializing with the other kids. The day after I lost my Holden and Vivian to college, Jeremy and I were going on a walk around the school to give him a break from the classroom. As we walked, he whined to me, "I don't want to be here."

"You know what Jeremy? I don't want to be here either." I didn't have the patience for his incessant complaining today.

"Yeah," he sighed, dragging his hand along the wall absently. "You and me are a lot alike."

For all his quirks, Jeremy sure knew what he was talking about. It was true I had trouble following directions, sitting still, paying attention or socializing with the other kids. "We sure are, Jeremy." I sighed in return. "We sure are."

I got home from work around 3:00 and started to clean the house again for the lack of something better to do until Alex came home. When the kids were younger, after three was the time I'd be running them to dance and karate and scouts and whatever other activities their little hearts desired. Once they got their licenses, my 3:00 duties were significantly reduced. If

I was really lucky, Holden needed help with his homework, or Vivian had nothing to wear to school the next day which would create some sort of crisis that, though it annoyed me at the time, I realize now, made me feel blissfully needed. Now they were gone. They didn't need me to drive them anywhere, or do their laundry or help them with their homework or hold them when their hearts were broken.

What a fool I'd been when they were toddlers and I longed for their independence. I'd taken it all for granted. If only I'd known then how terribly useless I'd feel without them. Sometimes now, I hear people say things like, "Thank god, those days are over," which is a complete lie. The truth is most of us would give our pinky toe to go back to those times for just one day. I would definitely be willing to part with my left pinky toe if it meant I could have just one more day with my kids as snuggly, playful, needy, clinging toddlers.

I managed to talk myself out of calling Holden and Vivian that afternoon, though it wasn't easy. It was hard work trying to switch off the blades of my helicopter parenting that had been spinning for the past eighteen years.

So, now I rattled around our empty house, hoping Alex would come home early. My writing for that afternoon consisted of jotting down what Jeremy had said to me. I don't know if I thought it was so damn funny or so damn sad. Either way, it seemed like good dialogue. I was thinking of writing something to go with it while I was cleaning the dining room.

I did a lot of writing in the dining room. Probably because we didn't do a whole lot of dining in the dining room. It was the one room Alex didn't mind if I let get a little cluttered (or a lot cluttered). And cluttered it was with pages and notes and scribbles all over the table. I enjoyed sitting in a mess that was all mine. After cleaning up after everyone else all the time, sometimes, it felt good to just flat-out refuse to put my things away. I would have to be sure to put it all away before the kids came home for Thanksgiving so we could have a proper family dinner together.

The Woodpecker sat on the dining room table practically begging me to finish it, but it didn't offer me any insight on exactly how to do so. I certainly wasn't looking forward to getting back into a story about a mother losing her son. When I really thought about it, there was no way I was going to be able to finish it now. Not when the pain of losing my own kids was so fresh and raw. I had to put it away, at least for a while. And I knew I had no ending. I could torture poor Emily and Daniel all day long with awkward silences and conflicts with Emily's husband. But how could I get to their happily-ever-after? Or even their not-so-happily-ever-after?

Now that I could no longer stand to look at it, there was no place else for it to go. I had to put it away. *I was close this time*, a voice said inside my brain. *Maybe I'll finish it later*, I consoled myself. It was as close as I had ever come to finishing one. But it had taken so long. At this point, I'd lost interest in the characters. I didn't care what happened to them, which probably meant that I wasn't a very good writer to begin with. God, I hated the feelings of loathing and self-doubt that accompanied all my failures.

Anyway, I pretended I was doing just plain old house straightening, not shelving my dreams once again. I gathered my notes and notebooks from the dining room table and put them into a tidy pile, then into an empty box that I had in my closet, a box that had been sitting on the shelf just waiting for my next disappointment. That's right. I already had an extra box. It was almost as if I knew I would fail again. On the side, I carefully wrote, *The Woodpecker*. I almost put a date on it, but then I thought it would look too much like a tombstone.

I carried the box up the stairs, down the hall, sighing as I passed Holden's room, choking back tears on the way past Vivi's room, and into my own room. I opened my walk-in-closet, sighing once again, as I looked up at all the neatly labeled boxes. I dropped "The Woodpecker" box on the bed behind me to make room for it in the closet. Damn, there were an awful lot of boxes up there. Five of them in all. Just the ones I'd made any significant progress on. There were countless others that never made it far enough to earn themselves a box.

I slid the box that said "Mercy" on its yellowed label down the shelf, and put the box that said "Kip & Bridget" on top of it, making a perfect slot for "The Woodpecker" box. I marveled at the organization of my closet. All of the boxes matched and were labeled oh so neatly. If only I labeled my successes as well, but then again I didn't have any of those.

Anyway, there was the perfect spot for "The Woodpecker" box, just sitting there, tailor-made for my next disappointment. It was amazing how utterly prepared I was to fail once again. It made me wonder if I should even start again. I slid the box into place and though it was just a box made of nothing but cardboard, somehow in my head, it sounded more like a prison door sliding and then slamming closed.

"Quitting again, eh?" a voice startled me just as I slid "The Woodpecker" box into its rightful place in my archives.

I turned around quickly, clutching the closet doorframe for support. There was a man right in the middle of my bed, laying there like he'd been there all along, like he belonged there. I use the term "man" loosely, as this guy looked to be just a few years older than Holden. His feet were crossed at the ankles and his hands rested behind his head, the torn sleeves of his grungy flannel shirt hung in his long, somewhat unwashed hair. He had a strange familiarity that kept me from dissolving into full-on panic mode. I knew I should've been more afraid, but I felt like I knew him from somewhere, or sometime.

"W-who are you?" I whispered softly, almost too terrified to get the words out. My gut was filled was a mixture of panic and bewilderment. My hands trembled as I put one to my forehead to see if I had some sort of raging fever.

"Who am I?" he laughed. "Have you forgotten me already?" He joked, shaking his head as he got up off the bed and approached me. I backed away until I was actually in the closet and started looking around for a weapon, not because I was really afraid, but because that's what you do when you find a strange man in your bed.

"Stay away from me," I said, trying to sound like a tough girl, but realizing the only thing I could arm myself with was a wire hanger. (Clearly from my side of the closet – Alex would never have a wire hanger on his side.)

He sighed and shook his head with a pout. "You put me up there and forgot all about me, didn't you?" He gestured towards the shelf.

"Who are you?" I repeated even though, by this point, I had a pretty good idea of who he was. What I didn't know is how it was possible that he was standing in what appeared to be the flesh, in my bedroom. I almost reached out to touch him, but I was afraid of what he might feel like because he couldn't possibly be real.

"C'mon. Quit messing around. You know who I am." He told me knowingly.

I shook my head. It was not possible that he was who I thought he was. He didn't exist anywhere outside my own mind. He barely existed on paper. This was a real person standing in my bedroom. I could see him and hear him. For god's sake, I could smell the stale stench of smoke on him.

"OK, OK. I'll give you a hint." He clapped his hands and rubbed them together as if he were preparing for some sort of magic trick. "I'm an actor, who works as a bartender…and I HATE high-pitched sounds."

"Kip," I whispered, finally, admitting what I had known since I'd heard his voice over my shoulder.

Kip was a character from the first book I attempted to write after college. His best friend/love interest, Bridget, was a writer who took a job that she hated in the real world and gave up her aspirations of being a writer. (Sound familiar?) Kip was secretly trying to get her fired so she would be forced to pursue her dreams. And there he was, exactly as I had written him, in my bedroom.

"Give the lady a prize!" Kip cheered. "So, now my question to you my dear lady is, why are you quitting this time?"

"What?"

Kip eyeballed "The Woodpecker" box I had just placed on the shelf.

"Oh, that." I shrugged. "I'm not quitting – I just have some other things I need to take care of. I'll finish it later." I lied to him, like he would believe me.

"Oh, I am so sure that you will." He nodded a little too emphatically and rolled his eyes.

"What is that supposed to mean?" I didn't like his tone. But his sarcastic bite was exactly how I wrote him. It seemed that Kip was indeed in my bedroom. He was as real to me as Alex though I still didn't dare touch him. My brain finally started to process the idea of a figment of my imagination, laying on my bed, as being completely crazy. Seriously, mentally-ill crazy. "Why am I even talking to you?"

"Maybe you missed me," he smiled in his brazen, flirty way, and I couldn't help but be ever so slightly sucked in by his charm.

"I doubt that," I retorted anyway.

"Maybe, just maybe, it's because you need to talk to me."

"You know what?" I snapped, his brazenness now scraping on my last nerve. "You're not real. You can't be here." My head started spinning and my heart hammered in my chest as the reality of the situation started to sink in. I was having a real conversation and could physically see and hear someone who I knew wasn't really there. I was officially going crazy.

To be fair, it wasn't the first time I'd spoken out loud to one of my characters. I often spoke to them when I was writing. It was part of my process. Was it weird? Sure, but it worked for me. Sort of. But none of the imaginary conversations I had had in the past were like this. Normally, (and I use that term loosely) I would write dialogue and sort of review it out loud with my imaginary characters. This little scenario, where Kip seemed to have his own words, was completely nuts.

"I may not be 'real,'" he put the word 'real' in air quotes. "But I feel pretty darn real to you right now – don't I?"

I didn't want to answer that question. He did feel entirely and completely real to me, but I wasn't going to give him the satisfaction of telling him that.

"What was it that stopped you from finishing me again?" he continued.

"I don't remember," I lied.

"I do. It was your wedding…remember? You put away all your writing notebooks and took out all those shiny bride's magazines."

I smiled at the memory of being newly engaged. How excited I was when Alex proposed. And, of course, Kip was right. Our engagement was exactly what stopped me from finishing Bridget & Kip. I had far too much wedding planning to do then to concern myself with Bridget and Kip's little melodrama. So, I shelved them.

Kip's uncanny ability to be right about me was getting on my nerves. I decided maybe if I played along, whatever neurosis or mental breakdown I was having would resolve itself. That was my strategy, anyway. "What do you want, Kip?" I asked him.

"What do I want?" He pointed to himself in a grand gesture. "Nothing, babe. I just got lonely in that box up there. It's kind of confining for a guy like me to be trapped in a box for, what has it been, ten years."

"Twenty," I whispered.

"Twenty!" Kip yelled. "God, I thought you looked old."

"Shut up!" I snapped at him.

"Damn, girl," he sighed and sat back down on the bed. "Where have you been?"

"I've been busy." I shrugged.

"Busy?"

"Yes, busy. Raising kids. Working."

"Oh, please, let me guess. You have some crappy job that you just hate, but you go there every day anyway."

"Shut up, Kip. I don't have to justify myself to you," I said, echoing something Bridget might have said twenty years ago.

"No...you have to justify yourself to you. But, hey, you're the one who has to live with yourself." His smugness just about killed me. I wondered what would happen if I attempted to slap him, but was afraid to try because if I could actually make contact with his face, what exactly would that say about my sanity, or lack thereof.

Instead, I took a deep breath and ran my hands through my perpetually messy hair. "I'm arguing with a figment of my imagination."

Kip laughed, "Yeah, you keep telling yourself that."

I was about to say something, I don't know what, when my phone rang in my pocket. The sound of it brought Kip to his knees. His disaffected arrogance melted away and he crumbled at my feet. I laughed at Kip's aversion to high-pitched sounds, "I always loved that about you."

"Make it stop," Kip groaned from the floor.

"Welcome to the twenty-first century, Kip." I laughed as I stepped away from him and answered my cell. "Hello?"

"Mom?" It was Vivi.

I couldn't help but look back over my shoulder. Kip had disappeared.

"Mom?" As excited as I was to hear Vivi's voice, I was a little disoriented by Kip's sudden disappearing act. I looked around for a moment, but he was gone. "Mom?"

"I'm here." I shook my head back into reality, trying to clear my brain.

"You sound weird. Are you writing?" Both kids knew well my propensity for being spacey and distracted when I was writing.

"Uh, yeah, kind of." I closed my eyes tight and shook my head, trying to focus on the concreteness of Vivian's voice.

"I'm just finishing up. How are you? How's school?" I asked cheerfully.

"I only have a minute, but I wanted to tell you that I aced my first Spanish test!" Surprise, surprise. Vivian was one of those kids that everything she touched turned to gold. She was like her father that way.

"Already? I just dropped you off two days ago."

"It was a placement test. But I got the highest grade in the class."

"That's great, honey," I said, probably with not enough enthusiasm.

"Are you sure you're ok, Mom? You sound so far away."

"I am far away, Viv. You're away at school, remember?" I said, snarkier than I meant to.

"I know that, Mom," she answered me with perfect teenage attitude. "I meant you sounded different."

I stared up at the boxes in my closet and shook off my crazies. "I'm fine. I just miss you, Viv." I tried not to sound whiney and pathetic, but I think I failed. "How's everything else going?" I folded my legs underneath me and settled in for a nice, long chat with my daughter.

"Awww, I miss you, too, Mom. Oh! I gotta go! Love you!"

"Love you, too," I answered, but she was already gone. So much for that.

Sliding my phone back in my pocket, I looked back up at my closet of failures with a sigh and pulled down the box that said "Bridget & Kip" neatly on its side. Putting the box on my bed, I sat down and tucked my legs underneath myself again and stared at the box. Opening the box slowly, half-afraid that something might jump out at me, I pulled out the orange binder that sat on top of the collection of scraps of paper of all different sizes and shapes, all with my scribbled handwriting on them. For as neat as the outsides of all the boxes were, the insides were more like construction zones filled with receipts, napkins, newspapers, whatever paper I could find to scrawl ideas on whenever they occurred to me – on the train, while I was at work, or driving in my car.

The orange binder was cracked on the corner and split down the seam and when I opened it, the first yellowed page stuck to the inside cover. The ink peeled off the paper and imprinted itself on the cover, a tattooed reminder of how I'd neglected my stories. I started at the beginning, reading through Bridget's misery at her job, and Kip's frustration when she completely turns her back on all her dreams. I found the scene where Kip steals Bridget's key during dinner and makes a copy so he can sneak inside her apartment. The high-pitched sound of the key machine nearly killed Kip. The scene starts at a payphone, which made me chuckle. When was the last time I saw a payphone?

****

Kip returned to the restaurant, his new copy of Bridget's key tucked safely in his pocket. He tried to sneak in all stealth-like so Bridget wouldn't see him, but just as he began to cross the restaurant back to their table, a waiter slipped and dropped an entire tray of food at Kip's feet. Bridget turned with a start as Kip hung his head and returned to their table. He slid into the booth, picked up a menu and began to read it like he hadn't just been gone for twenty minutes.

"Kip?" Bridget pulled down the menu and peeked over.

"What?" he answered, annoyed, like he was really trying to figure out what to order.

"Where did you go?"

"The phone," he answered, matter-of-factly.

"Is in the back of the restaurant," Bridget continued.

"Oh, right. It was broken, so I ran across the street to use the phone over there. There was a line. A really long line."

Bridget looked at him skeptically. She knew his nervous babble well enough to know when he was hiding something. "I didn't see you leave," she said.

He shrugged and avoided any eye contact with her, "You were probably reading the menu." Kip looked around the table and suddenly ducked under to pick something up off the floor. "Hey, Bridget, are these your keys?" He asked when he emerged from under the table. He had keys in one hand and his napkin in the other.

"Where did you get them?"

"They were under the table, on the floor."

Bridget took them, "They must have fallen out of my pocket."

"You should be more careful," Kip scolded.

"I know...I don't even have a spare." She dropped her keys in her purse and zipped it up while Kip stifled a giggle.

"I'm starved, let's order," Kip said, still looking at the menu and not at Bridget.

"Oh, yeah. I already ordered." Bridget answered.

"You ordered for me?" Kip asked, clearly annoyed, just as their food arrived.

"Every time we come here, you always have the Chicken Quesadillas with extra sour cream and guacamole."

"Maybe today I didn't FEEL like having Chicken Quesadillas with extra sour cream and guacamole," he whined.

"Maybe you shouldn't have left me sitting her for twenty minutes."

"Still doesn't mean you get to order for me." He sulked.

Bridget rolled her eyes at his complaining. "Shut up, Kip."

"You know that's just the kind of thing that drives me crazy," he muttered, as he took a big bite of his quesadilla.

"I know, dear. How is it?"

"It's delicious," he answered with sour cream dripping off his chin. "Hey, Bridgey. How many times a week do you think we argue?"

"I don't know." Bridget shrugged and then quipped, "How many times a week do we talk?"

Kip drank the last sip of his beer as he pondered her answer, then looked at his glass quizzically. "Didn't I order another beer?"

Bridget didn't answer him. Now it was her turn to avoid eye contact with him. She cut her food meticulously and avoided his gaze. "Bridget, where's my beer?"

"You were gone a long time..."

Kip dropped his silverware on his plate loudly and sat back in the booth. "You KNOW, that's just the kind of thing that drives me nuts!"

Bridget smiled coyly at him. "I know."

CHAPTER 3

I DON'T KNOW HOW LONG I sat there reading a story from so long ago. It wasn't half bad. But it wasn't half good either. It was clearly written by a miserable, naïve twenty-something. God, remember when I was a twenty-something? Still, there was something very endearing about Kip trying to get me, I mean Bridget, fired. I was almost to the end. When I say the end, I mean the part where I stopped writing, because of course, *Bridget & Kip,* like all my other stories, had no ending. It didn't even have a real title. *Bridget & Kip* was just a working title. My inability to come up with a decent title for any of my stories is a story for another day.

Anyway, I was at the end of what I'd written when I heard a voice whisper in my ear, "So, what happens next?" I didn't turn around, but I could feel Kip sitting behind me. This time I wasn't scared, or startled. He wasn't real, but I could still feel him sitting there. I could smell him, patchouli oil and cigarettes with just a hint of Dial soap. I put my head in my hands to stop myself from turning around, because I really wanted to. Part of me really wanted to know exactly how crazy I was.

"C'mon." He prodded. "Do they admit they love each other and live happily ever after? Starving artists to the end?"

"I don't know." I whispered through gritted teeth. I didn't know. Having them live happily ever after seemed too cliché. But not having them live happily ever after seemed pointless. What was the point of their story if they weren't going to end up together?

"Creating this story without an ending is really downright irresponsible of you." I could practically hear Kip smirking on the bed behind me.

"Gimme a break, Kip. Don't be so melodramatic." I said, finally prying my head out of my hands.

"Oh, you're one to talk about melodrama." He laughed at me. My own imagination was laughing at me. "Why don't you just finish it now?" he said softly, switching gears away from teasing me.

"I'm not sure I can. It just seems so long ago. I don't know what's going to happen to you guys," I admitted sadly.

"Well, Bridgey and I control what happens in our lives." He air quoted when he said 'lives.' "And you control us. Right?"

"In theory." Though that did very little to explain what Kip was doing on my bed.

"So, what do you think we'll do next?"

I answered him with a shrug of my shoulders, not wanting to say "I don't know" yet again.

"C'mon," he pushed, growing exasperated. "No one knows us better than you do. What do we do next?"

I closed my eyes and thought, rolling through the options in my head. The happy-ending would be that Bridget quits her job and realizes she loves Kip and they live happily ever after. But then there was the unhappy-ending where Bridget kept her job, gets promoted and had a super successful career, but barely sees Kip anymore.

"What if the ending means you don't get to hang out with Bridget anymore?" I turned around and asked him.

"Hmmm," he pondered. "That doesn't sound quite right. Try again."

"It doesn't sound right for you, but it might be just perfect for her. Maybe she marries someone she works with, and has her own happily-ever-after…without you."

"Whatever, Bridget." Kip shook his head and rolled his eyes at me.

"I'm not Bridget," I protested.

"Sure you are," he insisted with a scoff, as if it was so obvious to everyone, but me.

"No. I'm not."

"Aren't you the writer who gives up all your dreams for one stupid job after another?"

"Yes," I relented. "But not like Bridget."

"Really? In what way are you not like Bridget?"

I was going to answer him, because there really were plenty of ways I was not like Bridget, but Kip didn't give me a chance.

"I bet if you continued our story, end it the way you're saying, then fast forwarded twenty years, you could easily find Bridget standing right where you are now. Hating her job. Still wanting to write, but being too afraid to fail. Wishing maybe, just maybe, she'd done things differently twenty years ago."

"Shut up, Kip," I whispered fighting back the tears. I was not going to let him see me cry.

He smiled, knowing he'd won without even seeing a tear.

Suddenly, I heard footsteps on the stairs and I prayed it wasn't Bridget coming to tell me that Kip was right and I screwed up my life twenty years ago.

It was with great relief that I heard Alex's voice. "Bella, honey? Are you up here?"

I wiped the tears brimming out of my eyes and ran out of the bedroom and to the landing, running to him and away from Kip. "You startled me!" I jumped into his arms.

"I'm sorry, honey. I didn't mean to scare you." Alex wrapped himself around me and I collapsed into him, not wanting him to see my red nose and splotchy cheeks, not wanting him to see the evidence of me crying. "Jeez, Bella, you're shaking like leaf. Are you ok?"

"Yeah." I sighed. "I'm fine. I'm just really glad you're home." I curled further into him relishing his warmth and the solidness of him.

I felt badly for Alex sometimes. What a pain in the ass it must be to be married to an emotional train wreck like me. Someone who almost always took the path of most melodrama, who thrived on over-reacting to things. Someone who was always running out of the room for a piece of paper to write down the most brilliant thought ever. How annoying it must be to sleep in a bed next to someone who was always scratching away in some notebook in the middle of the night. Someone who was half a world away half the time, tangled up in my now completely insane brain.

Then again, Alex was often far away in his own way, too. Thinking about his job that I knew so very little about. I honestly wasn't really sure what he did all day. He sells something that's part of something else. I'm not exactly sure. I used to ask him about work when he came home, but he was never one for rehashing his day. I used to try to tell him about what I was writing or whatever project it was that was currently holding my attention, but he was usually too busy to pay attention, so eventually I just stopped talking to him about it altogether. I didn't blame him. He worked hard to take care of all of us. He devoted himself to taking care of his family. I worked hard volunteering for the PTA and for whatever committee needed a chairperson. But somewhere along the way, it seemed we got so busy taking care of "things" that we stopped taking care of each other.

Alex held me another moment before he stepped back, looking at me suspiciously. "Tough day at work?"

I took a deep breath and contemplated telling him about Kip. But he wouldn't understand. It was hard enough for him to understand the writing side of me. My actually seeing Kip would cross the line between eccentric and crazy. He, quite simply, wouldn't get it. So, I shook my head and shrugged. "You know, same crap, different day."

Alex kissed the top of my head. He knew I hated my job. And I knew he felt badly about me having to have a job that I hated so very much. But deep down, I think he thought it was good for me to have the structure of a workday. "So, what are you doing up here? I thought I heard voices."

I looked up at him, trying not to look totally panic stricken. Could he have heard Kip, too? Of course not. He couldn't have heard Kip because Kip wasn't actually here. "I was on the phone with Vivian." I stretched the truth just a smidgen.

"How is she?" Alex asked, as we lapsed into the very familiar business of raising a family.

"Great. She aced her first Spanish test."

"Of course she did." Alex went toward the bedroom loosening his tie and my heart fluttered nervously, thinking that I was going to get caught with Kip in our bed.

"I know. But you know her, she ties herself up into knots beforehand and then gets everything right."

"Whose kid is she?" Alex laughed. Vivian was so much like Alex – ambitious, solid, normal.

"I have no idea." I looked for Kip in our now empty bed and my gaze accidentally fell on the *Bridget & Kip* box. And Alex's eyes, of course, followed.

"Are we shelving something?" 'Shelving something' was Alex's way of saying I'd given up again. A chill went down my spine as the echo of Kip's words "Quitting again?" whispered in my mind. I shook his voice out of my head.

"No." I lied, not wanting to let Alex down, yet again. "I was just looking at some old notes for reference."

"Reference?"

"Yeah, I'm kind of stuck and I was referring to old notes."

He nodded before chiding me, "Just don't get distracted by your old stories. Focus on your work and finish it." He always simplified things like this. It made me crazy. He honestly thought if I just worked a little harder that the endings I was seeking would magically come to me. As if I hadn't spent hours staring at blank pages, staring at one sentence over and over again, trying to find the sentence to follow it. His formula was simple. Work hard. Success follows. It always worked for him. But not for me. It was never that simple for me.

"You are a great writer, Bella. You can do this," Alex said, ever supportive. Yet as supportive as he was, I couldn't shake the feeling that I was always, in some way, disappointing him. I knew he didn't quite understand my "process." The idea of putting words on paper and making them into something was a completely foreign concept to him. I knew it hurt him when I retreated into myself to find those words. I knew that Alex thought that sometimes, my writing sent me a little bit off the deep end, which he may have been right about. OK, he was definitely right about that. I also knew that Alex truly believed I was a great writer. And every time I didn't finish, I failed him on top of failing myself.

"Hey," he said as he lifted my chin and forced me to look at him, eyeing me suspiciously again. "You sure you're ok?" Alex was no dummy. We'd been together more than 25 years. He knew something was up. And I so wanted to tell him. *No. I'm not ok. My children have gone to college and taken my identity with them. I'm a complete failure without them. And, oh, by the way, honey, I think I may be losing my mind.*

I took a deep breath and looked right into his soft, chestnut eyes. His eyes were so downy-looking they reminded me of cashmere, gentle and warm and safe. I just wanted to climb into them and hide away from the rest of the world. "I'm fine," I whispered and curled into his chest once again.

Fortunately, Alex made good on his promise to take me out to dinner. If I had to spend one more minute in that house with Kip lurking around, I was going to scream. But as glad I was to be out, part of me wanted to be home and hiding under the covers. Being out I felt exposed and naked and strangely alone.

We went to a local favorite restaurant. Good food. Good service. But my head was swimming with the events of the afternoon and I was having trouble making conversation. My gut was just filled with emptiness, like something was missing and I couldn't quite put my finger on what it was. I knew I had bigger problems than the children being gone, but I was ignoring them. The reality was, I would've rather thrown a pity-party about missing my children than deal with the fact that I had a ten-minute conversation with someone who doesn't actually exist.

"You are a million miles away from me, Belly." He was right about that. I wasn't quite sure what planet my brain was currently residing on. "Belly," Alex repeated since I didn't answer him the first time.

"I know. I'm sorry," I said. I was sorry. It wasn't his fault I was a basket case.

"You know, they're only two hours away. They'll be back for Thanksgiving in just a few weeks."

"I know." A few weeks? Was he kidding? That was a lifetime from now.

"Kids go away to college all the time, Bella. It's not the end of the world."

And that, ladies and gentlemen, is what I hated about my husband. Literally hated. He always said that whatever particular thing I was feeling at any particular time was no big deal. He was so nonchalant about his feelings, and mine for that matter, that sometimes I really wanted to kill him. Or at the very least, throw something at him.

My temper flicked on like a switch, and it took every fiber of my being to resist the urge to throw my drink in his face. "You know, Alex. It is a big deal to me," I barked at him in a hushed whisper. "I know it is," he said. "But it's not like they've joined a cult and we're never going to see them again, they're just in college." He laughed, amusing himself, and sipped his wine, miscalculating my anger.

"It's not funny," I sneered.

"I know it's not funny, hon," he tried to backpedal. "I just think you're overreacting a bit." Unfortunately, for Alex, he backpedaled himself right off a cliff.

"Overreacting?"

"You know what I mean, Bella." He reached across the table to take my hand but I pulled it away. Of course I was overreacting. I always did. I was an over-emotional kind of girl. I always have been. But if there was one thing I hated, it was being called out on my hyper-reactivity. We'd been married so long I couldn't understand why Alex kept trying to change this one thing about me. We should've put it in our vows: Love, Honor, Cherish, and Tolerate her drama. He looked at me kindly, but I think he knew the damage was done. "I don't want to fight with you, baby. I just don't want you to let this get you too crazy, ok?" He didn't know how poor his choice of words was.

A better woman would've just let it go. But, unfortunately for Alex, I'm just not that good of a woman. "You think I'm crazy to be missing my children."

He rolled his eyes, knowing right then our evening was over. "That's not what I meant and you know it," he said to me sternly, like he was talking to a petulant child. Which is, of course, exactly what I was acting like, but it annoyed me nonetheless.

"I'll tell you what I know. I know that you haven't mentioned either of their names since they left." That was true. He hadn't said the words "Holden" or "Vivian" since before we took them off to school, like maybe I'd forget them if he didn't bring them up.

"It's only been two days, Bella," he answered reasonably, calmly.

I barely heard him. I was far too busy trying to get him to react to my drama. "I know that what really makes me crazy is you not having any emotions!"

"Really? I have no emotions? That's what you think?" he asked me evenly. Still so damn calm.

I was about to tell him he was so shut down he reminded me of a robot, when I caught a glimpse of a familiar face sitting at a table across the room. She looked kind of like me. Or a younger, prettier, taller, thinner, better-haired version of me anyway. It had to be Bridget, wearing her 1990s office wear, a light blue silk blouse with black, wide-leg pants. She was sitting alone at a table for two, checking her watch like she was waiting for someone. I closed my eyes tightly to see if she would go away, and was surprised when I opened them to find she was gone.

"Do you really think I have no emotions? Do you honestly believe that I don't miss them too, Belly?" Between the brief appearance of Bridget and the softness in Alex's voice, my anger evaporated just slightly. But I still wanted to be mad at him. I wanted him to hurt the way I was hurting. "Mirabelle?" Again, he tried to take my hand, and this time I let him. He pulled me toward him and then leaned over the table. "I do miss them. A lot. Just because I don't wear my heart on my sleeve like you do doesn't mean I'm made of stone."

Of course, I knew he wasn't made of stone. I never would've fallen in love with him in the first place if he was. Though I was still mad, I contemplated apologizing. I hated the way he made me feel ashamed of being outwardly emotional, like there was something wrong with feeling and reacting to those emotions. But I knew I was the one being difficult here, as always. I sighed and got ready to tell him I was sorry, but when I looked up, I saw Bridget over his left shoulder, waving frantically to me from the ladies' room doorway. She was desperately trying to get my attention and since I didn't really want to apologize anyway, I said, "I need to go to the ladies' room. I'll be back in a minute."

"What?" Alex looked at me with crinkled eyebrows.

"I'll be right back." And I ran off before he could stop me.

In the ladies' room, Bridget was fixing her face and fluffing her "Rachel" hair in the mirror. "Oh good. I was afraid you wouldn't come." This was perfectly normal, right? Chasing an imaginary person into the ladies' room.

"I almost didn't." I said as we looked each other over. She looked like a 1990s version of me, though she had an air of confidence about her that made her seem like she knew what she was doing. I was pretty sure I never had that. "So, um what do you want?" I asked her. "I'm kind of in the middle of something."

She sat down in the chair in the corner. "I just wanted to tell you not to let Kip bully you. Don't let him tell you when to write. He doesn't understand that the words don't just appear on the page. I understand you. I know you can't write when you don't feel like it."

"Ok. Thanks for the warning. I guess."

"Just be aware. Kip is a giant pain in the ass when he gets something in his head and right now that something is you. He will ruin everything for you."

I was beginning to see that Kip was right. Bridget was like me – just all the things I hated about myself. Blaming other people for her failures. Taking things out on everyone else. Turns out, all my flaws make for one annoying character. Her whining and melodramatic warnings were not what I wanted to hear right now. Suddenly, I just wanted to get back to Alex and tell him how sorry I was. "I can handle Kip," I told Bridget.

"He's going to put a lot of pressure on you to start writing again."

"So, I'll deal with him. Now, I really need to get back to my dinner."

"I'm not kidding. He will fuck up your life and tell you it's for your own good." Nice mouth, Nineties-Bella.

"Listen, Bridget. Being that neither you nor he actually exist, I'm quite sure I can handle him." I turned to leave the bathroom, having had quite enough of this nonsense.

"This isn't just about Kip. It's my life, too. You'd better think really hard before you change *my* life forever." She said as I walked away, the door closing slowly behind me.

Ugh. No wonder I never finished that book. Was I that bitchy in the nineties? I'd have to ask Alex next time he was speaking to me.

I sat back down at the table with Alex like nothing had happened. "Are you ok? What was that all about?" Alex asked, clearly confused by my rapid exit.

"Would you please stop asking me if I'm ok. You know I'm not." I pleaded with him, but the damage had been done.

"That's *why* I'm asking, Belly." He growled back, "Your emotionless husband actually understands that you're not doing ok and, god forbid, I want to help you. I actually care about your well-being."

I said nothing. What could I say? He was right and I was wrong. If I didn't feel crappy before, I sure as hell did now.

"Talk to me, baby." He ordered me. But not in a comforting way that made me want to tell him what I was feeling. He said it in a way that I knew he had already lost patience with me, and no matter what I said now I couldn't get it back.

"Can we just go home?" I choked out, doing my very best to keep my emotions under wraps.

"Fine." Alex said, taking my failure to communicate as rejection.

****

We drove home in absolute silence. I could feel Alex's anger steeping like a cup of tea. It wouldn't boil over though. He'd keep it all under control, like he always did. I was sorry that

I had ruined our evening. I didn't mean to. That wasn't my intention. But, honestly, Alex's anger invigorated me.

Sometimes, I really enjoyed the roller coaster of emotions that an argument brought to our marriage. I didn't purposely try to get him mad at me, but arguing with him made me feel more connected to him somehow. Though, I was pretty sure it made him feel more disconnected from me. But when I got mad at him, it gave me an opportunity to say things in the heat of an argument that I wouldn't say to him otherwise. Sometimes they were things that needed saying. Sometimes they weren't.

At least I wasn't feeling so badly about the kids anymore. And I had almost completely forgotten that I was going crazy.

Alex didn't wait for me or open the door for me when we got out of the car. He just walked right in the house without a backward glance. Sometimes, like right now for instance, I wondered why he put up with me. I followed behind him, watching my footsteps. Hating myself for being who I was, the way I was. I walked a little faster, trying to catch him before he went upstairs. I was done with him being mad. Now, everything just felt wrong.

"Alex," I called from behind just as he got to the stairs. He kept walking. I lunged for him and managed to catch his hand before he got more than a few steps up. He stopped but didn't turn around. "I'm sorry," I whispered. I searched for the words that would earn his forgiveness. But I didn't really have any. I didn't know why I started an argument. Maybe I just wanted to feel something other than loss. And anger was better. Or it felt better at the time. Nothing felt better now. "I didn't mean to," was the best I could come up with.

I watched his shoulders rise and fall as he took a deep breath before turning to me.

"I'm sorry I hurt your feelings." I said meekly.

He came down two steps, so now he was only one step above me, but he still didn't say anything.

"I just feel sort of alone in this right now," I told him, the first truly honest thing I'd said to him all night. That was exactly what I felt. Alone. And if I had to get him angry at me to get him to say out loud that he missed them too, the evening wasn't a total loss.

He pulled me up a step so I was standing on the same stair as him, though I was still a great deal shorter than he was. "Mirabelle, you are not alone in this. You have me. Always." He pulled my hand to his lips and kissed it softly.

"I know. I just forget sometimes." I told him, just to end the fight. I was lying. The truth was I *was* alone in this. Of course Alex missed the children. But it wasn't in the same way I did. Alex's identity was never dependent on the children, or even on me. Alex was always *Alex the Account Manager* or *Alex the Product Manager*. I was the one who was defined solely by the people around me. The best I could do was *Bella the Crazy Lunch Lady* and that certainly didn't help to define me. At least, I hoped it didn't.

Alex wrapped his arms around me. "Don't forget, okay," he whispered into my neck. I sighed, still feeling alone, but relieved to have his forgiveness. He turned to head upstairs, but I couldn't crawl into bed. Not now. My head was busy hating myself for being such an awful wife. I heard the familiar monologue in my head that made me long for my notebook and favorite pen.

He sensed my resistance immediately. "Come to bed, Bella." He snaked an arm around my waist, and tried to will me upstairs.

"I'll be up soon. I need to do some scribbling." Which was code for "I need to put my neurotic thoughts down on paper."

I watched him swallow his words, his frustration. I wondered if it burned his throat. Finally, he sighed. "Don't be too long."

I turned away from him, but he grabbed me harshly and kissed me hard on the mouth with so much passion, I almost changed my mind. Almost. "I'll be up soon," I lied again.

****

I kept all my journals in the dining room china cabinet. I know some people who actually keep china in their china cabinets. Mine was stocked with old notebooks, filled with every emotion I'd ever had since high school. My current journal was a recycled purple marble notebook that Vivian needed for some class in middle school, but had never used.

From the silver drawer, I pulled out the special pen that I bought myself as a "writer's gift." I had a teacher in college who told me that every time I started a new project, I should buy myself something as a reward for beginning such an undertaking. Given my track record, I probably should've waited until I actually finished something before buying myself a treat. I curled up with a blanket under the front window and opened my notebook, pouring out my head onto the paper.

I was writing about how when the kids were little, the weight of the fear of losing them almost brought me to my knees. I remembered one morning, putting them on the bus and just feeling crippled that something was going to happen to take them away from me. I loved them so much, but I could never understand what I had ever done to get so lucky. It seemed inevitable that sooner or later I would lose them.

When did they go from needing me for everything to needing me for nothing? I mourned the loss of those toddler days. Sure, I complained *then* about never having a break, never getting any sleep, never being able to even go to the bathroom alone. Still, I would go back to the sleepless nights and those chaotic days in a heartbeat. I missed being needed. I missed being wanted.

Tears were blurring my words as I scrawled away. I was oddly happy in my misery. I loved having a good cry. It was such a release. Sometimes, I thought, maybe I started arguments with Alex just so that I could have a good cry. I really wasn't a very good wife. I found myself feeling so tired of the mediocrity in my life – mediocre wife, mediocre mother, mediocre writer. As I sniffled away, I reached for a tissue and realized that I was not alone.

For a fleeting moment, in the dim lighting, I though maybe Alex had come down to attempt to lure me upstairs, but it wasn't Alex. It was Emily. Poor, sad, pathetic Emily, sitting on the couch.

"I know how you feel," she whispered. Emily's voice was so sad, it almost always came out as a whisper. "There's nothing worse than losing a child."

I looked at Emily, her shoulders hunched with the burden of her loss. I didn't want to find myself in the same category as her. She was so limp and lame looking. Worn down miles beyond her years, I pitied her, so lost and lonely. I wondered when in *The Woodpecker* this Emily was from. "Have you seen Daniel?" I asked her.

She closed her eyes tight at the mention of his name and shook her head violently. "Not since he was three."

I was glad this Emily was from early in the story. Daniel would visit her soon and things would get better for her. A little better for a little while anyway.

Turns out Emily had very little to say. She just sat there while I scribbled away. It shouldn't have surprised me that Emily was so quiet. I made her that way. Resigned and sad. Bridget and Kip had been so insistent on me, so combative. Their visits were irritating and harassing. But I really didn't mind Emily sitting there in solidarity with me while I missed my children.

CHAPTER 4

ALEX WAS MAD AT ME in the morning for not coming upstairs until very late, but he pretended he wasn't, which I found even more annoying than if he just acted pissed off to begin with. He always did this when he was angry with me. He was never unkind or nasty. He never told me that he was mad or what he was mad about. He just had a certain coldness about him that if you weren't married to him for twenty years, you'd probably never notice. I'm not sure even he noticed. But I noticed. He was distant and aloof, which accomplished very little except make me mad at him in return.

So, he left for work in his passive-aggressive state and I did some of my daily crap, I mean, chores. I was folding already-wrinkled laundry due to my terrible habit of letting things sit in the dryer until they wrinkled beyond recognition. I pulled out a t-shirt that I expected to be Alex's, but turned out to be Holden's. My knees buckled just a bit as I held it to my face. Even though it just came out of the laundry, it still smelled like him. I couldn't name a distinct smell, it just seemed to have Holden's essence imbedded in its fibers. I folded it neatly and ran my hands over it to press out the wrinkles. Sighing, I picked up something else to fold, part of me hoping I would find another stray object of Holden's or Vivian's, part of me hoping I wouldn't, when I heard a crash from the kitchen. I dropped Alex's favorite grey t-shirt back in the basket and went to investigate, though I was pretty sure I knew what I was going to find there. I just wasn't exactly sure who.

Tiptoeing into the kitchen, I called out "Hello?" as I peeked around the corner. "Is someone there?"

On the floor sat a young man, maybe nineteen years old. Tall and lanky, he scrambled to his feet and picked up the garbage can. "Uh, sorry. I tripped over the bin. I'm a bit clumsy," he said with an English accent.

"Daniel," I whispered. I knew him immediately. Even before he spoke in that ever-so-charming accent, I knew him. He had a sadness behind his eyes that none of my other characters did, except maybe Emily.

"You recognize me, then?" he said, reciting a line of dialogue directly from *The Woodpecker* as he got up off the floor, wiping his hands on his jeans.

I nodded, with a smile, glad to see him despite his appearance's implications regarding my mental state. Daniel was one of my all-time favorite characters. He was warm and funny and sensitive. He was sweet and vulnerable, yet had a quiet strength to him despite, or maybe because of, the difficulties in his life. He was just a nice kid stuck in a super ugly situation. If only I had been able to flesh Emily into some sort of interesting character, instead of the needy, pathetic, wimp she turned into, I might have actually finished their story.

"Are you surprised to see me?" he asked.

"A little, I guess." The truth was, I wasn't surprised at all. I was starting to get used to my little friends showing up and scolding me for not finishing any of my books, for forgetting about them, abandoning them.

"I thought you'd be shocked," he said, just a little bit disappointed. "My mother was shocked."

"I know she was." I knew well how shocked Emily was when Daniel showed up on her doorstep after being missing for fifteen years. In fact, that was the scene I wrote first when I started *The Woodpecker* – Daniel ringing Emily's doorbell and Emily trying to process the reappearance of her son. Poor, poor victim Emily. Her Daniel taken away by her bastard ex-husband and she goes on to marry yet another bastard and takes on the care of his ill-behaved children.

"So I've been living with my mother and her git of a husband for a few weeks now."

"How's that going?" I asked, but immediately regretted it. I knew it wasn't going well. I knew that Emily's husband was indeed, in Daniel's words, a git.

Daniel shrugged and jammed his hands in his pockets like he always did when he was nervous, or had something he didn't want to say. Come to think of it, that was something Holden did, too. "It's okay. Mum's great. I've been missing her my whole life…" he trailed off.

"And now?" I asked him, trying to find out how much he knew about his mother's husband.

"Well, it's just that…Thomas…isn't especially nice." He struggled to find the right words.

I couldn't help but feel badly for Daniel. I had such a soft spot for him, such a kind and gentle soul. He reminded me so much of Holden. I knew I had written his story out of my fear of losing my own children. I knew it wasn't just a coincidence that Daniel showed up right after I found one of Holden's shirts in the laundry.

"I know. I am sorry for that," I told him. Daniel didn't seem to have gotten to the point in the story where things get really bad for him and his mother.

"You do know, don't you?" he asked me, and I nodded. "Could you maybe tell me what happens next?"

I wasn't sure if I should. I knew that Daniel, Emily, Kip and Bridget were all appearing out of my own neurosis or imagination or whatever, but there had to be some sort of cosmic ramifications for messing with their stories like that. Sort of like time-travel and how you can't mess with things in the past without disastrous consequences for the present.

"I mean, right now," Daniel continued. "Thomas is away and Mum and I are getting along great, even with the kids." The kids. Emily's stepchildren, who were awful as a general rule. "I just can't help feeling that something really bad is about to happen."

Daniel's instincts were right on. I looked down at my slippers, ashamed of the torture I inflicted on this poor boy in my story. Something really bad was indeed about to happen.

"She's hiding something from me. I know she is."

I could only stare at him. He seemed so real, so sad and he was so bloody right.

"He hurts her, doesn't he?" Daniel asked me with a crack in his voice that told me he didn't really want to know the answer, or he already knew the answer. I couldn't lie to him. I had to prepare him at least a little bit for the ugliness to come. I nodded ever so slightly.

"I knew it!" He ran his hands through his disheveled hair as he so often did. "Why does she stay with him?"

"She loves him," was the only answer I could muster. It was exactly what Emily would say.

"No she doesn't!" he yelled. "You know she doesn't really love him! She just thinks she does." He gritted his teeth and shook his head. Daniel was right, of course. Emily didn't love Thomas. I didn't really have a good reason for Emily staying with Thomas. Maybe that's why I didn't finish them.

Shifting gears on me, Daniel whispered, "Is something bad going to happen?" A solitary tear drifted down his cheek.

Daniel clearly hadn't gotten to the big fight and the moment Thomas tells him he has to leave. I almost reached out to hold him and tell him everything was going to be ok. But then I remembered that he wasn't real. God, he was so real to me, though. I could feel his sadness overwhelming me. I ran my hands through my own hair. "I don't really know, Daniel."

"You don't know?"

"I'm sorry. I don't."

"I don't understand, why don't you just finish us? How can you stand it…not knowing what happens?" He looked at me with such honest confusion, it hurt.

And all I could do was shrug and watch the confusion on his face melt into disappointment.

"Is she going to be okay? Mum, I mean?" he said, looking down at his shoes. "Can you at least tell me that?"

I toyed with the idea of lying to him, but figured he would know a lie from the truth.

"You'll just have to see, Daniel. I can't tell you what happens next." I was far too cowardly to tell him that he was going to ask Emily to leave Thomas and go away with him. I was too afraid to tell him what Emily's answer was going to be. I so wanted to reassure him that everything was going to be okay, even though it wasn't. I had no happy ending planned for Emily and Daniel. I had no ending at all.

****

I wandered into work totally absentmindedly that day. I was glad, for a change, that I had no classroom hours that day. It allowed me to be completely checked-out. I had the luxury of not having to make any kind of cognitive connection with anyone. I mostly ignored the children in the lunchroom, with the exception of little Billy Finnegan, a first grader diagnosed with Oppositional Defiance Disorder, meaning he was constantly oppositional and defiant. I caught him in the bathroom, punching other first graders. But I barely had the energy to punish him. It wouldn't make any difference, anyway. Billy would come in tomorrow with some new, even more troubling behavior.

Daniel's appearance weighed on me like an anvil around my neck. It was getting harder coming face-to-face with my demons like this, and it was getting more and more difficult to convince myself that I wasn't completely psychotic.

On my way home, I stopped at the grocery store figuring it wouldn't be a bad idea for me to make a nice dinner for Alex and me. The way to his heart had always been through his stomach, and I hoped it would be a nice peace offering.

Unfortunately, every face I saw in the grocery store reminded me of some character I had written somewhere in my life, pesky reminders of everything I hadn't accomplished. I was positive I saw Julia, Emily's pink-haired friend from *The Woodpecker,* hovering in the meat department and Jack, the John F. Kennedy, Jr./Bridget's love interest character, from *Bridget & Kip.*

I kept my head down and kept moving so as not to engage anybody. "I am definitely losing it," I told myself. But if I was really losing it, I wouldn't be so aware of the fact that I was losing it, would I? I felt far too sane to be crazy.

The only person in the store who didn't seem to be a ghost from my past was a little old lady in a lime-green dress. Her dress was covered in white polka dots and had a plunging neckline you don't often see on a woman in her eighties. I so wish I had written this character, that she had come from my imagination. Her white hair was perfectly coiffed in tight, but soft curls. Her skin was translucent, wrinkled and covered in brown spots, but this woman was absolutely radiant. Her elderly husband, though not as flamboyantly dressed, doted on this lovely woman as they did their shopping, reaching things on the high shelves for her. Though, he shuffled when he walked, his shuffle had a bit of a strut. He was so clearly pleased to be with this beautiful woman. Their obvious enthusiasm for life was so adorable I wanted to follow them around the store. Here was this old woman in this crazy dress with her sweet husband looking completely…happy. Was that what happy looked like?

I sat in my car for a few moments after finishing my shopping, stalking the elderly couple through my windshield as they walked to their car. I was lime green with envy. I wanted that. I wanted to be so comfortable in my skin that I could wear whatever I felt like wearing, be whomever I felt like being. I wanted to be a writer, even if it made me feel weird and different. I wanted to be who I was with no apologies. And I wanted to live to be a hundred with Alex walking proudly by my side. If only I knew how to get there.

****

Alex returned from work that night, his warmth restored. As I stood stirring my caramelized onions on the stove, he came in, hugged me from behind and nuzzled my neck. He had apparently forgiven me at some point during the day or had forgotten that he was mad at me in the first place, or maybe it was the onions. I was glad he was done being mad. And I was really glad that he didn't ask me if I was ok. As great a job as I was doing keeping it together, I was still feeling like I was falling apart on the inside.

We made idle chatter while I finished making dinner. He told me stuff about his work that I didn't quite understand, but pretended I did. I told him about Billy Finnegan punching kids in the bathroom.

"You may hate your job, but at the end of the day, you have way better stories than I do," Alex commented, grinning.

"I guess that's true." I agreed with a small smile. "Sit down, dinner's ready."

He sat at the table and I served and joined him. I waited for him to make some awkward comment about how we were going to be eating dinner alone for the rest of our lives because that's what I was thinking.

"Mirabelle, can we talk?"

Uh oh. My full name was never a good sign. Perhaps I hadn't been forgiven for last night after all.

"Of course."

"I mean talk. Not fight." He reminded me.

And with that, my shame for last night's argument returned. Part of me wanted to slap his pretty face for bringing it up, but a bigger part of me knew that he was right. He usually was. I did have a propensity for starting fights with Alex when I was upset about something that had nothing to do with him. I loved that he knew that about me. I loved him and hated him for that at the same time. I loved that he was my strength, my rock. But I hated that I needed a rock in the first place. I loved that he knew when to walk on eggshells around me, but hated that I was such an emotional wreck that he had to walk on eggshells around me. None of that was actually his fault. When it came right down to it, Alex was everything to me. He always had been and I didn't want to be alone in this. I didn't want to be alone at all. So I nodded silently and was careful not to start a fight.

We talked, and ate, and drank and even laughed. We talked about the kids and what we missed, and what we didn't miss. We talked about when they were babies and what we used to call the golden years, when they were eight or nine and old enough not to need us for every little thing, but not old enough to be getting into any kind of trouble.

"Do you remember when Holden colored himself brown?" Alex asked.

I laughed. "He wanted to be a reindeer." We'd actually missed the entire coloring event itself. He had brought markers up to his room and was supposed to be sleeping. By the time we checked on him, he was entirely brown and sound asleep.

"Everything was brown except for his little nose." Alex reminded me, wrinkling his own nose. "Which was red, of course, so he could be like Rudolph."

I thought, at first, talking about them, Holden and Vivian, was going to make me sad. But it didn't. It filled my heart with warmth remembering the toddler stories I'd almost forgotten, or at least hadn't thought about in a while. It connected me to Alex in a way I could never be connected to anyone else. Ever.

"I know it's hard for you with them gone, honey," Alex said as he took my hand.

"You know, it's not so much that they're gone. I mean it is, but it's more than that." I sighed and drank some more wine. "I just feel like I should be more than I am right now. I feel like first, I was 'Alex's wife' and then I went to being 'Holden & Vivian's mom' and now I'm just Mirabelle."

He chuckled and drank some wine himself. "Darling, you are never 'just Mirabelle.'"

"You know what I mean. It's not so much about the kids. It's about me, and not knowing who or what I am without the kids. I feel like I just got laid-off from a job that I've had for eighteen years."

"You're still their mother, Bella. You will always be their mother. And I know it doesn't feel like it now, but they will always need you."

"That may be, but who am I supposed to be now?"

"Sounds like it's time for you to write another book." Alex looked at me in that way he does when he knows more about me than I know about myself. What he didn't know was that this was quite possibly the worst suggestion he could possibly have made to me.

"Another book to not finish." I sighed and finished what was left in my glass.

"What?" He looked at me funny, like he was afraid I was going to start another fight.

"Alex, it's just that, I've started so many things I haven't finished. I'm just tired of it."

"Well, if it bothers you so much, then you should finish them." He said matter-of-factly with a shrug.

Oh great, not you, too, I almost said, but then I'd have to tell Alex about my delusions, which I just couldn't bring myself to do. Instead, I said, "I'm just so damn afraid, Alex. I'm terrified that I missed my chance. All the years I poured into everything else, saying my career didn't matter to me. All the time I poured into children that no longer need me. What am I left with?"

He scooted his chair closer to me. "Well, first and foremost, you're left with me." He put a hand on my cheek. I leaned into it as if he could hold up my entire frame with his fingertips, and my anxiety melted away.

"I suppose that's not so bad." I told him. The great thing about being with the same person for twenty years is that sometimes, all they needed to do was touch you for you to know exactly who you're supposed to be.

CHAPTER 5

I WOKE UP FROM A DREAM with a start. I couldn't remember the dream, but whatever it was, it yanked me out of a deep sleep and into the darkness with a pounding heart, sweaty hair and a completely unsettled feeling. Beside me, Alex slept peacefully, with his back to me. I rolled toward him and tossed an arm over his bare shoulder, hoping to wake him or fall back to sleep myself, whichever happened first. I listened to Alex's soft breathing, his chest rising and falling rhythmically, but it did little to settle my nerves. My heart still thundered and my hands were shaking.

I rolled onto my back and stared at the ceiling for a moment, trying to recall what had frightened me so much in my dreams, but yet, not really wanting to know. Finally, resigned to wakefulness, I threw off the covers, wrapped a robe around me and headed downstairs for some water.

Down in the kitchen, I eased the dimmer switch up really slowly. I hated that pain you get in your eyes when the light comes on too brightly, too quickly, so Alex installed dimmers for me on all the light switches in the house. As the lights came up slowly, I recognized a familiar figure leaning against the sink.

"Well, I'll be damned. I thought I'd never see you again," he said, dressed in a tuxedo, the bow tie undone, sipping an amber liquid from a crystal glass. Same guy from the gas station. Same tux. Same swagger. "So, uh, what's a pretty girl like you doing in a dump like this?" he asked flirtatiously.

I sighed, loudly. I had been dreading the reappearance of Cody and was hoping that his cameo at the gas station was all I was going to see of him. He was so cliché, so poorly written. No story I wrote around him could possibly save him. I sometimes toyed with the idea of bringing in a woman to save him. Or maybe turning him into a vampire or an alien. But I also thought killing him off just might be the best option. I just couldn't think of a good enough reason to keep him alive. "What do you want?" I growled at him as I went to the cabinet for a glass.

Cody took a swig from the glass in his hand. "Now, is that any way to greet an old friend, beautiful?" he drawled in his stupid, cliché bad-boy kind of way that was supposed to be irresistible, but was really just irritating.

I rolled my eyes and filled my glass with water from the dispenser in the refrigerator door. "I'd hardly call you an old friend, Cody." Seeing Kip, Daniel, and Emily, and even Bridget for that matter, was fine. But Cody, not so much. I was starting to get a little bit annoyed by, and just a little bit scared of my crazy brain.

Cody moved smoothly from the sink to the fridge, in what seemed like one giant, slithering step. He leaned in real close to me, "Well, what would you call me then?"

"Ugh." I recoiled at the odor of him. "Someone who's had too much single malt." I waved my hand in front of my nose to diffuse the smell of him and marveled at the power of my own imagination that made it possible for me to smell the scotch on his breath.

Cody smiled crookedly. "You got me there, gorgeous." He took another swig and swallowed, finishing with a sharp exhale, like he just drank cold lemonade on a really hot day, not throat-warming scotch. "So, aren't you going to ask me what I'm doing here?"

"I know what you're doing here. You're here to remind me of all my failures. Blah blah blah." I knew I was being a little snarky with my bad-boy character who had some dangerous proclivities, but it was the middle of the night and I was half-asleep and very cranky. Not to mention, I was growing more and more curious with each visit as to how far each character would go to get an ending out of me. Cody, temperamental, over-reacting Cody, was just perfect to find out exactly what I was dealing with. He could show me just how crazy I really was.

"Your failures?" he wrinkled his forehead and scoffed in disgust. "What makes you think this is about you? I'm here to talk about me."

"Of course, you are." Leave it to Cody to make everything revolve around him.

"So, tell me," he leaned over the counter, "What's next for me?"

There it was. The $64,000 question. "I don't know." I shrugged off his question, filled my water and placed the glass on the counter. My eyes were starting to blur with exhaustion and I tried unsuccessfully to suppress a yawn.

"You don't know? What the hell does that mean, you don't know?" he raised his voice to me. Always so quick to anger.

"Shhhh. Don't yell at me." I scolded him.

"Why not? Who the hell is going to hear me?"

He had a point there. It's not like Alex was going to hear him. But I still didn't want him yelling at me. "I hear you," I said firmly. "And I don't like being yelled at." I just had no patience for his bullshit, because that's exactly what it was: no depth, no substance, just arrogant bullshit.

"Well, I don't like being left alone, unfinished for years. It's been *years,* hasn't it! Years stuck alone!" He screamed. "Why the fuck didn't you finish me?"

"Stop it, Cody!" I said to him in the voice I generally saved for the second-grade lunch wave. "If you want to talk to me, you have to stop yelling."

Cody moved in even closer to me. He was short and strong and he smelled of sweat, cigarettes, and whisky. "I'll stop yelling," he whispered coldly, "as soon as you tell me what happens next."

I shivered, finally fully awake. He was so close and so real. He was suddenly less cliché and more terrifying, and I hated him more than ever. One part of my brain told me he wasn't real, he wasn't there. But the other part of my brain was sending panic impulses through my whole body, starting to feel very afraid of Cody. "I don't know. I didn't get that far," I said softly and looked at the ground, feeling the shame of my failures on my shoulders yet again.

"You don't know?" he growled quietly through gritted teeth. "We'll see about that." He stared at me so coldly it made me shiver.

I slowly lifted my eyes to meet his gaze, his eyes filled with fury, my knees buckled ever so slightly. Still, I refused to let my own imagination bully me like that. "Is that a threat?" I asked him incredulously.

"Take it any way you want." He rocked backward onto his heels, smiled creepily and sipped more scotch from his glass that never seemed to empty.

"You're not real," I reminded myself and him. "You can't hurt me."

"Can't I?" he answered, staring me down. And before I could respond, before I could even think, he backhanded my water glass clear across the kitchen. I turned away to shield my eyes and when I turned back, he was gone.

"Bella?" Alex called from the top of the stairs. "Is that you down there?" I heard the rhythmic thumping of his feet bouncing down the stairs. "Are you OK?"

I was too stunned to answer him. I stood there, my heart galloping in my chest. That did not just happen, I told myself, trying to convince myself it was just my imagination. Yet, when I looked around, there was glass everywhere. And I do mean, everywhere.

"Honey?" Alex's voice grew closer.

In a panic, I stepped forward to pick up the shards that were sprayed all over the kitchen. I stepped squarely on a piece of glass and cried out.

"Bella?" I heard Alex's footsteps quicken. My brain scrambled to think of an explanation for this mess.

"I'm ok! Stay out, I broke a glass." I called, trying to buy some time. I needed a few more moments to collect myself before facing him.

"It's ok, honey, let me help you." Before I knew it, he was standing behind me, bare-chested in his slippers and pj pants. He stooped down beside me and picked up a big piece.

"Jeez, Belly, what'd you do? There's glass everywhere." He stood up and looked around, puzzled.

I shook my head, fighting back fear, holding back the tears until finally, I came up with a quasi-plausible lie. "I tripped." I choked out. "I tripped and the glass flew out of my hand."

"It looks like you threw it across the room," Alex said with a chuckle as he pulled the broom out of the crevice between the fridge and the pantry.

His laughter was enough to break me. Tears flooded out of my eyes.

Alex's laughter turned to alarm. "Belly, it's just a glass. Don't cry."

"It's not that, I –" I looked for the words to tell him what happened. I wanted to tell him, I didn't want to be alone in this mess. I wanted someone to tell me I wasn't as crazy as I felt at that very moment.

"What is it then?" He looked at me with such kindness, such concern. I just couldn't do it to him. I couldn't burden him with this much crazy. I had to do a better job dealing with everything I was going through. I had to try and control these things that kept showing up in my head, or in my kitchen.

But how was Cody able to hit that glass? Or did he? Was I so crazy that I threw the glass myself? I tried to remember throwing a glass across the room because that truly was the only logical explanation for what just happened. All I could remember was Cody's rage and the back of his hand flying through that glass. Whatever it was that had just happened in the kitchen was too crazy for Alex. I couldn't tell him. I had to protect him from this.

"It's nothing." I shook my head. "I just had a bad dream, so I came down for a drink. I'm still half asleep, I think." I tried to smile, but I don't think I did.

Alex stroked my cheek and smiled at me like I was a little girl. Normally, I hated when he did that. It made me feel like a child, but right now, that was what I needed. I needed someone to take care of me. "Let's take a look at that cut," he said.

I sat down at the table and Alex crouched down to look at my injured foot. He carefully pulled the sliver of glass out and pressed a towel on it to stop the flow of blood. "It looks ok. Just keep pressure on it," he said before grabbing the broom. I watched the blood soak through the towel. Real blood. My blood. My head spun with the impossibility of it all.

"Why don't you go back to bed, Bella? I'll clean this up."

"N-no. I'll help you." I stammered in a panic, standing up on my non-injured foot, unwilling to be left alone.

"Really, honey. I've got this. Go get some sleep." He tried to push me toward the door.

"No!" I resisted firmly, stopping in my tracks.

He stopped and looked at me strangely. "Are you sure you're ok?"

"I'm fine. I just...I just don't want to be alone right now."

He wrapped his long arms around me and I felt completely safe. My heart settled back into a regular rhythm and I thanked my lucky stars for Alex. No matter how many times I pushed him away, he always fought his way back to me. Though I often wondered why he put up with me.

"OK, then. Let's clean this up and go back to bed together." He winked and smiled and this time I managed to muster a smile back. For him.

CHAPTER 6

OVER THE NEXT FEW DAYS, I was visited by all kinds of friends. I started thinking of them in terms of "friends" and "visits" because, outside of Cody's tantrum in the kitchen, that's what they seemed like and it seemed less frightening than calling them the "hallucinations" and "delusions" that they really were. They were just old friends, popping in to catch up and relive old times and maybe offer me some un-requested opinions on just how badly I'd screwed up my life. Bridget came by again with her annoying rants about what a pain in the ass Kip was, as if I didn't already know that. Kip showed up to defend himself, and nag me about my job. Emily sat on the edge of my bed last night, just to make sure I didn't get any sleep.

Monica came by in the middle of my yoga class wanting to know if she was going to end up with Peter. It was more than a little awkward having her yapping away in the middle of my downward dog.

"I just met him and yet I feel like I've known him my whole life," she babbled on giddily as I looked at her upside down through my legs.

I, of course, didn't tell her that she didn't know him at all. She thought she knew him because she was his landlord and she had been creeping around his apartment, going through his personal items, reading his mail and just generally being a snoop. Little did she know that Peter was a sub-letter, and all the exciting things she thought were his really belonged to a friend of his who was currently sailing around the world. Peter wasn't even his name. She called him that because that was what she read on his mail and on his lease, so she just assumed that was his name.

Monica was so blissfully in love with the idea of Peter that she didn't even notice that his quirky personality didn't even remotely match up with the world traveler things she found in his apartment. You'd think she would've guessed something was amiss, but she just didn't want to see it. Instead, all through my sun salutations, she begged me to keep writing so she could have the fairytale wedding she'd been planning since she was eight. I wanted to tell her that she should want me to write more so she could learn more about the man she was supposedly in love with, not for a wedding scene. But I didn't know how to talk to her without the rest of the people in yoga class noticing, so our conversation remained one-sided.

After days of everyone I encountered telling me to write, it was a marvelous change of pace when Peter was waiting outside the yoga studio after class to beg me NOT to finish his story which would reveal to Monica that he was nowhere near the person Monica thought he was.

"Please don't write anymore." He pleaded with me as he followed me to my ginormous minivan, my last bastion of motherhood.

"You want me to not write?" I said with a laugh. "That's refreshing"

"Don't you see?" he whined. "If you finish, she'll find out the truth about me."

"And what truth is that?" I asked, looking over my shoulder to make sure there was no one else in the parking lot to witness me talking to myself.

"That I'm not who I say I am. That the person she's in love with is not me. I'm not adventurous or passionate. I'm just sub-letting a better man's apartment. And his life."

Poor Peter, so sweet, and insecure and quirky. He was handsome enough, but not exceptional. He was super smart and warm and a just a little bit funny. He deserved better than a life where he spent all his time and energy pretending he was someone else.

"We could just stay right where we are in the story. Nothing has to change. Ever. She could just be in love with me forever," he explained matter-of-factly.

"True, but wouldn't you rather she love you for who you are and not who she thinks you are? Wouldn't you rather have someone who loves you just the way you are?" I asked, playing my own devil's advocate.

He looked at me like I'd just asked him the dumbest question ever. "No. I just want Monica." He was hopeless.

"Don't you feel badly about lying to her?" I asked him.

"Everyday. But sometimes we tell lies to protect the people we love...don't we?" He said knowingly before disappearing from the parking lot.

Peter had hit a nerve. I was wracked with guilt over not telling Alex about my so-called visits. I hated keeping things from him. I felt like a liar, even if it was only a lie of omission. But every time I got close to telling him, the whole story stuck in my throat. It just wouldn't come out.

I was getting used to them, my visitors. I know how crazy that sounds, but I was getting used to talking to myself. I just didn't feel all that crazy. I felt completely sane. And while many of my characters were annoying in their insistence that I finish their stories (yes, that means you, Kip), I was actually starting to look forward to seeing some of them. Was I that lonely? Maybe I was. Maybe I was just so damn lonely without my kids to hover over that I was having fun talking to my imaginary friends.

It was a Saturday when Kip came by for the third time. I wasn't sure why Kip seemed to appear more often than the others. Other than the fact that I created him at a time in my life when I hated my job, and I certainly found myself in that place again, in that ugly and confusing place where I constantly questioned my purpose.

Anyway, it was Saturday and Alex had to meet some clients for golf, so I was home cleaning my house that was already pretty darn clean. But sometimes I liked cleaning my house. It made me feel grounded and connected to my home, blasting music and scrubbing the layers of dirt off my life.

"Oh, that looks fun," came a caustic voice from behind me, as I scoured the kitchen floor on my hands and knees.

"Jeez, Kip!" I said, jumping out of my skin. "Do you always have to sneak up on me?"

"I think that is the nature of our relationship, isn't it?" Kip tossed his head back to get his long hair out of his eyes.

I dropped my scrub brush in the bucket. "I suppose so," I said with a half-sigh, half-smile sitting back on my heels. I know, I know. I shouldn't have been smiling. I should have been worried about my recently diminished mental stability. But Kip was familiar, and friendly, and funny. And I was tired of cleaning, anyway.

"So, how are you?" he jumped up on the kitchen counter, a maneuver I would have scolded Holden or Vivian or even Alex for attempting. But Kip wasn't real so it didn't matter if his butt was on my counter, did it?

"How am I? Aren't you going to ask me about my job?" I asked, getting to my feet. Kip never started a conversation without asking me (or Bridget) about work…unless he was up to something.

"Nah. I'm tired of hearing about your job." He answered, apparently forgetting that I knew he wasn't to be trusted.

"Okay, what are you up to, Kip?" I asked him.

"Nothing." He shrugged. "I just don't want to fight."

"But, you love to fight." It was true. Kip was one of those people who truly enjoyed arguing and forcing other people to defend their positions.

"I do not." He denied it, but I knew he knew I was right. "Can't we just talk, you know, like friends?"

"I think I'd rather fight," I said with a wink.

He stuck his tongue out at me. "OK, fine. Listen, I was thinking about something."

"Were you?" Here it comes, I thought. Kip's rationale about why I should quit my job, shrouded in concern for my well-being.

"I was thinking about why you wrote that story. My story."

"It's actually Bridget's story, but who's counting."

He looked at me, wounded, and said. "Whatever. Can I help it if I'm a scene stealer?"

"You probably could if you tried, but you won't."

He glared at me as though he was insulted, but I knew he really wasn't. Kip always enjoyed a good-natured ribbing. "Anyway," he continued, "I was thinking about the story and I was thinking about why you wrote it."

"Were you?"

"Why do you think you wrote that particular story at that particular point in your life?"

Just so we're clear here, I was not unaware that these were my thoughts that Kip was articulating. It was his tone, but the questions were all mine. I was baiting myself into analyzing my own actions.

"It just came to me one day…at work." I humored him.

"Uh huh. And you were how old when you started it?"

It was so long ago, and god, did I hate that job (see a pattern here?). It really wasn't a bad job – I got paid a lot of money for not very much work. Unfortunately, the people I worked for were abusive, disrespectful, and borderline psychotic. They'd go out for lunch at 11 and return at 3, drunk and disorderly. They lied to their clients and blamed me for it. But they brought money into the firm, so any complaints I made were largely ignored. I know it sounds like I'm making this up, but I'm not. It was my first job out of college and a true rude awakening to the ways of the real world. "I was twenty-one." I said softly, just slightly lost in my memories.

"Twenty-one, wow. Barely legal."

"Legal enough." As I recall, I was legal enough to drink myself silly when I came home from work every night. When I finally quit, Alex and I burned my Rolodex, card by card in some sort of rebellious cleansing.

Kip shrugged. "Anyway, I'm assuming you wrote that story because, at that particular time, you would have killed to have someone force you to quit your job or get you fired." Kip may have been sitting on my counter, but he was definitely starting to climb onto his soapbox.

"And?" Of course, I knew where he was going with this, but I indulged him anyway.

"Am I right?"

"Yes, Kip, I was desperate for someone to fire me because I was too gutless to quit. Happy?"

"Interesting." He stroked his goatee like a professor. Professor of what, I don't know.

"What are you getting at, Kip?" I asked, knowing exactly what he was getting at.

"Nothing, nothing. Just thinking out loud."

"I swear to god, Kip, if you touch one of my shoes, I will kill you." I told him, referring to the time he stole one of each of Bridget's shoes so she couldn't go to work. "I could just kill you, you know," I said, relishing the power of being able to destroy him. "That would end your story pretty damn quickly."

"Oh, I know that. Though, death might be preferable to living my life in a box."

"You don't have a life." I said, finally losing patience with him.

"But, wouldn't it be great if I could get you fired," he said wistfully. "Wouldn't you just love not having to go to that awful place every day? You could live the life you've always wanted. Imagine it. Writing, all day long." He looked off into the distance as if he could actually see it: me, writing all day long.

I had to admit, it was tempting. I did long for that life where I could just write all day. If I could remove all the other distractions in my life and just write, all day, every day. I might actually be able to accomplish something. Something real. Something that was mine.

The thing was, and I don't think Kip had this figured out, but I was pretty sure it wasn't my job that stopped me from writing.

"I can help you, you know." He jumped off the counter and spoke in a soft voice that would've made me swoon in my twenties. "Let me help you."

I shook my head, almost laughing at his naïveté and mine. I remembered, wistfully, my twenties. What a great time, when I thought everything was so hard, but it was really so very easy. That perfect time of your life between childhood and adulthood where could do whatever you want. Your only responsibility is to whatever job you had, crappy or not. Everything else was playtime. Kip represented all that. His enthusiasm for life was endearing. As big of a pain in the ass as he was, I couldn't help but enjoy his ideas that if you chucked your job and did exactly what you wanted, your life would be perfect.

"Thanks for the offer, Kip, but I'm fine just where I am."

"You lie like a rug," he said, shaking his head. "If you're so fine, why are you talking to me?"

I sighed. I hated when my subconscious was utterly and completely honest with me and even more, I hated when it was right. "I'll give you that," I agreed.

"Let me help you," he pleaded. "I can get you out of your job. You know Alex will never let you quit."

Flag on the play. "Yeah. Let's leave Alex out of this, ok." I wasn't about to let Kip bring Alex into this insanity.

"Leave me out of what?" Alex's voice cut through the room as he entered the kitchen. Though I didn't turn to face him, I knew he was scanning the room. "Who are you talking to?"

I was busted and there was no way out.

I was caught by my husband, talking about my husband, to nobody, in the middle of my kitchen. Kip vanished like the coward he was. Alright, that's not fair. He vanished like the figment of my imagination that he was, but I still couldn't help but feel ever so slightly abandoned. I stood alone, my back to Alex. For the first time since my visions started, I felt just plain old ordinary crazy. Not just eccentric, talking to myself crazy. But full-boat lunatic.

"Belly? Hello?" Pretending nothing had happened seemed like the best, and most sane course of action. I turned to him. "You're home early," I said brightly.

"Yeah. We only played nine holes." He looked around the kitchen intently. "Who were you talking to?"

"What?" Playing dumb always worked. Right?

"I just heard you say 'let's leave Alex out of this.' Who were you talking to?" he pressed.

I don't know how long I stood there trying to find an answer to that question that didn't sound completely nuts. It must've been a while, because Alex grabbed my arm and pulled me to the couch. He sat me down firmly and sat down next to me. "Bella. Talk. Now." He actually looked really mad. Alex never looked really mad and I knew I couldn't lock him out any longer. I had to tell him. I had to tell him his wife was losing her mind.

I exhaled slowly, blowing air out like I was blowing out candles on a birthday cake.

"What's going on, Bella?"

"Nothing." I shook my head and looked away from him. I couldn't look directly at him. If I did, I'd melt into a puddle right there on the couch, like a snowman sitting in the sun.

"You've been acting skittish for days," he pressed. "Every time I walk into a room, you jump out of your skin. C'mon, Belly." He stroked my hair, his annoyance with me fading into concern. "What is going on in that head of yours?"

I laughed on the inside at his choice of words. "If I tell you, you have to promise you won't be upset with me."

"Why? What did you do?" he said, only half-concerned. As if he couldn't wait to see what his crazy wife had done next. I felt like Lucy to his Ricky. Except Lucy wasn't certifiable.

"Nothing."

"Then, why would I be upset with you?

"Because."

He took a deep breath, trying to regain his patience. "Belly, you know you can tell me anything. I love you no matter what." He took my hand, making it impossible for me to keep my walls up.

"I know you love me, Alex. But…"

"But what?"

"It's just…" His damn caramel eyes were just killing me. "Something has been going on with me and I have been afraid to tell you," I said, looking away from him, but then quickly looking back.

"Why?" he asked, honestly confused as to why I'd be afraid to tell him anything.

"I'm afraid you won't understand." It sounded funny and contrived when I said it out loud.

"Try me," he said patiently and stroked my cheek.

I took a deep breath, feeling like I was about to dive off the high dive. Head first. Into a waterless pool. Filled with shards of glass. Finally, I said it. "I've been seeing things."

"Seeing things?" he asked. "You mean like things that aren't really there?"

I nodded, but offered no details.

"OK." He nodded. "What kinds of things?"

I bit my lip, still terrified, but finally whispered. "People."

"People?" I could tell he was trying really hard not to react to anything I was saying, though his eyebrows were starting to twist.

"Characters," I continued. "From my books."

"Characters from your books?" He repeated before shaking his head and laughing just a little, sounding almost relieved. "But you've always done that, Belly. I've seen you talking to yourself a hundred times when you're sitting at your computer." That was true. I'd caught myself more than once gesturing or whispering at the screen as I pounded out dialogue on the keyboard. But this was different.

"It's not like that. It's not like when I'm writing. It's all the time. They just show up out of nowhere. I can hear them. I can smell them. I can talk to them and they answer me!" I started to ramble, because quite honestly, it felt just spectacular to get it all out. I stopped short of telling him about Cody and the glass because I didn't want to scare him. "I see them everywhere," I continued. "They're in the grocery store and the gas station, and my yoga class. And they all have opinions about what I should be doing with my life."

Alex nodded patiently, taking it all in. "So, when I heard you before, you were talking to…" he waited for me to fill in the blank.

"Kip, from the first book I wrote after college."

He sat there for a while, staring out the window over his shoulder. I watched him looking at something in the distance he couldn't quite see. I could almost see the wheels turning slowly in his head, processing the idea of being married to a complete lunatic.

"Say something," I said when I couldn't stand his silence anymore.

It was his turn to exhale. “I don’t really know what to say.”

“I know.” I pushed my hands through my hair and dug my fingers into my scalp. “Tell me I’m crazy.”

Alex shook his head. “I don’t think you’re crazy.”

“What do you think then? I mean, clearly there must be something wrong with me, Alex.”

“I think you just need to spend more time writing and less time talking to yourself, and I’m not saying that to nag you. I’m saying that because maybe you’re imagining these things because you’re not using your gift. You have no creative outlet right now and maybe it’s making you just a little bit… crazy.”

“A little bit crazy?” I stared at him. The irony was not lost on me that he was telling me to do exactly what all of my characters were telling me to do (with the exception of Peter). “Who are you and what have you done with my very normal husband?” I said, relieved at how well he was taking my news.

“What?”

“I thought you’d want to have me committed.”

“Do you think I don’t know you? Or understand you? How long have we been together, Bella?” he ran his hands through his own hair, frustrated by me, once again. It was amazing he hadn’t pulled all his hair out by now. “We’ve raised children together. We’ve been together since we were kids ourselves. I know you. I know your writing makes you just a little bit crazy sometimes. Do you think I haven’t heard you talking to yourself in all these years?” He took my hand. “Bella, I love all of you. Even the crazy parts.”

Virtually paralyzed by his words, I couldn’t do anything but nod.

Alex tugged me forward and I fell into him. "Just promise me you'll stay in control here. Don't let these things control you. They're yours. You wrote them. You're in charge of them."

CHAPTER 7

ALEX LOVED ME IN SPITE of my lunacy, which was a good thing. A great thing really. Having told Alex my deepest, darkest secret I felt much less alone. I can't deny feeling a little bit exposed having told him everything... well, almost everything that was happening to me. But he was probably right. There was an awful lot going on in my brain and I didn't have an outlet. Unfortunately, I also didn't have any ideas, so I was a little concerned about how I was going to channel all this nervous creativity into something productive.

I started out scribbling in my journal. And that's what it was. Just scribbles. You'd think for a person losing her mind, I would've had far more interesting thoughts. Usually when I journaled, I would reread my ramblings and find some tiny kernel of something that could be brilliant in some lifetime. But now it just felt forced and uninspired.

One day, before going to work, I thought maybe I'd start a new story. Write what you know, I told myself as I caught my own reflection in the screen of my laptop. I was on the brink of starting a story about a writer who couldn't finish her stories. But in the end decided no one wanted to read a story about someone so uninspired. Write what you know they say, so I tried writing about a woman whose children have just left for college. But I couldn't get my emotions in enough of an order to get them down on paper. It just hit way too close to home for me. Write what you know? But what if you don't know anything?

At a loss for new ideas, I pulled *The Woodpecker* box down from the shelf and out of the closet, but I couldn't get poor, pathetic Emily to make any kind of a decision to save my life or hers. It just seemed so out of character for her to make any kind of positive change in her life. No matter how much abuse Thomas sent her way, it just seemed in Emily's nature to sit there and take it like the perpetual punching bag that she was. Sitting on my bed, surrounded by scraps of paper, I searched for a clue to the ending. Just when I was so frustrated I wanted to throw the whole damn box in the fire, I heard a light tapping on my bedroom door.

"Come in?" I called, questioning who was going to be there.

"Hello?" Daniel entered timidly. "I hope I'm not disturbing you." Leave it to Daniel to knock before entering my fantasy world.

I patted myself on the back for creating such a polite young man, hoping I had done half as well with my own children. "Come on in, Daniel. I was just thinking about you."

"Um, good. I've been thinking about you, too." He stood awkwardly, looking at the mess on my bed while obviously trying not to stare. He was definitely looking for answers.

"How are you doing?" I asked him, trying to draw his attention from the papers on top of the covers.

"Hard to say," he answered succinctly. He clearly had something that he wanted to ask me, but was afraid to, leaving me to carry the conversation.

"Is everybody getting along ok?" I said, nudging him along.

"For now. But Thomas is coming home soon."

I closed my eyes and looked down at my notes. He was getting to the really rough part of the story. Soon, Emily would choose Thomas over Daniel and the lovely boy that stands before me would be gone, replaced with a hurt, angry and abandoned Daniel. I wanted to tell him not to go back. He could move into Holden's room and stay here with me. I wanted to spare him the pain he was about to endure. Maybe I could rewrite it, so it wouldn't be quite so painful for him. But that wouldn't make for much of a story, would it? That raw, fierce agony that Daniel was about to experience was the best part of what I'd written.

"Have you come up with an ending for us then?" Daniel asked me, for the first time, about his end.

With a sigh, I answered him, failure crushing my spirit again. "No. I'm sorry, Daniel. I haven't." Having to tell all of these characters that I was too incompetent to finish them was getting really old, really fast.

"Would you please come up with one?" he pleaded with an urgency that was not quite like him.

"I'm trying, Daniel, I really am. I just don't know what to do with your mother. She's not one for making big decisions, you know."

"I know that," he said bitterly. "Why don't you just write what you would do?" He continued with a shrug.

"Because I'm not Emily," I answered matter-of-factly.

"Aren't you?"

"No." I bristled at his suggestion. If anything, I was the anti-Emily.

"Aren't you? Just a bit perhaps?" he asked unsurely.

Was I? Good god, was I as spineless and weak as Emily? I hoped not. But if I was being completely honest with myself (which I absolutely hated being), I did tend to stay in a bad situation longer than I needed to. I was desperately afraid of failure, like she was. And I was obscenely terrified of losing my children.

"Well, maybe a little –" I finally answered Daniel.

"So then, what would you do?"

"Me? I would kill Thomas," I said without a doubt.

"No, you wouldn't." He shook his head, calling my bluff.

He was right. I wouldn't kill him. As much as I would like to, I wouldn't have the guts. It just wasn't in me to kill anyone.

"I would leave him," I said, offering Daniel the next best solution.

"Would you?"

Would I have the guts to leave him? Would I? If I had been crapped on by as many people as Emily had, I hoped I would have the guts. But I honestly didn't know. "I hope I would, Daniel, if he gave me a good enough reason."

"What kind of reason would you need? How far would he have to push you?" he asked me.

I thought about this question long and hard. "What is my breaking point?" I asked myself out loud.

Daniel nodded. "What would he have to do to you to make you leave? How much would he have to hurt you?"

That was the question. That was what kept me from letting Emily leave. She needed a straw to break the camel's back and I didn't give her one. I was afraid to give her one. I didn't know yet what that straw was going to be, but that was what she needed. I smashed my hands down on the piles on the bed, looking for a pen that had to be buried under there somewhere. I jotted down: *Emily's reason for leaving. Straw that breaks.*

When I looked up, Daniel was gone.

CHAPTER 8

I STOOD AT THE FRONT OF the school cafeteria, hands on my hips, surveying the noise. Two hundred kids and me. My co-worker, who was supposed to help me with the second-grade lunch wave, was off because her grandmother died (again), which left me alone and in charge of feeding time at the zoo. God, I hated it in there. I counted every second of every day until summer when I could leave that room. (163 days, 3 hours, 48 minutes and 27 seconds left).

I used to love being around children. That was why I applied for this job in the first place. I was hoping to get a position working in a classroom helping kids. I looked at this job as a foot in the door of that classroom. Instead, I got a room where all I could see were the troublemakers – the rotten ones. I was so busy keeping tabs on the food flingers, the cheese stick stealers, the screamers and the tattlers, I never even noticed the good kids. I'm sure they were in there, but my position left no room for forging relationships with the good kids. It was kill or be killed in there, and I really didn't want to be killed by a bunch of obnoxious second graders.

After telling Kyle not to get out of his seat for what seemed like the forty-seventh time that day, I sighed and tried to decide if I should quiet the cafeteria down, or just let them make noise. Sometimes, I just didn't give a crap how much noise they made, and that day, they were plenty loud. Then the percussion section of the school band started to practice behind the curtains, on the stage behind me, as if there wasn't enough noise in there. "Are you fucking kidding me?" I muttered to myself, not expecting to hear an answer from over my shoulder.

"Seriously, like it wasn't loud enough in here."

I knew Kip was standing next to me, but I wasn't about to acknowledge him.

"Are you in charge of all these kids?"

I breathed in deeply and rubbed my temples, ignoring him.

"Oh, fine. Don't answer me. Pretend I'm not here. Pretend you don't want me here."

I continued to act like Kip wasn't there, though the truth was I was actually grateful for the company.

"You know what you should do? You should quit this job and finish one of your books. Preferably mine, of course."

I looked down at the ugly shoes I wore. There was no point in wearing cute shoes there because of all the crap on the floor. "Why are you such a pest?" I said to my shoes so no one could see my lips move.

"Because you made me that way." Kip beamed proudly. "Damn fine job you did, too. Hey! I was thinking about maybe some ways I could get you fired. What if I stole money from the register? Or if I…"

I glared at him wordlessly. So much of me wanted to let him do his worst, get me fired, let me write all day. But a bigger part of me knew I needed this job, for money and for Alex.

"Ok fine…it was just an idea." He relented.

I looked up at the clock on the wall and walked away from Kip, intent on doing my best at my loathsome job. I clapped my hands in the rhythm that was supposed to quiet the children and make them echo me. Unfortunately, the noise of the drums escalated along with the voices of the children until it was so damn loud in there, most of them didn't hear me clapping and those who did just didn't care.

I clapped my hands again, louder this time, but the massive roar of their two hundred tiny voices continued. A third time I clapped and this time got the attention of about half of the little monsters. The other half continued to buzz away.

"Second graders!" I yelled. At least I thought I yelled. I sometimes felt like I was screaming at the top of my lungs but no one else seemed to be able to hear me. It was so loud in my head; how could the world not stop and listen to me when I screamed that loud?

"Second graders!" I yelled again only this time I banged my hand on the table in front of me. My wedding ring dug into the back of my ring finger, making a horrible clanging noise as I hit the table. Finally, the children stopped talking and froze, as shocked by my outburst as I was.

I glanced up at Kip whose mouth was wide open in disbelief, astonished and maybe a little bit afraid of the level of my temper. Shame filled me up and reddened my face. How did I become this wicked, yelling shrew? This wasn't me. I was gentle and soft-spoken and creative and eccentric. I was a mother, and I would've killed any mother who spoke to my children the way I was speaking to these children. But right now, I was nothing more than the "Mean and just a little bit Crazy Lunch Lady," and I hated myself for it. My cheeks flushed and I took a deep breath before continuing calmly. "Second graders, it's time to clear your places and go out to recess. When I call your table, take all your garbage with you and line up quietly. And stay quiet."

The children mostly listened now, afraid of the crazy lunch lady.

I felt a burning in my chest that was rising up in my throat. For a moment, I thought I might throw up. My hands were shaking and my face felt hot with embarrassment over my behavior. I felt more insane now than I ever felt talking to my little friends that don't really exist. How did I get here? How had this become the way I spent my days? Yelling at children. Banging my hands on tables. Where did all this rage come from? What happened to all my dreams? I was going to be a semi-famous novelist, not some old battle-ax of a lunch lady who did nothing but yell at little children all day. I was embarrassed and ashamed of myself and there was Kip watching it all.

I hung my head and walked back to the front of the cafeteria. It was silent now as the children all left for recess. I could hear their happy voices through the windows. They sounded so sweet and joyful. My hand stung from where it hit the table.

"Don't say anything," I said to Kip. "Not one freaking word."

"I wasn't going to," he said softly.

I closed my eyes and exhaled in relief. Kip had a habit of beating a dead horse.

"Not much to say after that little display." He chuckled. "It looks like you won't need me to get you fired after all."

"Damn you, Kip," I said through gritted teeth, but he was already gone.

****

I went home after work that day and crawled straight into bed, pulling the covers over my head and blocking out the whole world. All of it. Even the crazies in my head stayed away. That's right. I was such a mess even my own demons didn't want to deal with me. I cried myself to sleep and stayed there in a dreamless state until Alex came home.

"Bella," he whispered and pulled the covers back gently. "Bella, wake up."

"I don't want to." I yanked the covers back over my head.

"What's the matter, honey? Are you sick?" He asked, half-concerned and half-amused by my theatrics.

"No." I muttered from inside my self-made cocoon.

"Then, sit up and talk to me." He patted my blanket-covered legs. "What's wrong?"

"Nothing. I just had a crappy day," I growled, still under the covers.

Alex wrestled the covers away from my head again. "Aww. I'm sorry, Belly. Was your day crappy in a 'you hate your job' kind of way or crappy in a 'you're talking to people that don't exist' kind of way?"

"That's not funny," I pouted.

"Come on. It's a little bit funny." Alex gave me an irresistible smirk, stroking my cheek, and my walls started to crumble.

"Fine. I hate my job. I hate it every second and I want to quit," I whined. I knew I sounded like a four-year-old. But I didn't care. I spent enough time around children; I had earned the right to act like one.

Alex smiled and nodded patiently. He'd heard my 'I hate my job' tirade so many times he could probably recite it himself.

"I know you hate your job, honey. I know how awful it can be."

"No, you don't. It's more awful than you could possibly imagine." I sat up in bed and crossed my arms over my chest dramatically, in defense of whatever logic he was about to throw at me.

"I doubt that. I'm sure it could be worse. I'm sure there are plenty of people in this world who have far worse jobs than you do."

Oh great. He was going to be rational with me. I wasn't in the mood for rational. I was in the mood for melodrama. I rolled my eyes at him.

"Mirabelle, my love." He brought my hand to his lips and gave it a gentle kiss. "I know you hate your job. But the bottom line is, we have two kids in college for the next four years. Believe it or not, that $600 a month that you bring in does help."

I knitted my eyebrows at him and kept my arms crossed.

"It's only a few hours a day," he continued softly.

"I know that," I snapped. "I tell myself that thousands of times a day. Thousands, Alex."

"I know you hate it. And I know it takes a toll on you, I know that, but the reality is, we need the money."

"It's hard." I frowned some more.

"If it wasn't hard they'd call it play and not work," he said, and I wanted to punch him. "My work is hard for me, too, you know. It's not how I would choose to spend my days, but I don't have a choice."

I should've felt guilty right about then, but I didn't, really. Alex was more suited to working. The structure made sense to him and he was good at his job. I wasn't. "I know." I continued my whining. "But I'm so tired of it. I just don't want to do it anymore."

"I know, Bella, I do. But sometimes we have to do things we don't want to do. Until you can sell a book or make some money writing, we need you to work at least part-time." He brushed the hair out of my eyes. "I can't do this without you, Belly."

When he put it like that, how could I deny him? This was how Alex and I worked. I loved him more than I knew I was capable of loving anybody or anything, and I knew he loved me in the same way. I loved him more than I hated my job.

But some days, I just hated him. I hated his rational thinking. I hated the way everything he said always made sense. I hated when I knew he was right but I wanted to argue with him anyway. Why did everything have to make so much sense when he said it? I hated when his logic made me feel stupid and petty.

I thought back to when we were in college and we would stay up all night talking about whatever I was writing. Alex would play devil's advocate to my stalwart optimism. He would force me to defend my characters and their choices, keeping me honest to their nature. Those days, his rational thinking was a helpful contrast to my ridiculous melodrama. It helped keep my stories real.

These days, Alex was too focused on other things, like reality or his job or whatever it was that he sold at work everyday, to be my sounding board. Somewhere along the way, Alex had gone off and become a grown up. I was glad, mind you. Someone had to be the grown up and it certainly wasn't going to be me. But every now and then I missed the Alex who lived in that tiny room in the back of that crappy apartment. I sometimes longed for the Alex who was content to spend a Saturday afternoon smoking pot and playing ping-pong, instead of entertaining clients and being attached to his Blackberry.

"Bella? Are you still with me?" Alex gave my hand a little squeeze and I blinked myself back to reality. Alex smiled at me and I forgave him for being a grown up.

"Of course, I am."

"Good." He kicked off his shoes, untied his tie and crawled over me into bed, putting his arm around me protectively. I curled into him instinctively. "Did you write today?" he asked, always checking up on me.

"A little. Baby steps, you know?" was the best explanation I could come up with for what I had written with Daniel this morning.

Alex nodded. But I knew he didn't really know what I meant. "Did you…uh…see anyone?" he asked.

It was sweet the way he was trying to understand me, trying to understand something that was so far outside of his comfort zone.

But, ah, to tell him or not to tell him? That was the question.

"You don't want to know."

He shook his head, frustrated with me, as always. I couldn't blame him. I was awfully frustrating. "Don't do that to me, Bella. Don't shut me out. I'm asking because I do want to know."

I believed him. Alex wasn't one for lip service. So, I answered him. "I saw Daniel and Kip today."

"And what did Kip have to say?"

"Not much. He just got to witness my epic meltdown in the caf today."

Alex opened his mouth to ask "What epic meltdown?" but must've decided either he didn't want to know, or he didn't want to send me into a tailspin because he changed the subject.

"Daniel's the boy from *The Woodpecker*, right?"

I nodded, just a little surprised and pretty impressed that he remembered.

"What did he have to say?"

I squeezed my forehead with my hand. "He thinks I'm like Emily."

"Emily, the pathetic one who won't leave her abusive husband?"

"That's the one." I nodded, impressed again by his knowledge. Clearly, I wasn't giving Alex enough credit.

"Do you want to know what I think?" He held me just a little tighter.

"I'm not sure."

"I think that you're afraid of being like Emily. You're afraid you're not strong enough. Afraid you're not a good enough mother. Afraid you're not a good enough wife."

Ugh. There he goes being right again.

"But you're wrong." He kissed the top of my head. "You are so totally wrong," he whispered, and I believed him. For just that moment, I believed him.

CHAPTER 9

OF COURSE, THAT NIGHT I had no chance of actually sleeping since I slept all afternoon. I tossed and turned for hours, Alex breathing peacefully beside me. I had always envied his sleeping ability. Alex could sleep through anything. I never was much for sleeping. I tossed and turned all night, making lists in my head of all the things I didn't accomplish that day.

After tossing and turning for a solid twenty minutes, I figured I might as well try writing something, well aware that my writing alone at night was bound to bring some characters out for a visit. I just hoped it wasn't going to be Cody. I hated that bastard. Though, sometimes, I wasn't quite sure I could explain my venom toward him. You'd think it would be Emily, whose weakness I feared was really mine, who I hated. But there was something about Cody that rubbed me in all kinds of wrong ways.

I took out my laptop and curled up under a blanket in front of the downstairs window. I liked sitting in front of the window when I wrote. It kind of made me feel like I was in front of a big screen TV. Not that there was anything good on, but sometimes someone would walk by or the trees would blow in just such a way that it gave me a snippet of inspiration. A very tiny snippet.

Endings. What was it about endings that gave me such a hard time? Did I have some issue with closure that made me refuse to write an ending to anything? How cruel was it that I had this gift for writing but no ability to actually come up with an ending that wasn't contrite or predictable in some way? It weighed me down with sadness. My eyes filled with tears, not for me (well, ok, a little bit for me), but for the characters in these stories I had created with no conclusions. I knew they were only characters, things that existed only in the confines of my brain, but to me, they were people I knew. People who had problems that I couldn't help them with.

"Life sucks, doesn't it?" said a voice from across the living room.

I had almost forgotten about my brief foray into serial killer darkness in college. Sitting in my tiny single dorm room in darkness, the only light coming from the glow of my MAC SE, burning incense in front of the screen and listening to the Cure over and over again. It's a wonder that I'm not crazier than I am, with that kind of ritual.

Ever-despondent Detective David Mitchell sat in the white chair in my living room. I poured so much loss into him. Nothing but death and violence surrounded him until he was so forlorn, he didn't want to live anymore. He sighed loudly and I felt obligated to answer his question optimistically, not wanting to send the suicidal cop over the edge. "It could be worse," I told him cheerily.

"Oh yeah, how?" he snapped.

"Oh, I don't know, David." I sighed, not having the answers that he needed. "But I'm quite sure it could be worse."

"Hey, hey, can you help me catch him?" he leaned forward eagerly into the moonlight pouring in through the front window and I could see the deep lines etched under his eyes. He looked like he hadn't slept for days. The whites of his eyes were so bloodshot you could barely call them white. They were more like yellowish-pink. His hands were clenched into tight fists as if he was trying to prevent them from shaking.

"Catch who?" I asked, even though I knew damn well who.

"The Mercy Killer. Can you help me catch him? Do I know who it is?" he asked breathlessly.

I sighed and looked out the big front window for an answer. Of course, I knew who the Mercy Killer was. I'm not sure you could even start writing a serial killer book without knowing who the murderer was. I just never quite figured out how to tie David to the Mercy killer in a way that would make for an interesting finale. But I always knew who the killer was. Finding the killer wasn't the end of the story. It was how David found the killer and what he did when he found him that was the end.

Poor David – another tortured soul for me to jerk around for 300 pages and then leave in the dust with no resolution. I couldn't help but feel a little bit guilty for all the bad things I inflicted on this poor man.

"You must know something," he pleaded. "Help me catch him. Help me stop all this killing."

David was so desperate, it was creepy and a little scary. He was even less fun than Cody, and I made a mental note to not complain about Kip ever again.

I wondered what would happen if I just told David who the killer was right here and now? Would his ending just write itself? Or would there be a consequence for interfering in David's life like that? Were there ramifications for how I handled these characters? Would doing so change something in my own life? Could it change something real?

"Bella, are you down there?" David and I both looked towards the stairs as we heard Alex's voice and footsteps. When I looked back to the white chair, I was greatly relieved to find that David was gone.

"I'm here," I answered in a whisper.

Alex came down the stairs in the same plaid flannel robe I bought him the first year we were married. That robe was so old it could walk around by itself. It was torn on the sleeves and the belt was frayed. Every time I saw that robe hanging on the hook, I wanted to throw it out. But when I saw it on Alex, somehow it looked like new.

Alex looked over my shoulder at the blank screen on my laptop. "How's it going?"

"It's not. But I couldn't sleep. All that self-pity sleep I got this afternoon messed me up."

"Do you want me to leave you alone?"

"No. I definitely don't want that." I shook my head.

He smirked. "Oh wait. Were you not alone?" His eyes grew wide and he suppressed a chuckle as he looked around the room.

"It's not funny." I scolded him, but he laughed again. He always had the strangest sense of humor. "Seriously. It's really not funny, Alex." I looked out the window for more answers.

He squished me over on the couch and curled up next to me. Damn that robe was soft. "I know you hate when I ask this, but are you ok?"

"Yeah, I just…" I trailed off. I just what? I just don't know how to handle the fact that I'm going completely crazy? I just don't think it's funny that my suicidal cop friend can't catch a serial killer? Jeez, I couldn't even write my own dialogue.

"Come back to bed?" he asked me, grabbing my hand, pulling me to my feet and interrupting my disjointed thoughts.

Not that I had high hopes for sleeping at this point. But I was pretty sure as long as I stayed with Alex, no one would visit me. I could be normal. For a little while anyway.

CHAPTER 10

THE NEXT DAY WAS SUPER Nachos day at school. I hated Super Nachos day above all others. And not because I was outraged that mystery meat, a bag of "baked" chips, and some sort of gelatinous cheese-colored substance was considered a healthy school lunch (which I was, of course). But mostly because when it was time for the little beasts to clear their places, they all insisted on holding their trays upside-down over the trashcans and the sight of that yellowy-orange goop dropping slowly into the garbage turned my stomach.

However, my nighttime visit with David gave me something I didn't have on my last Super Nachos day. Optimism. Life could be worse. Don't get me wrong. I fully enjoyed feeling sorry for myself about my miserable little existence and horrible job. But when I was forced to remove the melodrama and look at my life, it really wasn't so bad. At least I wasn't a cop who couldn't catch a serial killer. I was merely a wife, mother, and a writer with a bit of an identity crisis.

I managed to remain calm, cool and collected throughout the day, barely giving the cheese goop a second thought. Every time a little monster irritated me, I told myself, I'd rather do this than be a cop who couldn't catch a serial killer. David's pain was my gain. Though, at every lull between lunch waves, I weighed the pros and cons of telling David who The Mercy Killer was.

What if I wrote an ending, even a bad ending that revealed the killer to David? Wouldn't that put him out of his misery?

Would it make him less suicidal? How drastically would that change the course of his life? Would it change the course of mine? And what if I didn't have to write the great American novel every time I sat down at my computer? What if I could just write a story? What if I took the pressure off myself to make things so perfect and just wrote like it was the first and last time I was ever going to write anything? What would be the harm in that?

****

Later that week, Alex left for a business trip. It was only overnight, and no place interesting or exotic. It still bothered me. I hated being left alone. And even though I never wanted to go with him, I still felt somehow abandoned. Of course, I knew I was being irrational, but that didn't especially matter to me.

He called me before dinner and told me he was going out with a colleague. Rebecca. Ick. I'd met her at some stupid, boring, holiday party. She giggled too much and was always touching Alex on the arm.

It wasn't that I didn't trust him, because I did. I completely trusted him. There were some women I didn't trust. Rebecca was one of them. I knew Alex wouldn't cheat on me. But he was just so damn nice all the time, I didn't trust him to reject them hard enough. Forcefully, enough. Something ugly in me wanted him to shut her down and make her wish she never flirted with him in the first place. But he always said that he felt badly for her because she was obviously so lonely. It didn't mean anything. My assertion that it meant something to me didn't seem to matter much to him.

"Would you rather I just ate alone in my room?" he asked in that impatient way he spoke when he thought I was being ridiculous.

"No, of course not." I said, when I really meant, "Yes, I would. Very much so."

"Then please stop making such a big deal out of this, Bella. It's just dinner."

"I don't want to fight, Alex."

"Yes, you do, Bella. You do want to fight. I'm here for work, because I have to be, not because I want to be. I'm not going to let you bait me into some silly argument over something that doesn't mean anything."

I said nothing. I knew he was right. But I certainly wasn't going to tell him that.

"Good night, Bella." He sighed, clearly having had enough of my antics.

"I love you, Alex," I sniffed into the phone like a heartbroken teenager.

"I love you, too, Bella," he said, but not in a way that sounded like he meant it. He said it in such a way that I could practically feel him rolling his eyes through the phone.

Of course, I was overreacting and I knew I was wrong. But still, I wanted Alex to fawn over me and cater to my insecurities, not brush them aside as if they didn't matter. Crazy as they were, my feelings did matter, to me anyway. I hung up feeling alone and misunderstood, as I stood in the blackness of the empty kitchen.

"Well, hello there," Cody's husky whisper cut through the darkness. The way I was feeling, I should've expected it, but it startled me anyway.

I was in no mood for Cody. I was surly and angry, though maybe that was exactly the mood I needed for Cody. But instead of flipping on the light, I turned and walked right out of the kitchen hoping to avoid him by ignoring him. I went, instead, to the family room and turned on the TV, trying to distract my brain from creating its delusions. The TV flicked on with a pop, and then promptly turned off.

"Uh, hello? Did you not hear me?" Cody said, appearing next to the TV.

I turned the TV on again. And Cody reached over and turned it off.

"You don't get to just ignore me, you know. It doesn't work like that."

"How does it work?" I growled, losing my temper and taking my anger with Alex out on Cody. I stood up and put my hands on my hips. How does it work? Like I expected Cody to have the answer to that. Like I expected myself to have the answer to that.

"I dunno. But if I'm here, I'm obviously here for a reason. And you, my dear, are the only one who knows what that reason is." He sipped from his ever-present low-ball glass of amber liquid, clearly amused by my irritation.

"Is that blood?" I said, gesturing to the crimson stains on the front of his tuxedo shirt. I racked my brain to remember when I gave Cody a reason to have blood on him.

"Relax, it's mine. Your glass, remember?" he held up his hand that now had a deep cut on it. "I guess I deserved that." He looked at his hand almost sadly. I almost grabbed it for a closer look, mothering instinct taking over, wanting to clean it and bandage it. Then I remembered Cody wasn't really there and even if he was, he certainly didn't want to be mothered.

"How can you bleed?" I softened a little. From what I could see, it looked like a pretty nasty cut.

He shrugged and tucked his hand carefully in the pocket of his tuxedo pants, wincing ever so slightly, almost imperceptibly. "I don't know. You seem to like to hurt me, so it's probably because of you." He half-laughed, like he was kidding, but not really.

"I don't like to hurt you." I was offended…sort of. I didn't like being told that I liked hurting anyone, even imaginary people. But I knew I had a nasty habit of torturing my characters, especially those I didn't like, which was a category that Cody fell squarely into.

"Really? Then how do you explain how I am, *what* I am?"

"That's not my fault." I shrugged, as if Cody was someone I just met and not someone who came from my own imagination.

"Isn't it? Isn't everything I am because of you? Didn't every little detail of my existence come from your twisted brain? From my crooked nose to this cut on my hand. It all came from you, baby."

I couldn't deny that. I also couldn't deny that I felt a strange sense of power about this level of creation. It was one of the things I enjoyed most about writing. The complete sense of control that came from creating an entire world and its inhabitants was staggering sometimes. I was the puppet master. I could manipulate instead of being manipulated. I was in charge and strong and powerful, instead of sweet and soft-spoken. Coming from the wonderful world of motherhood, a place where everything else I did was dependent on someone else's needs, I had to admit, I loved the power writing gave me.

"So why, baby? Why is it that you like to hurt me so much?" he asked in a way that made me think he already knew the answer.

"I don't know." I shrugged cavalierly, trying to ignore him, knowing full well he was baiting me into an argument.

"Ha," he scoffed. "Your favorite answer. I can tell you why, you know."

"Of course, you can. You know everything." Smug bastard.

"Well, thanks to you, I do." He bowed to me in mock gratitude.

"OK, so why did I make you the way I made you?" I asked, hoping my own psyche could explain itself to me. I flopped down on the couch.

He sat down in the brown leather club chair opposite me on the couch and smirked. "Because I am the person you want to be, the person you wish you could be."

I laughed out loud. "Right." Or maybe it couldn't.

"Think about it," he said and, never one for sitting still, he got up and started to pace in front of me. "First of all, look at me. I'm gorgeous."

"And modest."

"No…you're modest," he corrected. "I'm not. I'm just astoundingly good looking." He smiled and I had to agree with him. He was terribly handsome. "You would love to feel as good looking as I feel."

I shrugged as if I was unimpressed and completely disinterested in being beautiful, which was, of course, a lie.

"Secondly, I have an astoundingly glamorous life. I do whatever I want to do whenever the fuck I want to do it. I am accountable to absolutely no one."

"Yes, yes, Cody, you're fabulous. What does any of this have to do with me?"

"You? I'll tell you." He continued knowingly, like he was a teacher and I was his student. "You wish for a more glamorous life. You wish for the freedom to do whatever you want. And there are so many days you would just like to tell everyone in your world to fuck right off."

"You are not even close," I said firmly.

"Really? Can you honestly tell me there haven't been days that you've wanted to walk out on every single responsibility? Every single chore? Every single job? Every single expectation that people have of you?"

"Of course, there are days..." I started to justify myself but Cody wouldn't let me finish.

"You made me because some days you want to be that person who says: 'You know what? That's mine, I want it,' and then you just fucking take it. Some days you want to be that person that says 'fuck you and the horse you rode in on' and just bail on everything and everyone."

"Everybody has days like that."

"Do they? Have you had that conversation with someone? Have you spoken to anyone besides me who wants to tell the entire world to go right to hell in a hand-basket?"

"No, but..."

"How sure are you that everyone feels that way?"

"Pretty sure."

"Pretty sure? That's bullshit."

"I don't fucking know!" I barked.

He smirked like he just won something. "Well, I do." He jingled the ice cubs in his glass. "You have a real dark streak, you know. Darker than most people and you made me like that...dark and ugly. And then you beat up on me because you feel guilty about having that dark streak. You want to kill it, ergo you want to kill me."

"That's pretty deep, Cody." I laughed at him, at me. It was ridiculous to even consider myself in the same class as Cody. Wasn't it?

"Don't mock me," he said through clenched teeth. "You know I hate that."

"Really?" I rolled my eyes at him.

"Yes, you know I hate that. Because you know that you hate to be mocked, too."

I yawned in defiance of him and because I knew it would piss him off.

"Am I boring you?"

"Of course not," I said, my words reeking of sarcasm. "But being psychoanalyzed by my own self-conscious is exhausting." So was being told that the person you hated most was just like you.

"I saw you in that lunchroom. I know what kind of anger you have inside you. I can feel your temper raging. That same blood flows in me. I know how ugly you can be." I shook my head as he ranted on. I wanted him to stop talking now. "When you are frustrated with everything and everyone and you just want to walk, you think of me. Why?"

I shrugged, looking down at the floor. I had a fleeting thought that maybe Cody wasn't the one I hated, maybe it was myself. I pushed that thought to the furthest recesses of my brain.

"Why am I here now, Bella? When you're feeling like this, why am I here?" he said softly and sat down on the couch next to me. It wasn't lost on me that it was the first time any of them had used my name. It was also the first time Cody called me something other than 'baby' or 'honey.'

Covering my ears as if that could keep out his words, I yelled, "Stop it! Just stop it! It doesn't matter why or how I created you. I just want you to go away. Tell me what you want for the rest of your story, and I'll give it to you." I cried, my anger now morphing into fear, not fear of Cody, but fear of me.

"Aww. I can't tell you that, baby."

"Well, now you really do sound like me. What do you want, Cody? Do you want to end up dead, in jail or a changed man? You choose."

"I don't get to choose. You do. You're the writer, remember? You have to decide. Do you want to see me dead? Suffering in a cage? Or do you think maybe, just maybe, I might have a light side to compensate for my dark side? You're the one who has to decide." It was true that being the writer gave me phenomenal cosmic power. I got to choose what happened to them. All of them. But maybe that power was what scared me away from finishing them. Maybe it was just a little too much responsibility for my taste.

"What do you want for me?" Cody asked in a tone of voice I hadn't heard from him before. I looked into his beautiful blue eyes, and for the first time I saw fear and sadness behind them instead of arrogance and spite. Suddenly, Cody didn't seem like such a bad guy. Maybe he was just a lost soul. Maybe he *was* like me.

"I don't know, Cody. I just don't know." I said sadly for what seemed like the thousandth time. I don't know. I don't know. I don't know.

"Well, I suggest you figure it out, soon." He stood up. The harshness had returned to his voice. "You're the one who knows what I'm capable of."

I did know what he was capable of. There was no awfulness that I could write about Cody that would surprise me. He was ruthless and selfish and cruel and sometimes violent.

He had nothing to lose and would do whatever he had to to get what he wanted. "What? Is that supposed to scare me?" I asked him, trying not to let my voice quake.

"What do you think?"

"I'm beginning to think I might want to see you dead."

He laughed at me and shook his head. "Atta girl. But do it soon, will ya? You know I'm not a very patient man." He glared at me with his beautiful, piercing eyes. And with a chill up my spine, he was gone.

What did I want for Cody? Part of me hated him now more than ever before. He was absolutely right about me and about him. I couldn't remember where or why I had created him, but he was the absolute physical manifestation of every dark thought I had ever had. So what do you do with your dark thoughts? Destroy them? Keep them locked away inside? Or try to turn them into something good?

Suddenly, finishing my books became less like accomplishing something and more like fixing myself. Were all my characters manifestations of something inside me? And did I really need that much fixing? Was I really that broken?

The room started to spin as I contemplated all my characters and where they came from. I held my head to stop the reeling. They all existed because of something I'd felt at one time or another. Cody was for every time I felt rebellious. Daniel was when for when I felt alone. Emily was when I felt weak and scared. Kip was when I felt afraid that I couldn't be what I wanted, and David was for when I felt I had nothing to live for. Monica was for the time I was searching for something and Peter was for all the times I was hiding something about myself. And they were all parts of me that I didn't want to deal with. All things that I didn't like about myself. It wasn't just Cody. I hated all my weaknesses and character flaws.

I always knew there was a little bit of me in each of my characters. I never realized how much. I honestly had never given it that much thought other than to avoid an obvious comparison between me and my characters. (I never wanted to write any character that was even remotely close to me, or people might think it *was* me.) I just wrote what was in my head and never looked back. Suddenly, all my stories felt like looking in a big, ugly funhouse mirror and quite honestly, I was pretty horrified at what I saw. Maybe I couldn't finish my damn stories because I didn't want to deal with my own flaws, my own shortcomings. Maybe it wasn't my characters I didn't know how to fix. Maybe it was me.

CHAPTER 11

ALEX RETURNED FROM HIS BUSINESS trip the next day. I was glad to see him, but part of me just wasn't. I had just gotten used to him being gone and now he was back. I was glad to not be alone, but in light of my latest revelation, I needed some more time alone with my introspection. So, as glad I was that Alex was home, I wished I didn't have anyone watching me. Anyone real anyway. There was a strange relief in being home alone with my demons, and being able to talk to them without someone looking over my shoulder. As hard as Alex tried to be ok with me being not ok, and he was trying, I could tell he was trying and sometimes that just made me feel weird. Weirder. Weirdest. Alex with his damn normalness and perfection. And me trying not to hate him for being the person he was, as much as he was trying not to hate me for being the person that I was.

"I need you to come to dinner with some clients on Thursday," he told me without asking, which totally annoyed me, as if I wasn't already annoyed enough by his mere presence.

"Thursday? Thanks for the notice." It was Wednesday. Realistically, plenty of time; it's not like I had to prepare anything, but I hated these dinners and was just itching for any excuse to be difficult about it.

"I just found out about it myself. I didn't think it would be a problem to fit it into your busy social schedule." He grinned at me and I wanted to slap him.

"Ouch." I told him, instead, as if he had slapped me.

"Sorry, Bella. But it's just a dinner." He picked up my hand and kissed it. "And I need you." He knew how much I loved to be needed. But I didn't love that he was manipulating me. Successfully.

I just didn't feel like putting on the whole dog and pony show. Sitting at a table with a bunch of guys and their over-made-up, high-heel wearing, over-plucked, manicured, Botoxed wives with Alex trying to impress everyone, and me just trying not to offend anyone by saying something stupid. It was harder than it looked. Especially when you were totally overwhelmed by a series of hallucinations haunting your every move. Not to mention, the revelation that I had created representations of all of my very own personal issues in my characters.

"We've done this a hundred times before. Why are you making such a big deal out of this?"

"I'm not." I said, though I knew I was. I hated myself for being so petty.

"It kinda seems like you are." He lifted my chin and tried to get me to look him in the eyes.

"It's just a lot of work. That's all." I whined and squirmed out of his gaze.

"I know that. But will you do it? For me?" he kissed the inside of my wrist as if a kiss could make me do what he wanted. I didn't say anything else. I knew it was no big deal, but I wanted him to think it was a big deal. I don't know why.

"Of course, I will." I sighed unhappily.

"You ok, Belly? You seem…" Alex trailed off. I wondered what he was going to say. He didn't seem to know either.

"I'm fine. I just have a lot on my mind." I said, stating the obvious. Easing him into what I knew he wanted to ask me about.

"Do you want to talk about it?" He pulled me onto the couch and put his arm around me.

I shrugged. I did, but I didn't.

"You seem a little high-strung today."

"I'm always high-strung." I looked at him like he should've known that.

"That's true," he agreed.

"But in a good way, right?" I joked.

"Yes, dear." He half-smiled in the way he did when he was nervous. I dropped my defenses and put my head on his shoulder, giving him the ok to ask me what I knew he was just dying to ask. "So, uh, did you have any visitors while I was gone?"

I wasn't sure whether I should tell him or not. Do I share my breakthrough with him? Do I tell him that every one of the characters I've ever written is a direct reflection of me and my tragic flaws?

"What do you think?" I asked him, still trying to figure out how much to tell him.

He sighed. "I'm guessing that since someone pretty much shows up every time you're alone that you had a whole boatload of friends stop by while I was away."

"I wouldn't say it was a boatload."

"No?"

"No."

"A small boat, maybe? A row boat, perhaps?" Alex teased. I liked it when he teased me. It reminded me of when we were young and in college and he was always teasing me in some desperate bid to get my attention.

"Just a canoe," I told him.

"Anything interesting you'd care to share with me?"

And I was going to tell him. I wanted to tell him. But quite honestly, I didn't want to ruin the moment. I was just getting back to the point where I could tolerate his presence back in the house with me. I was even enjoying having him there. My gears had switched. Back to wife and mother. Away from part-time writer and full-time lunatic. It felt good and safe and warm under Alex's arm. I didn't want to ruin it with my insane revelations.

If I did tell him, he would get that far away look in his eye, like he was trying to understand me, but just didn't quite get it. I was trying hard not to give Alex too much crazy at one time. If I measured it out in small doses, maybe he would continue to tolerate me. If I gave him too much at once, he might run.

I don't know why I was always afraid of him running. We'd been together forever and never once did he give me any indication that he would ever be anywhere, but right by my side where he'd always been. We'd been partners for more than twenty years. Partners, friends, lovers and parents for longer than I could remember. We were together for our entire adult lives. Yet, somehow, I was still afraid. Still afraid I would say something stupid to scare him off. I don't know why. Insecurity, I guess. Stupid, I know. But obviously, in a lot of ways I was stupid about a lot of things.

And then sometimes, I just didn't feel like sharing. Sometimes, I just felt like keeping secrets for myself. They were the only thing I owned that was one hundred percent mine. Not ours. Just mine. Sometimes, I just felt like keeping things inside me. Sometimes, I just didn't want him to know every single thing that was going in my brain. When someone knows all of your stories already, at the end of the day, sometimes it's nice to keep a few things inside, so when you get to one of those moments, one of those date nights or special dinners, that you have something to reveal. Granted, I was not very good at keeping things inside. I had a habit of chucking every little thing that entered my crazy brain right out there on the table. But these characters were mine. They were part of me and if I didn't feel like sharing them right now, I didn't have to. It was ok to keep a couple of secrets from Alex. Maybe even necessary.

So, instead of telling him my deep, dark secrets, I sank into him and just tried to enjoy his affection. I would tell him about my revelation later. I would have to. Sometime. Not today.

****

We arrived first at the stupid client dinner just as Alex planned, taking seats next to each other at a large table. The ladies would sit on my left and the gentlemen would sit on Alex's right so I could make idle chatter with the wives while Alex talked business with the husbands. I dressed myself up in appropriate attire and put on way more make-up than I ever wear in some vain attempt to fit in with these ladies. I'm sure I failed miserably, but I made the effort and that must count for something.

"Do me a favor, Alex," I said.

"Anything for you," he answered giddily, resting his arm on the back of my chair. He was enjoying this way too much. I think he enjoyed making me jump through hoops for his clients.

"Don't mention my job." I told him.

"Why not?"

"I don't know." That was a lie. I did know. I was embarrassed. Not that I had any reason to be. But these women didn't work at all, ever. How could they possibly understand doing a job you absolutely hated because you had to? For money. I'd rather they think I was a homemaker than the crazy lunch lady. "I just would rather not discuss it with them."

"If that's what you want…"

"And don't talk about my writing either." I hated telling people I was a writer. People usually responded in one of two ways. Either, they would ask me what I was working on and I would tell them and then they would get at look in their eyes that said they didn't know what to say next. That look that said they thought I was weird. Or they would tell me how amazing and wonderful I was for writing, when I'm not. I haven't accomplished anything. They make some little quips about how when I'm famous, they'll be able to say they "knew me when." They assume I'm actually a good writer and will actually publish something, someday. Either way, I didn't like the responses I got about my writing, so I tended to keep it to myself.

The rest of our group arrived together and the once quiet restaurant erupted in noise. I was sweet and charming and pretty, like I was supposed to be, though I lacked the spray-on tan and designer shoes of the other ladies at the table, and I thought their heavy make-up made them look like some weird caricatures of themselves. I managed to carry on the conversations I needed to hold so Alex could do his job of schmoozing.

It always made me smile/cringe to watch Alex with his clients. He was so different with them than the quiet, reserved Alex that came home to me at night. Watching him manipulate/entertain his clients was terrifying and exhilarating at the same time. He flirted just enough with the wives to make them feel attractive and wanted without being lecherous. He talked sports with the men, adding just enough controversy to make him not seem like a suck-up. It was quite a show watching him work the room all while I struggled to stay afloat with the wives.

"So, Mirabelle, how are the kids doing at school?" asked one of the wives whose name I could not seem to remember, even though I'd known her for years. Karly or Kayley or something. Her kids were a few years older than Holden and Vivian. She was nice enough. She always seemed to ask just the right questions to keep the conversation going, a skill I lacked.

"They're doing great…I think. They're kind of hard to get a hold of these days."

"Isn't that amazing? They go to college and forget they ever had parents." Lori said bitterly. Never really liked Lori. She was far too abrasive for me and was so openly flirtatious with Alex it made my skin crawl. "Until the tuition bill comes. Then they remember you," she continued bitterly.

"And how are you doing? Do you miss them?" Karly or Kayley grabbed my hand in faux concern. Ok, it may have been real concern. I was too socially incompetent to know the difference.

"I do miss them…" I confessed and was about to commiserate when Lori cut in.

"I bet you don't miss them one bit, now that you're alone with that gorgeous husband of yours." She winked at me and then proceeded to eye Alex like a piece of meat.

Alex curled his foot around my leg under the table as if he knew what I was thinking. He was carrying on an entirely separate conversation but knew exactly what was going on on my end of the table. I'm sure he thought I was going to say something irrational and somehow violate that whole "the client is always right" thing. As much as I wanted to tell Lori exactly where she could shove her fake nails, I didn't. I looked sideways at Alex who was pretending he wasn't listening, when I knew he was. "There are definitely advantages to them being gone," I responded with a smirk of my own. Alex rubbed my thigh under the table, still pretending he wasn't listening, and I had to stifle a giggle.

"I wish I had your advantages," Lori whined and took a big slug from her wine glass, staring at Alex over the top of it. When she finally caught his eye, she winked at him. God she was gross! *I'm sitting right here! Stop hitting on my husband!* I wanted to scream at her, but for Alex's sake I responded with a silent smile, screaming on the inside instead.

I excused myself to go to the ladies' room just as the dessert menus arrived. I prayed the other three ladies wouldn't attempt to join me. I know this may go against some woman credo, but I hated the whole 'group go to the ladies' room' thing. I just wanted to go to the bathroom and catch my breath without having to make idle chatter between the stalls. Why would you even want to talk to someone while you were going to the bathroom? It made no sense to me.

Fortunately, the other ladies at the table were more interested in talking about all the things they would never eat off the dessert menu than to tag along to the rest room with me, so I managed to make my escape unscathed. Alex stood as I did, showing off his impeccable manners and squeezed my hand, giving me a wink and a grin as I walked away.

I exhaled heartily in the bathroom, blowing out all the pretense that I'd been wearing for the past two hours. I let my fake smile fall as I peed away the four glasses of wine I drank.

When I bent over the sink to wash my hands a familiar voice came from behind me, "Nice dinner." I closed my eyes. Not now, I told my brain. For Alex, not now.

My brain had other ideas.

"I particularly like the one with the nails. I bet she's all kinds of fun." I looked at my horrified reflection in the mirror and Cody smirking over my shoulder.

"Dammit, Cody, what are you doing here?" I turned away from the sink to face him.

"Like you need to ask."

"Not now." I dried my hands on a paper towel and headed toward the door, hoping I could just run away from him. But Cody was faster than me and was able to jam the door with his patent leather wingtips before I could open it.

"I cannot talk to you now," I said softly, turning to face him slowly, then leaning on the door. "Come back another time, ok?" I whispered, hoping that if I was nice to him, maybe he'd just leave nicely. No such luck.

"Oh, so you do want me to come back later then," he put his hand on the door over my head, preventing my escape, and leaned in so close that I could count the stubbly hairs on his chin. Of everyone that had come to visit me, no one appeared more real to me than Cody. I wondered why that was. It seemed strange being that he was the least developed of all the characters I'd written. Was it because he was special to me in some way? Was it because he was right and I really wanted to be like him? Or was it simply because he was the only one who just completely invaded my personal space?

"What do you want? Why are you here now?" I whispered, barely out loud, my nerves rattled by the nearness of him.

"I think I'm here because you're pissed off at someone… maybe Mrs. Slutty Nails?" He purred and looked at me like he was going to kiss me.

I turned my head away from him since the rest of me was now pretty much pinned against the bathroom door. Clearly being nice to him was not working. "Back the fuck off, Cody," I snarled at him and hoped he couldn't feel my heart leaping out of my chest.

"Nice mouth," He smiled slyly and leaned his elbow on the door over my head, practically on my shoulder.

"I mean it. Back off!" I growled, trying to sound tough when I was truly terrified.

"Oh, I'll back off, baby. I'll back off when you tell me what happens next." He placed his palm gently on my face and stroked my cheekbone with his thumb.

As soon as his hand touched my face, his mood switched from snarky to soft. "I just needed you to help me, honey," he whimpered ever so slightly. I didn't know if I was more astounded by the fact that I could feel his touch on my face, that it felt good, soft and gentle, or that Cody was asking for help. All of it scared the crap out of me. "Pretty please," he pleaded tenderly.

Suddenly, I heard voices outside and was snapped back into reality. I had to get rid of Cody before someone came in. Even though, for the very first time, there was a very tiny part of me that didn't want him to go. Part of me was enjoying being locked into his blue-eyed gaze.

But, I couldn't stay there, hiding in the bathroom with someone who wasn't there. Alex needed me back at the table. If I was gone much longer, it would look suspicious. "Cody, you will back off right fucking now or I will end you." I whispered sharply.

Cody eased off just a bit, just enough for me to breathe and regulate my heart rate. "You wouldn't." He laughed uneasily.

I made him nervous and I knew I could get rid of him. "I will end you in the most horrible, painful, disgusting way I can think of. Don't think that I won't. I don't like you. You're a sleaze and a rip-off." I could practically feel my words hurting him, and it was hurting me to say them, but I had to make him go. I felt badly about it, he was human after all. Kind of, anyway. Berating him into oblivion was just my best option right now. And so I continued, "I never liked you and I don't give a shit about what happens to you…which is why I couldn't be bothered to finish you before," I was just getting rolling when I heard Alex's voice.

"Bella? Are you ok?" Alex tapped lightly at the door.

I stared long and hard at Cody who relaxed and grinned like the Cheshire Cat, either at the sound of Alex's voice or the panic on my face. "Go. Now." I said firmly before I turned my back on him and tugged on the door again.

Thank god it opened. Cody was gone. "I'm fine, honey," I said to Alex waiting for me on the other side of the bathroom door.

Alex looked at me skeptically. "Who were you talking to?"

"No one." I lied. I tried to walk past him, heading straight for the table, but he grabbed my hand and pulled me back a little harder than I expected.

"Bella?" he said sternly, still holding my hand. "Who were you talking to?"

"No one," I answered equally sternly, having no interest in discussing any of this here and now. "I'm fine. We should get back." I tugged him along with me and returned to our guests, apologizing for my delay and making some excuse about getting a call from one of the kids having a crisis while I was in the bathroom. Everyone laughed it off and started yakking about issues with their own kids. Everyone except for Alex who looked right through me.

****

We drove home in silence. Usually after one of these client dinners, we would open up another bottle of wine and stay up late being catty about our dinner cohorts and rehashing the evening. Our own personal after party was one of the only things that got me through these damn dinners. But tonight, Alex had nothing to say to me. I was sure no one noticed that I was arguing with Cody in the bathroom. They couldn't have heard me (though Alex may have) and if they did hear me, they would assume I was on the phone, not talking to someone who didn't actually exist. Why would they think otherwise?

But Alex knew. And his silence told me I had given him more crazy than he could handle. I could feel him seething on the car ride home, but I knew he wouldn't say anything. He was just so damn non-confrontational.

"I know you're angry with me." I forced the issue when we got home as I poured my own glass of wine and kicked off my high heels.

Alex stood at the table and stared at me for a moment. I think he was trying to decide whether to argue with me or not. "I'm not angry." Alex said matter-of-factly as he poured a glass for himself.

"Liar…" I whispered.

He shook his head, grabbed his glass of wine and walked away in his typical passive-aggressive fashion.

"You should be!" I called after him.

He returned a moment later, his lips folded inside his mouth like he was trying not to say something. "You should be angry with me, Alex! I'm being a royal pain in the ass!" I continued.

He crinkled his brows together and shook his head almost laughing at me in disbelief. "You want me to be mad at you? Is that what this whole thing is? Are you just in some desperate bid to get my attention?"

"No." I wished. Wouldn't it be nice if all this was just a bid for attention and not the full-blown psychosis I was truly experiencing. "God, I just can't stand you being so perfectly in control of all your emotions all the time."

Alex rolled his eyes, "Well, somebody has to be." He growled in a tone I hardly ever heard from him. I must've struck a nerve.

"Nice one." I was always a sucker for a good zinger.

"Look, Bella." He sat down at the table with me and took my hands. "I accept you the way you are and god knows that is not always easy for me. You have to take me the way I am and if that means watching me bury my feelings, so be it."

"It's not healthy –"

"Yeah, well, you're not exactly one to talk about healthy, are you?"

I accepted that as I tiptoed across that fine line of sane/crazy. All the same, I could tell Alex regretted saying it.

"Do you think anybody noticed?" I asked, changing my tone and swirling my wine around in my glass.

"That you were in the bathroom having an argument with yourself?"

"Yeah, that." I sighed. It sounded so stupid when he said it. It sounded stupid when I said it, too, I guess. But it stung more when he said it.

"No, I don't think anybody noticed. I just got nervous when you were gone for awhile so I went after you. I should probably tell you that I could hear you outside the bathroom."

"I'm sorry."

"I know." He sipped his wine. "So who was it?"

"What?"

"Who was it? Who were you swearing at?"

I suddenly remembered Cody's gentle touch on my cheek and shivered. "Cody." I rubbed my temples. Just saying his name made my head spin.

"Cody? I never heard of him. Is he new?"

"You never heard of him because I hate him."

"OK. What's his problem?"

"Cody's an asshole, that's his problem. He wants me to make him less of an asshole or something. But I can't stand him and I really don't give a shit what happens to him."

"Apparently, you do." Alex said with a tilt of his head, like he had just said the most obvious thing in the world.

"No, I don't. He just comes around a lot because he likes to annoy me."

"Bella, he's not real. He comes around because your brain makes him come around. He's whatever you make him. You are the one that wants to change him. He has no wants. He comes around because you want him to."

The voice of reason strikes again. I shook my head. "They seem so real. It's so hard to remember sometimes..."

"That you're going just a little bit crazy."

"I think I'm already gone," I put my hands on my face just a little to cover the fact that I was more than a little embarrassed that I momentarily forgot that Cody wasn't a real person. The fact that I actually felt Cody touching me made me understand that I had taken another step down into the basement of crazy. I left eccentric in the dust back there at the ladies' room. I got up from the table, not wanting to confront my level of insanity anymore. Alex followed me.

"Maybe we should put that crazy to good use." Alex whispered in my ear from behind me as he brushed his lips softly against my neck.

I turned to him and stared into his eyes. "I'm sorry I'm crazy." I really was sorry and scared and maybe just a little bit sad that I was so freaking crazy.

"You can make it up to me." He snaked an arm around my waist and pulled me close to him.

"Oh, really?" I couldn't help but smile at him. He was so damn cute when he was trying to get something from me.

He nodded, placing a finger on my lips, tracing them with his thumb before kissing me softly. I closed my eyes and sighed, Alex's warmth erasing my memory. Forgetting about Cody and Kip and Daniel and David, and all the other characters, memories, visits – whatever I called them. They drifted far from my mind now.

Alex brushed my hair out of my face and danced his fingers down my shoulder, pulling the edge of my blouse off and running his lips along my collarbone. I grabbed his too-long hair and brought his lips to mine. He kissed me again the way he had a thousand times before, but it still made my knees quiver. He pulled away just long enough to push me toward our bedroom, stopping in the doorframe of the kitchen to kiss me again and to unbutton my blouse while I took off his tie, and again on the stairs, kissing me again while I fumbled with the buttons on his shirt.

By the time we made it to the bedroom, I was so completely lost in him I barely knew what room we were in. When we were done, we curled up naked under the sheets, too tired to talk, too tired to think, too tired to be crazy.

CHAPTER 12

I WOKE EARLY AND HAPPY. Alex and I were still curled together like young lovers, not like old married people who all too often retreat to their separate corners of the bed. This morning, for once, I was glad that the children were gone.

Watching Alex sleeping contentedly with a hint of a smile on his resting face, I reminded myself again that he needed attention, too. Our world was about us. Not me and my crazies. At that moment, I felt more connected to the real world than I had in months. This was my real world. Not my stupid job, not my writing or lack thereof. This was one hundred percent mine. I just prayed I could keep my demons at bay enough to not destroy the only thing that really mattered. I wasn't a hundred percent sure I could do it.

Still, I woke resolved to keep my feet firmly on the ground and firmly entrenched in my relationship with Alex. I felt so good, I actually felt like writing, which was weird. Usually it was misery that made me want to write. But this particular morning, I was feeling loved and I sort of felt like shouting it from the rooftops, which was generally not my style, but maybe it was time to turn over a new leaf. Right now, I felt like Alex and I had come through a bit of a storm and had emerged on the other side, stronger and closer. (I ignored the little voice in my head that told me that this could be the eye of the hurricane and there was more rain and high wind to come.)

I snuck out from Alex's grasp long enough to throw on his 1992 US OPEN t-shirt that was the softest thing we collectively owned, and pulled a notebook out of my night table. Putting my pen to the paper, I wrote softly, not in manic scribbles like I usually did. My handwriting was clear, legible and flowy. I was at peace for a change. And I wrote that. I felt serene and settled. While I'm quite sure my manic writing was generally more interesting to read than this happy drivel, it felt good to say something positive for a change.

"What'd I do this time?" Alex whispered into the back of my neck.

"Good morning." I turned slightly to him and kissed him softly.

"Am I in trouble?" He snuggled into my back.

"Why do you say that?"

"Because the only time you write in your notebooks is when you're mad at me."

"Well, this time I'm actually writing because I'm happy."

"That's weird." He looked at me skeptically.

"I know, isn't it?"

Alex looked at the clock and sighed.

"Wanna call in sick?" I asked him, hoping he'd say yes. I would've gladly called in sick, of course.

"Desperately." He swung his bare leg over me, straddling my waist. He nuzzled my neck and moaned. "But I can't. I have three meetings today." He said, climbing off me and out of bed, heading off to the shower.

"You're no fun." I pouted.

"Are you going to work today?" he called over his shoulder, knowing all too well I was itching for any excuse play hooky. I hated being such an open book to him.

"Of course I am." Truth be told, I was thinking of skipping and just writing about how darn happy I was all day. It seemed a shame to waste such a good mood on a work day. But I knew Alex wouldn't like that idea. And I wanted to make him happy. For the first time in a long time, I was more concerned with Alex's happiness than my own.

I was in such a good mood that even work couldn't bother me. It was Friday. I just had to get through today and I could spend the rest of the weekend with my adoring husband. I felt untouchable. The kids didn't bother me one bit. Even when I caught them stealing yogurt from the salad bar, it didn't bother me in the slightest. I pretended they were adorable little imps instead of future juvenile delinquents.

My classroom time on Friday was after lunch duty. I got to go down to Kindergarten and spend more time with Jeremy. All I needed to get him to do today was to write the letter 'b' five times and then draw a picture of himself. Seemed simple enough. But for poor Jeremy nothing was ever simple. There was just some disconnect in his brain that wouldn't let him write the letter 'b'. I managed to get a small circle and a line out of him. But I wasn't sure it qualified as a 'b'.

My patience was wearing thin with Jeremy. I wished I had more patience for him, but it just wasn't my strong suit. Alex was the patient one. I remember one night when the kids were in third grade and Vivian had a friend sleep over. The girl lost her tooth and I put it aside in a bowl for her mom. Alex dumped the bowl promptly down the garbage disposal not realizing it was holding such precious cargo. And of course, we had corn for dinner. Guess what corn looks like when you pull it out of the garbage disposal? Little baby teeth. I tried for a few minutes to find it, but gave up right away. Not Alex, he spent an hour picking through every little piece of corn from the disposal. Sure enough, he found it, much to the delight of the little third grader. Alex would probably have Jeremy writing his whole name by now. I couldn't even get the letter 'b' out of the little guy.

It was a relief when the kindergarten teacher asked me to make copies for her instead. I loved going to the copy room. It was warm in the winter from the heat of the machine and the air conditioning ran in the spring to keep the machine from overheating. I loved the smell of the ink and the slam of the built-in stapler. I loved the feel of warm copies when I held them against my chest. Best of all, there was hardly anyone in there, ever. Going to the copy room was, for me, like a little vacation in the middle of my day.

So there I was, making sure my double-sided copies weren't coming out with one side upside down.

"Wow, this takes me back," Kip said, referring to a scene he'd had with Bridget at a copy machine years ago. In the scene, he apologized for being a jerk and promised not to bother her about her job ever again. He lied.

"What, no flowers?" I asked just to prove that I knew what scene he was talking about.

"I wanted to, but it proved to be logistically…difficult," Kip said looking around the copy room. "So whatcha doin'? Makin' copies?"

"You just love coming to visit me at work."

"I was actually hoping to find you writing at home, but when you weren't there, I came here."

"That's a record," I said and looked at my watch for effect. "It took you only eight seconds to mention my job."

He just smiled, looking guilty.

"What are you up to?" I asked.

"Nothing. Why do you think I'm up to something?"

"Because you look guilty."

He sighed and hopped up on the counter. It would never occur to Kip to sit in an actual chair. He was always jumping on some type of counter surface, swinging his feet merrily. "Guilty? Me? You're paranoid," he said in a half-mocking tone that may or may not have been covering up his actual guilt.

"I'm not paranoid," I answered him. "Borderline psychotic, maybe. But not paranoid."

"Borderline?" He raised one eyebrow at me.

"True…" I laughed at myself. It felt good to laugh at me after spending so much time feeling guilty and sorry for being insane.

"Why are you in such a good mood today?" Kip asked me suspiciously. "Usually you're miserable here."

"I'm just happy today. Turns out my life isn't so bad after all," I put new originals in the copy machine and programmed the screen.

"*Hmmm*. Sounds complacent."

"Nothing wrong with that," I said, not wanting to let Kip ruin my good mood.

"Isn't there? Complacency is the enemy of study," he said, playing professor again.

"Who said that?"

"I dunno." He shrugged. "But it sounds about right."

"I'm just happy today, Kip. Let's just leave it at that."

"OK, then. I gotta go." He hopped down.

"Where are you going?" Kip never left me or Bridget until we begged him to leave us alone.

"There's something I've got to do." He called over his shoulder as he disappeared.

****

My good mood almost faltered when I got called to the principal's office after Kindergarten. Something about getting called to the office made me feel like a child...a child who was in trouble. When I was a kid, there was something so ominous about being called to the principal's office, but somewhere along the way, getting sent to the principal became unscary. Our principal in particular was not especially threatening and had no sense of discipline. I used to send kids to him from the cafeteria for disciplinary reasons (food flinging, cheese stick stealing) and he just sent them right back with no consequence or punishment. If the kids didn't take him seriously, I certainly didn't need to. So while I didn't particularly enjoy talking to him, I certainly wasn't worried about any consequences for me.

"One of our parents is concerned about the way you run things in the cafeteria," he told me in a voice that if I didn't know him better, might have sounded stern.

"Really?" I answered, but I couldn't say I was surprised. The only surprise to me was that it hadn't happened sooner. I knew I tended to be more on the strict side in the cafeteria. I tried warm and fuzzy when I first started, but those damn kids walked all over me, so I switched strategies.

"Yes. They say you run the cafeteria like a prison," he said with a wrinkled brow.

I pursed my lips together as tight as I could to stop myself from laughing. I know this accusation was supposed to be a bad thing, but I considered it a complement. "A prison? Are you sure they weren't referring to the food?" Probably not the time for a joke. But I couldn't resist.

"Mirabelle. This is serious." He looked at me like he was almost angry.

"I agree. And I run the cafeteria very seriously. I have two hundred kids in there. I have to stop them from running, yelling, fighting, throwing food, and stealing from the salad bar. Not to mention the accidents and spills. There has to be order, or someone's going to get hurt."

He digested what I said, clearly fearing confrontation, but knowing he had to give me some sort of a talking to. "These particular parents are concerned about you yelling at the children." Probably backlash from my hand-banging incident. I couldn't really blame them, but it's not like I tasered anyone.

"How else am I to be heard over two hundred little voices? If I don't raise my voice, then they can't hear me."

"Still, perhaps you could be more careful with your tone."

"OK, I'll try," I said with an apathetic shrug, even though I had no intention of trying. I tried a different tone years ago when I started this job. Back when I thought it would be fun working with children. Back before I was jaded and miserable. I hated what this job had done to me. I hated that it made me dislike children. I hated that I didn't care whether I got fired or not.

I really didn't give a crap that the parents didn't like what I was doing. I should have, but I didn't. If the parents really cared, they would do a better job parenting so their kids weren't disrespectful little snots, I told myself.

Sometimes I wondered where these horrible thoughts came from. I was a parent of two imperfect kids myself. I got it. I knew kids made mistakes and that mob mentality ruled.

But somehow, I forgot that I was a mother when I was in that cafeteria. "Just out of curiosity, which parent was it that called to complain?" I asked.

"They requested to remain anonymous." Of course they did. Their kid was probably a food flinging, cheese stick stealer…and therefore, often on the receiving end of my warden-like tone.

"Is there anything else?" I asked impatiently, anxious to start my weekend.

"What?"

"Is there anything else you want to talk to me about?"

"Oh. No. Just have a good weekend." He sighed, knowing that despite his best efforts he hadn't gotten through to me.

"I plan to." I smiled and walked out, leaving my job very much behind me.

The best thing about hating my job so very much was that I got a ridiculous, summer-vacation jubilance each and every Friday. The idea of two days of freedom made me positively giddy. So, even though I had just been reprimanded, I practically skipped out of the principal's office. Next weekend would be Thanksgiving. Vivian and Holden would be home Wednesday. I couldn't wait to see them. Though, I could only hope that my little friends would stay away. Or, at the very least, stay far away enough that my children wouldn't think their mother was a total whack job.

CHAPTER 13

"HI, BELLY," ALEX CAME IN from work quietly that night. Weirdly quietly. Not his regular, normal, reserved, rational quiet. Quiet in a way that said he had something to tell me that he didn't want to tell me.

I went to meet him at the garage door, but stopped as soon as I saw his face. "What's wrong?" I asked him.

"Nothing's wrong. Why would something be wrong?" he laughed weakly.

"Because you're acting weird."

He pulled flowers from behind his back. "For my beautiful wife." He smiled excitedly, but I didn't buy it. He was hiding something.

"Still weird." I shook my head, but took the flowers anyway. Flowers from Alex were immensely weird. In our twenty-plus years together, I could count no more than seven times he'd brought me flowers. Alex always said he didn't like spending money on something that died so quickly.

"Can't I bring you flowers without getting the third degree?" He kissed my forehead.

"You never have before…"

"I certainly have." He acted like he was insulted, but he knew I was right.

"Not in years, Alex. What's going on?" I demanded, officially losing my patience.

"Come sit with me." He sat on the couch with a sigh and put his arm out for me to cuddle under.

"Fine." I said as I sat down, resting the flowers in my lap and growing ever suspicious with whatever game he was playing. "Now, what's going on?"

"Well, I have a surprise for you," he began.

"A surprise?" Also weird. Alex liked surprises about as much as he liked flowers.

"You know that hotel on the ocean that you've always wanted to go to?"

"The one on the hill where each room has a private terrace?"

"That's the one."

"What about it?" I asked.

"We're going."

"We are?! When?" I'd been wanting to go to that place for years. Alex always said it was too expensive. So while I was super excited…I was also super suspicious.

"Next weekend. For the long weekend." And there was the kicker.

"Alex, that's Thanksgiving. The kids are coming home." But one look at his face and I knew. The kids weren't coming home…and they were too chicken to tell me themselves. They had Alex be their messenger. "Oh, wait. They're not coming are they?" Crushed. Literally, I felt my heart being mangled and mashed in my chest.

He shook his head. "They made other plans with friends for the weekend."

I sighed and tried to choke back my tears. Alex grabbed my shoulders and turned me to him. Of course, one look at him and I started bawling like a baby. I was pretty sure I saw a glimmer of a tear in his eyes, too.

"Listen, Bella. Our kids are growing up. We can't do anything about that," Alex said, which only made me cry harder.

"Belly, we had a life before we had them, we'll have a life after them, too. Come away with me."

"It's Thanksgiving…" I choked out through my sobs.

"We are not going to sit around here, make a turkey for the two of us and feel sorry for ourselves all weekend. Come away with me," he pleaded. "Like we used to."

Like we used to. A lifetime ago, before children, in what we called our DINKer days (Double Income No Kids). Back when we had plenty of cash to pretty much do whatever we wanted. Of course, now we were income and a half and two college tuition payments.

I sniffed back my tears and held my head high. He was right, this was what was supposed to happen. Our kids were supposed to grow up and make their own lives and we were supposed to grow old together. "They were too cowardly to call me themselves, huh?"

"They didn't want to hurt your feelings."

"So, they sent you to do their dirty work?"

He nodded. "I read the little bastards the riot act. I certainly didn't want to be the one to tell you."

"Very clever distracting me with a trip…"

"I'm smart that way. Are you going call them – lay the guilt on?"

I shook my head. "You're right, Alex. They have their own lives now…but they better freaking be here for Christmas."

****

In packing for our trip, I worked hard to keep thoughts of my absentee children away. I pretended they didn't exist anymore than my crazy delusions did. Cruel and unusual punishment,

I know. But I was royally pissed off at them and if I didn't do something drastic, I would've been completely consumed by my emotions – anger, excitement, betrayal, sadness – you name it, I was feeling it. I promised myself I would focus solely on the excitement part.

This trip had to be only about Alex and me. Not about the crazies in my brain and not at all about the fact that my children had abandoned me on their very first holiday since leaving for college. Though, my heart was heavy missing them, I was determined to keep my thoughts on Alex. This was a very romantic gesture from a very practical man and I had every intention of giving him my full attention in return. It was something I hadn't always been very good at for much of our marriage. One hand tending to the children, the other hand scribbling in a notebook, left no hands for paying attention to Alex.

This weekend could be, should be, a transition for us. The next phase of our life was to begin now. The phase without our children. Had I expected some measure of personal success for myself at this point in my life? Sure. But not attaining it was an even bigger reason to make sure that our marriage remained strong.

The glass half-full part of me felt like we were embarking on some new level in our marriage somehow. We'd taken each other for granted for a long time. And that wasn't ok. Me always looking at the children, at my feet, or looking off in the distance at some fairy tale of success I would probably never attain. It was time for me to spend some time looking at my husband.

I remember when we first had the twins. One night, they were maybe two months old, pj'd, fed, and we each held on to one baby dozing in our arms. I don't remember who had who.

Alex whispered, “Hey, have you noticed that we don’t look at each other anymore?” He didn’t say it in a bad way. More in a matter of fact, ‘ain’t life weird?’ kinda way. He was right. Once the children were born, our attention went from gazing into each other’s eyes to looking down at whichever kid we were holding, who was hungry, who needed to be changed. From there it turned to who needs help with their homework, who needs a ride to practice. Now, it was time to let them go. It was time to gaze at each other again…as terrifying as that prospect was.

Alex was positively charming from the moment we left the house, opening the door for me with his keys in his mouth and a bottle of champagne tucked under his arm. When he climbed in on his side, he exhaled, put both hands on the steering wheel before looking at me as if he wasn’t sure this weekend was actually going to happen. “Ready?” he asked, his always calm demeanor looking decidedly rattled.

I nodded and smiled. “Let’s go.”

At the first red light, Alex pulled his iPod out of his inside coat pocket and plugged it into the speaker dock in the car, smirking as he pulled up a playlist. “What are you putting on?” Usually, Alex and I didn’t agree on music. His tastes leaned towards the more serious jazz and blues music, where I preferred dancy, silly, poppy music.

“You’ll see,” he laughed, an oddly girlish giggle. And when the music started, I giggled too.

“You didn’t.”

“I did,” he beamed proudly. “I have compiled a playlist of various songs from our lifetime together, starting with this little classic right here.” The song was Bizarre Love Triangle by New Order. We had danced to it the first night we met…at a drunken fraternity party. God, college was so much fun. I wondered if Holden and Vivian were having as much fun as we did. I hoped they weren't.

By the time we got to the hotel after a lovely trip down memory lane courtesy of Alex's music mix, I had completely forgotten it was Thanksgiving. Alex jumped out of the car and ran around to my side, offering his hand to escort me inside. We checked in arm-in-arm and I remembered wistfully the very first time he put his arm around me.

We weren't even dating then, we were just friends, two people who happened to be randomly assigned to the same dorm. When he put his arm around me, it was meant to be a friendly gesture. But something about us fit together even then. His arm felt like it belonged there. In spite of our obvious differences, we seemed to belong together. At least we felt that way. Mostly everybody else told us we'd never last. We were too different to last. Shows what everybody else knows. For years we always walked with his left arm around my shoulders, my right arm linked around his waist. We had sides that we walked on just like we had sides of the bed. When the twins came along, we were too busy holding them to hang on to each other.

As soon as we got to our room, Alex popped the champagne as I sat out on the balcony overlooking the ocean. It was cold, but in a refreshing, invigorating kind of way. "For you, my dear," Alex passed me a glass over my shoulder. He pulled a chair close to me so he could put his arm around me. I let my head fall onto his shoulder. We fit together like pieces of a puzzle. An old, complicated puzzle where the edges were a little worn. But we still fit.

We sat there. Not needing to talk. Just listening to the roar of the ocean pounding onto the shore. I wondered what

Alex was thinking. If I had to guess, I'd say he was thinking of something to say that wouldn't mention either the children or my writing. I decided to put him out of his misery by starting a conversation. "I'm feeling very thankful."

"Are you? For what?"

"For you. No matter what, at the end of the day, I have you," I told him. And it was true…I just forgot it sometimes. Lots of times. Too many times.

"I'm thankful for you, too. Do you know that I still look forward to coming home to you every day?" He tilted his head and rested it lightly on top of mine.

"Every day?" I asked, staring out at the ocean waves crashing on the beach below us.

"Yeah. Every day."

"Liar."

"Well, there was that one day, back in '97. And then there was that Tuesday in '03. But other than that, every day."

When the champagne was empty, we walked the beach. The sand was cold. But it didn't bother us. Shoes off, pants rolled up. Alex was even bold enough to put his toes in, running out just as soon as the freezing water covered his feet. We danced on the deserted beach and laughed and talked and rejoiced in the freedom that came with your children growing up. Celebrating being on our own again. I have to say, it was pretty fun. Getting back to the place where we were the only ones who mattered. And yes, looking each other in the eyes again. Not being afraid of seeing each other's souls because deep down inside, our souls were one and the same.

****

The next day was Thanksgiving, though I pretended it wasn't just so I wouldn't be melancholy about missing the kids. Alex and I went out for a wine-drenched lunch and got caught in the rain. He held his coat over my head to keep me dry and pulled me into a doorway during a downpour. We huddled close in the freezing November rain and he kissed me with his soaking wet face. It was a movie-perfect scene…until I allowed my eyes to wander across the street.

Emily stood alone in the rain, looking like she had fallen overboard. Wet hair stuck to her sullen face, but she didn't even seem to notice it was raining. I wanted to help her, pull her in out of the rain. I wanted to save her from the rain and the storm that was her life. I wanted to help her be less pathetic, less weak, and for the love of god, less alone. I wanted to give her what I had with Alex – a moment in time where even though it was pouring rain and she was soaked to the skin she would feel safe and secure and nothing but happy.

Alex felt me drifting away. "Are you okay?" he asked, lifting my chin. He held my shoulders, grounding me to the world, keeping me with him.

I pulled my attention away from Emily and back to Alex. Reality. *Stay in reality* I told myself. "I'm good." I told him and myself. "Just wet."

He raised his eyebrows and smiled. "Then, let's get you out of these wet clothes."

When I looked back across the street Emily was gone.

****

Our faith in our marriage restored, we returned home on Sunday. Unfortunately, though my marriage was intact, my brain was not. I still saw not only Emily, but also Kip, David, Monica, and Daniel lurking on the peripherals of our weekend. I didn't engage any of them. Not once. I didn't talk to them, look at them, or make the slightest eye contact with them. As soon as I noticed them, I quickly looked away and pretended I didn't see them at all. They weren't there. They weren't real. Only Alex was real.

The problem was that I was sane enough to understand that these characters were appearing to me because subconsciously I actually wanted them there. And if that's the case, why did I want things to distract me from my weekend with Alex? I didn't. Did I? No, I wanted everything to be perfect on our trip just as much as he did. So exactly what part of my brain was trying to sabotage my marriage?

On the plus side, I did manage to control them – my friends. I ignored them and they went away. Temporarily at least. Of course, not actually being alone all weekend, with the exception of an occasional trip to the bathroom, helped. Keeping Alex close to me kept my demons away. All weekend I clung to him as hard as I could. I was not looking forward to Monday, to being alone without his presence to defend me and to keep me sane. I feared an onslaught of visits would be coming my way. I resolved to continue ignoring them. Refuse to engage them. Pretend they weren't there and they were bound to go away, permanently. Stay in reality. Stay in my marriage. Stay with Alex.

CHAPTER 14

MONDAY MORNING CAME TOO DAMN quickly. I woke up, thought of going to work, and felt like I had never been away in the first place with the exception that Alex lingered a little longer on his morning kiss than usual.

With a heavy sigh, I got myself moving and began the drudgery of my daily household chores. Today's chores featured the added bonus of unpacking and storing the suitcases from our trip. My suitcase was stored in "deep storage" in the bowels of our basement because, other than Alex's occasional business trips, we never actually went anywhere anymore.

Trudging down the stairs, dragging my suitcase behind me with a thud down each step, I descended the basement stairs. I figured while I was down there I should start pulling out the decorations for Christmas, so I pulled a box of nutcrackers from the top shelf.

"Pretty girl like you shouldn't be hauling such heavy boxes."

I heard Cody's voice, but I pretended I didn't. I didn't look at him leaning in the corner of the basement. I didn't need to look to know he was wearing a blood-stained tuxedo and carrying a glass of scotch. I returned to the storage room for another big box.

"Shouldn't your big, strong husband be carrying that for you?" Clever Cody, trying to bait me into talking to him by involving Alex. I further ignored him. Dug my heels into reality.

"Hello? Hey, I'm talking to you here." He started waving his hands in my face. "Hey? Hey? Can you hear me?" He snapped his fingers next to my ears as he followed me to the ping-pong table.

"I hear you!" I barked finally, as I dropped a box on the table with a clunk. "I'm just ignoring you."

"Yeah, you've been doing an awful lot of that lately. I don't like it."

"I don't care what you like." Then, it occurred to me. "Wait, when did I ignore you?" I asked, afraid of the answer and not entirely sure why I was continuing this conversation.

"You ignored me all weekend on your little getaway with hubby," he said, pouting.

"I didn't see you," I whispered.

"I was giving you some space from our, you know, relationship." He put air quotes around relationship.

"We don't have a relationship."

"Sure. You keep telling yourself that. Anyway, after our last encounter, I thought we could use a break." He gave my arm a little squeeze before plopping himself down on our nasty basement couch. He propped his fancy shoes up on our old coffee table that I used some weird spray paint on to get a leathery-type finish, but it ended up looking and feeling like sandpaper. Cody looked pretty ridiculous sitting in his formal-wear in the place where our old furniture goes to die. "But I was there. Nice hotel room. Big bed," he said with a smirk, crossing his ankles on our crappy table.

"God, Cody, could you be any creepier?" Mental note: If I ever get around to actually writing a story for Cody, give him some boundaries and maybe a filter.

"Probably. You tell me."

I shuddered in disgust and frustration. "What are you doing here?" I said, shaking my head, though it was a completely rhetorical question. I didn't really want him to tell me what he was doing here.

"Same as always, babe," he answered anyway. "I'm here because you want me to be here."

"You know what, Cody?"

"What?"

I was about to argue with him. About to tell him what I thought of him. About to beg him to leave me alone. Then I remembered my resolve to ignore them. Stay in reality. Stay with Alex.

Sprinting upstairs, I grabbed my car keys and bolted for the garage, slamming the door behind me. I settled into the driver's seat and began to back out of my driveway carefully.

"Didn't I tell you ignoring me won't work?" Cody's sudden presence in the passenger seat made me jump and slam on the brakes.

Still, I refused to talk to him. "He's not there. He's not real." I said out loud over and over again.

"And yet here I am." Cody said in response to my chanting. I wouldn't look at him, and I ignored the fact that I could still hear the rattling of the ice cubes in his ever present glass.

Accelerating, I drove myself to the grocery store hoping to lose him somewhere in the aisles, but he just followed me around, yapping in my ear the whole time. Generally, just annoying the crap out of me. I managed not to talk back to him in public. But he was still with me, no matter where I went. I couldn't seem to shake him.

I had to get to my safe place. To Alex.

Of course, the parking lot in Alex's office was full and it took me what felt like forever to find a spot. Up and down the aisles I drove with Cody babbling away the whole time. I don't even know what he was talking about. I didn't listen. But he kept talking and talking.

I walked quickly to Alex's office, and so did Cody, trailing behind me, practically skipping.

The door to Alex's office was open and he was on the phone. I stood in the doorway, wringing my hands nervously until he looked up. He almost smiled at the sight of me but instead frowned in confusion. He had a right to be confused. I was confused. I hadn't been in his office in forever and I certainly never showed up unannounced. He finished up on the phone and got up from his desk. Cody walked right between us and took a spot facing me, behind Alex's back. I tried my best not to react to him.

"Bella, what are you doing here?" Alex asked, taking my hand. I couldn't tell if he was happy I was there, annoyed that I was there, or afraid of why I was there.

I tried not to look as panic-stricken as I felt, but I doubt I succeeded. "Oh, I was just in the neighborhood and I wanted to see if you were free for lunch." I closed the door behind me.

But he stepped away, dropping my hand and gesturing at his desk. "Bella, I can't right now. I'm working."

I played the only card I had. "I know, but I missed you. Aren't you glad to see me?" Pathetic, I know. So damn needy. I hated myself for it. But I didn't have a choice.

"Of course I am," he softened for a moment, but only a brief moment until he realized what time it was. "Wait, aren't you supposed to be at work?"

Crap. In my frenzy to get rid of Cody, I plumb forgot to go to work.

And that bastard just sat on Alex's credenza laughing at me, sipping his scotch. "You should've just talked to me and saved yourself all this trouble," he said, grinning.

"I forgot," I told Alex sheepishly.

"You forgot?" He furrowed his brow at me.

"I was putting away the suitcases and getting out the Christmas stuff and I kind of lost track of time. I guess."

He didn't believe me. It was written all over his crinkly brow that he knew I was lying. "That's it. No visits?"

"Not since before the weekend." I smiled as I lied. "Maybe I'm cured."

Alex looked at me like he didn't believe me. "Really? Nothing's wrong?"

"Really." I reassured him. "I just got into the Christmas thing, and I missed you, and I just totally forgot about work." I babbled on.

"OK." He nodded, but still looked suspicious. "So, can I get back to work then?" He pointed at his desk.

"Of course. I'm sorry, honey. I should've called." I opened the door that I had closed behind me, quickly turning to leave before I could embarrass myself any further.

"Belly?"

I stopped, but didn't turn around.

"I am glad you came by."

Leave it to Alex to throw a little pity at me when I've just made a complete fool of myself. I muttered some sort of goodbye and high-tailed it out of there.

I managed to lose Cody somewhere between making a complete ass of myself in Alex's office and the car. How could

I have been so stupid? I felt more stupid than I ever felt crazy. Damn Cody pushed me too far. Too far from reality. Right off a cliff. Burying my face in my hands, I put my head on the steering wheel to regain my composure.

"That didn't go the way you planned, did it?" Cody appeared again in the passenger seat, scaring the crap out of me for the second time that day. Damn him.

"You know what, Cody?" I snarled at him as I lifted my head, started the engine, and put the car into gear.

"What's that, doll?"

"I think maybe I will kill you."

"That's my girl." He smiled as he looked off into the distance, sipped his scotch and vanished.

****

I was done. With Cody chasing me around all day yapping in my ear, or my head, whatever, I was enraged. He humiliated me in front of Alex and then relished in my discomfort. I couldn't take another visit from the bastard. I wanted to kill him, to end him. The guilt I felt for not telling Alex the whole truth about what had happened that morning settled in my gut like a rock, and I had every intention of taking it out on Cody.

I took the box labeled "Cody" from my closet shelf. Stupid Cody. I quite simply never wanted to deal with him again, and I was going to make it happen. I didn't want to hear his stupid theory about my so-called dark side ever again. He wanted an ending. Fine. I'd give him a freaking ending.

After flipping through the few notes I had on him, I found no place to start, so I started from nowhere.

KILLING CODY

I typed. Good start, I thought and then set my twisted imagination on a course of how I could end Cody. I'd read once, I can't imagine where, that the most painful way to die was to get shot in the abdomen and then bleed slowly to death. That sounded good. I was so angry with him. I wanted him to feel pain, lots of it, preferably for a long period of time.

"It won't work, you know." Cody's voice came from my left. I should've guessed any attempt to kill him would summon him to my side. There he was, stretched out on my bed, tie undone, crystal glass in hand, arms crossed over his chest.

I didn't look at him and just kept typing. "I don't care, it's going to be fun trying."

"You need to finish me first…then you can kill me."

Deliberately trying not to understand whatever the hell he meant by that, I ignored him.

Cody looked at Mark with his steely blue eyes. "You wouldn't dare," he growled at him.

"Who the hell is Mark? You can't just make this shit up as you go along, you know. You need to actually put some story behind it."

I sneered at him and went back to work.

"What makes you think I wouldn't, Cody? Do you think I don't have the guts? Do you think because you're my brother I won't spill your blood?"

"Oooh. Deep stuff, baby. Long lost brother comes to settle an old score? Been done. Do I even have a brother?" Cody mocked. I kept typing. The sooner I finished this, the sooner I wouldn't have to listen to his stupid, sardonic voice ever again.

I went back and changed Mark to Marcia simply because I wanted to picture myself pulling the trigger.

"Better. It'll be easier for you to put yourself in Marcia's shoes than Mark's. Mark's would be way too big for your cute, little feet. Though I hate the name Marcia…it's just too *Brady Bunch*, you know what I mean?" He rambled like I was looking for his creative input.

I stopped typing and looked at him.

"What?" he asked me. "I'm helping."

I checked my watch. I needed to kill Cody before Alex came home at five. Fifty minutes.

"You know, baby sister, I do think that. I do think that you don't have it in you to kill your own brother because you're not like me." She hated when he called her "baby sister," like after all these years and all the shit he had put her through that he somehow deserved the title "big brother."

Marcia gripped the gun tighter in her hands. Her mind raced with every crappy thing Cody had ever done. Her hatred for him boiled over.

"That's a cop out," Cody shook his head. "Show us the crappy things. Don't just tell us," Cody said and I glared at him. I hated when he was right.

She tried for a moment to remember some of Cody's redeeming qualities. Sure he had stolen thousands from her and their parents. And yeah, he beat up more people than she could count, including her husband, their cousin, and some poor homeless guy who just happened to be in the wrong place at the wrong time. And though she had no proof, she was quite sure he had killed her kitten when they were kids.

"Ouch. Kitten killer? Really? Am I that bad?" Cody asked.

I disregarded his questions and kept typing. Though even I knew he wasn't THAT bad, I didn't care. All that mattered to me now was ending him.

Marcia couldn't find one. Not one redeeming quality. She couldn't think of a single moment where he showed some level of conscience or the slightest bit of compassion toward her or anyone else. The gun grew heavy in her hands.

"You're not going to do it, baby sister, so why don't you just give me the gun?" He reached his hand out to her.

He wasn't even a tiny bit afraid. Here she was pointing a gun at his head, and he still stood there with that arrogant, cocky smirk on his face. "You're a sociopath," she told him and she meant it. She honestly wasn't sure if he knew the difference between right and wrong.

"You're the one with the gun and I'm the sociopath?" he laughed at her. "That's good."

"Fuck you, Cody," She hated when he laughed at her. Ever since they were kids, he mocked her, teased her, manipulated her, tortured her. She wanted him dead. No one would miss him. No one would even care he was gone. Her anger boiled in her veins and she squeezed the trigger, just a little...she wasn't sure how hard she had to squeeze to actually fire the gun.

"Marcia, don't..." were the last words he spoke before the blast from the gun shattered her ear drums.

Cody suddenly convulsed on the bed next to me, startling me out of my typing. He groaned and curled into a ball, grabbing his abdomen. Seeing him writhing in pain, I couldn't help but feel bad for the guy. He wasn't really any of the things I had just typed about him. He was a thief, and a grifter, and a master manipulator. But he wasn't a killer. He wasn't even particularly violent. Sure, he was an arrogant jerk, but he was no sociopath. I had been careless to kill him so quickly, so thoughtlessly.

"Oh, Cody." I said shamefully, feeling like I had indeed pulled the trigger myself. This wasn't what I wanted, not really. Wracked with guilt, I reached out for him and rolled him onto his back as he lay dying. But there was no fresh blood. Just the old stains from the cut on his hand. He winced and moaned some more.

Until suddenly, he bolted upright and winked at me. "Told you it wouldn't work."

"Fuck you, Cody." I swore at him, my heart pounding in my chest.

"Oh, come on, that was funny."

"No, it wasn't." Damn him for making me care about him.

"I did tell you it wouldn't work, didn't I?"

I turned my back on him so he wouldn't see the tears welling up in my eyes. I didn't know if I was crying because I was mad or happy or relieved or frustrated. Whatever the reason, I did not want him to catch me crying.

"I'm sorry, baby, you can't just kill me." He spoke softly, almost kindly, exhibiting the compassion I just accused him of not having. "You have to give me a story. Not just an ending, not just a death scene."

I shook my head. "I can't. I can't do it."

"Sure you can." He stroked my hair from behind and, though I shivered, I let him. "You already have an ending… though I'm not particularly fond of it, it's an ending…you have a character, that's for sure…you just need a beginning and a middle, and those are your specialty," he said with a chuckle. "You can do this, Bella. I'll help you," he coached and I realized how sweet he sounded when he didn't call me 'honey' or 'baby' or 'doll face.'

I looked back over my shoulder at him and for a moment I was locked in those beautiful, blue eyes and I almost believed him. I almost believed that maybe I could change him. Maybe I could fix him. Help him. Make him a better person. For just that moment, I forgot what a pain in the ass he was – until I heard the buzz of the garage door downstairs and he vanished again.

CHAPTER 15

THE FRENZY OF THE HOLIDAY season had officially begun and I was both thrilled and hopeful. Thrilled that my children would be home for the holidays… and hopeful that the business of Christmas would keep my little friends away. Despite what had happened with Cody, I wanted and I needed my lunacy to take a holiday. I needed to focus on the kids and on Alex. Not to mention, I was growing weary of being crazy and pretending to be normal. It was exhausting. So I figured, for the holidays I would try to be a little less crazy, or a lot less crazy. I equated it to giving up chocolate for Lent. I was giving up crazy for Christmas.

I dove into the holidays in full force and kept myself too busy to see Kip lurking in the back of the cafeteria, too tired to talk to David lurking around the house at night, and too filled with the spirit of Christmas to bring myself to talk to Daniel, who hovered everywhere else looking sad. Cody was nowhere to be found. I didn't know if he was hiding from me or if I was hiding from him.

Either way, I ignored them all and their realness seemed to fade. I could still see them, but they seemed somehow translucent, almost likes ghosts or some weird optical illusion that was there one minute and gone the next. Sometimes they were just blips or flashes out of the corner of my eye. And when I looked again, they were gone. I was relieved that they were fading. It was certainly better for my marriage to have them gone. But there was a part of me, a small part, but a part no less, that missed them. Just a little mostly. But, sometimes a lot. I missed Kip the way you miss that friend in college who always got you in just enough trouble. I worried about David, like he was a brother battling depression. And Daniel was almost like a son to me. I felt things that they felt. Hurt when they hurt. Rejoiced when they did. Though rejoicing was rare, of course, since none of them ever had a happy ending.

And I was just a little bit bored without them.

I'd be lying if I said I wasn't more than a little bit concerned about Cody. I hadn't seen him since I tried to kill him and that had been a few weeks earlier. I was haunted by his absence and tortured by questions about what I wanted for him. My own reaction to his fake death had me wondering. Killing him was clearly off the table.

One night, as Alex and I sat down to dinner, he asked me about my visits.

"You haven't mentioned your…uh…characters in awhile," he asked, but stammered as if he had rehearsed this beforehand but then suddenly forgot what he was going to say.

"I haven't seen them." I shrugged like I didn't care and moved my peas around on my plate with the tines of my fork.

"How come?" He looked at me quizzically.

"I don't know. Why do you ask?" I wasn't sure what he wanted to hear from me.

"I don't know. It just seems sort of odd, doesn't it?"

"It's always been odd, Alex." I said, irritated with all his questions.

"But isn't it odd that you haven't seen them. They were everywhere before and now they're just gone."

"I haven't seen any of them since Thanksgiving." I shrugged like I didn't care, not wanting to reveal the truth. Not wanting to let on that I really did care. Very much.

"Our weekend." He smiled. "Do you think that made them go away?"

"I guess." I didn't want to say too much. I didn't want to tell him that I saw them all through that weekend and have certainly seen them since but was trying desperately to ignore them for his sake. I didn't really want to talk about it at all so I changed the subject. "Are you ready for hosting duties this weekend?"

"Ah yes, the Annual Holiday Party. What time does it start again?"

"Alex, we've been having this party for fourteen years and you can never remember that it starts at 7:30."

"I knew that."

We'd been having a Holiday Party every year since the kids were old enough to help carry the coats up to our bedroom.

This year was different though. This year, I didn't exactly feel like having the party. The people we invited were mostly people we met through our kids and their soccer teams and drama productions. Since the kids left for college, I felt pretty checked out of that whole world.

But I had to have the party. If I didn't, people would ask why and what could I say? That now that my kids left for college I wasn't interested in hanging out with their friends' parents anymore? Or that this Christmas I was going insane so I certainly couldn't throw a party in the middle of all that? No, I couldn't say any of those things, so I told myself it would be good to see the old gang and went about planning a party.

I cooked and cleaned and listened to Christmas Carols. I set out my Nutcrackers and decked the halls with boughs of holly. And I enjoyed it. I allowed the holidays to consume me and it felt great. I almost forgot that I was losing my mind. I missed my characters less and less the busier I was. I missed my children less and less, too.

They came home the day before the party. Holden and Vivian, that is, not my characters. They got a ride from some friends who lived nearby, giving me the opportunity to stay home and make everything perfect for them. I baked their favorites, like I did when they were little. Banana Chocolate Chip Muffins for Holden and Cinnamon Crunch Bread for Vivi. In my stupidity, I assumed they were going to be excited to be home and that they might actually want to spend time with their mother. In reality, they walked in the front door and walked right back out again, anxious to see the friends from high school they had left behind. Holden grabbed a muffin on his way out the door. Vivi cited something about her skinny jeans, refused to eat anything, and went on her way.

I was so very jealous. And a little bit sad. And just a teensy bit bitter. They seemed so different than when we dropped them off. So independent. So mature. So adult. In three short months, they seemed to have aged years.

Seems like when your kids are little, you can't wait for them to grow up and not need you so much. And when they do grow up, and don't need you anymore, you would give anything for one more day of toddlerhood when everything they did was dependent on you. Every meal, every activity, every toy was all because of choices you made for them. Then they grow up and make their own choices. I was immensely proud to see them embracing their grown-up lives. But I did wish they needed me or wanted me more than they did. I knew they loved me and that was enough, mostly. I had hoped to spend more time with them during their vacation. But it became very clear very quickly that I was going to have to settle for a random conversation here and there and a couple of family dinners. It made me long for the days of baseball games and dance recitals that seemed to take up so much of our lives there was no room for anything else. They needed me then. Chauffeur. Chef. Costume designer. Counsel. Coach.

Our house was sparkling, the hors d'oeuvres prepared, and Alex and I were getting dressed for the party. My stomach buzzed with nervous energy, even though I knew I had everything well under control. All the food was prepared. Drinks were made. I just needed to plate and serve and entertain 40 people in my too-small house. And I had to make it look easy.

"You look beautiful," Alex said to me as he stepped out of the bathroom wrapped only in a towel.

"Why do you sound surprised?"

"I'm not. I'm not the one who forgets how beautiful you are. You are." He nuzzled my neck as I tried to put in my earrings.

"You're all wet." I pushed him away.

He just smirked.

"Get dressed…I need your help."

"Yes, ma'am."

Once the doorbell started ringing, it never stopped. I hoped to have the kids help with the coats, like when they were little, but they were out once again, so we were on our own. It was a bit frenzied collecting coats and serving drinks, but we settled into our roles as host and hostess quickly, as if we did this kind of thing all the time. Little did my guests know, the most entertaining I'd done in a year was hosting a parade of my imaginary acquaintances.

The party was going well. I was surprised at how easily I managed to make conversation after months of isolating myself with my characters. Most of the conversations at the party relied on safe topics like our children, reality TV or home improvement, which kept people from discussing truly interesting things like politics and religion. But that was probably for the best.

I was, much to my surprise, having fun. It turned out that almost all of the mothers were nothing short of devastated that their kids had gone off to college. All except that nasty Tammy McShane. She claimed to not miss her children one bit. Tammy was one of those moms that never remembered my name, but somehow always remembered Alex. You could tell that she was a mean girl in high school.

"I'm glad they're gone, honestly. They cramped my style," Tammy winked at me as if I could somehow relate.

"Stop it, Tammy," Maya Graham told her. "You know you miss Kaity just as much as we miss our kids."

"Maybe a little bit. But at least my kids came home for Thanksgiving."

"Tammy!" Maya scolded and slapped her on the arm. I'm sure it was all over town that my kids couldn't be bothered to come home for Thanksgiving.

"What? I just meant that must've been really upsetting. Right, Bella?" Tammy said, jabbing me with her elbow.

"Oh sure. I was definitely upset. So upset that Alex took me to Cliffside for the weekend." I bragged matter-of-factly. I know, it was kind of out of character for me. But it was my party and Tammy just made me so damn mad. Honestly, she was the one person that I would've loved to have left off the guest list, but if she found out I'd had the party and not invited her, she'd bad mouth me to all the other soccer moms. "I barely remembered it was Thanksgiving," I added with a smile and a wink to Tammy, just to twist the knife a little bit more.

Alex made his appearance right on cue, hooking an arm around my waist. "Hello, ladies. Anyone need anything from the bar?" A few drinks loosened Alex quite nicely into his hosting duties.

The ladies all fawned over and flirted with him and I managed to make my escape for a much needed trip to the ladies' room and a reprieve from Tammy. I climbed the stairs to the Master Bedroom bringing my wine glass with me, knowing full well if I put it down somewhere I'd never find it. I took care of my business in the bathroom noting to myself that the best thing about hosting the party was not having to worry about driving yourself home. The worst part was having to stop yourself from telling your guests exactly what you think of them. Well, some of them anyway. Most of them were perfectly lovely people.

When I came out of the bathroom, there was Cody. Passed out on my bed on top of all the coats. Snoring. Shirt unbuttoned to his waist, no longer tucked in. I know I should've just walked away. I know I should've just left him there to vanish into the recesses of my brain. But I didn't. I closed the bedroom door and went right to his side, giving him a little shake.

"Hey, baby. Merry Christmas," he yawned and stretched as his eyes fluttered open.

"Hey, yourself." I said, glad to see him even though he was a mess and he absolutely reeked of alcohol. "Wow… You're really drunk."

"Thanks to you, I'm always drunk. It's part of my character," he slurred so it sounded more like "characthpper."

"You're drunker than usual." I noted.

"Sorry. But if I'm not mistaken, you are, too." Mithtaken, he said.

"Fair," I agreed, but continued, "Cody, please, you have to go. You can't be here now."

"Don't you want me here?" he pouted and tried to stand up, but stumbled back down.

"No. I don't." I lied.

"You lie…you missed me."

"OK fine. I missed you. But you can't be here now."

"Why the fuck not? What the fuck is so important about this stupid party that I don't matter to you?" His temper flared as I knew it would, but hoped it wouldn't. 'Really drunk Cody' had no ability to control his rage.

"Of course, you matter." I whispered softly, hoping to settle him down into a rational conversation. But instead, he started to cry. Sob is probably a better word. He curled up into a little ball on top of the coats weeping, tears pouring from his beautiful eyes.

"I thought you would've ended me by now," he wailed.

"I haven't…I couldn't…" Excuses, excuses.

"Why not? Just do it already! Write my story and kill me already!"

"I'm going to…I just haven't…I can't…"

"What's taking you so long?" he yelled and then cried, looking down into his hands "Look what you made me do."

"Cody, what happened? What did you do?"

"I didn't do anything! You did it! You made me! You know what, just forget it…you get back to your party. You don't need me and I don't need you. I don't need anyone!" His usual crystal glass was now a bottle and he took a swig.

Cody was right about one thing. It was all my fault. I made him an ass, and then I made him do bad things and I gave him just enough conscience to hate himself. I had a responsibility to him. To all of them. I had to finish them. "I do need you, Cody. More than you know. I'm sorry I've been ignoring you. But I do need you." I reached out to wipe a tear from his face but stopped myself, suspending my hand an inch from his cheek.

"Do you, baby?" he slurred.

"Of course, I do. But right now…I have to be at this party. I'm begging you, please."

"I know, I know, go away." He sniffled resignedly.

"Just stay away until after New Year's. Then I can focus my attention on you again."

"You're not going to put me back in that fucking box."

"No. I'm not going to put you back in that fucking box. I'm going to help you, Cody. I'll finish you," I told him, sniffing back some tears myself. In this condition, Cody was almost as pathetic as Emily and it hurt me to see him this way.

"You'll fix me?" he asked softly, hopefully.

I nodded. "I'll fix you, Cody. But you have to give me time to get it right."

"Promise?"

"I promise."

Giggles. "I knew you liked me. Just a little." He kissed me softly on the cheek and vanished before the scotch from his lips dried on my cheek. I wiped my face and smelled my hand. Jack Daniels. Good thing I was at a party. Hopefully, no one would notice that I smelled like whisky when all I was drinking was wine.

I shook my head with a sigh and grabbed my wine glass. But when I opened my door to head back to my frolicking guests, Holden was standing right freaking there. "Mom, who were you talking to?"

"What?" I stammered, hoping to find out how much he heard before I incriminated myself too deeply.

"Nevermind." He shook his head. "I thought I heard voices."

I shrugged. "I'd better get back to the party."

"Yeah…I'm going to Mark's." he followed me downstairs and straight out the front door without a goodbye. I exhaled, relieved to have dodged that bullet. For once I was grateful for Holden's teenage oblivion.

I had to fight my way back into the spirit of the party. I couldn't deny that I had been worried about Cody since I hadn't seen him in so long. It turned out I really cared about the bastard; who knew? But I couldn't care now. I had to keep my feet in my world. And I certainly had to keep this craziness away from my children. Until New Year's. After the holidays, I would save Cody. I would give him the redemption he needed. I would save them all. I had to. I got them into all their messes. It was up to me to get them out. After New Year's. No time like New Year's for resolutions. What better time to make Cody a better person? And me.

CHAPTER 16

CHRISTMAS WAS DELIGHTFUL. I'M STILL naïve enough to believe that there actually is peace on earth and good will towards men on Christmas Day. And in our little corner of the world, there definitely was. Vivian and Holden were with us all day and were actually engaged with us for most of it. They barely even looked at their phones. We had a beautiful dinner, just the four of us, before the children scooted out with their friends for the night, leaving Alex and I curled up on the couch in front of a picture-perfect fire. It was amazing and yet all very, very normal.

New Year's Eve was nice and normal, too. The kids went out and stayed out, we went to Maya and Jeff's and enjoyed a champagne-soaked evening with them, culminating with watching the ball drop in Times Square with Ryan Seacrest.

I was completely engaged in my world and didn't even think about my characters. There was no sign of Cody, no Kip sitting on my counter, no sulking David, no Monica rambling about her dream wedding. I was beginning to enjoy being normal except for the fact that I felt like I had some good friends that had moved away. I certainly couldn't say I didn't miss them at all. I mean, I didn't miss the constant reminders of all my character flaws. But there was a certain comfort to most of their visits.

The kids went back to school right after the holidays and took with them any sense of normalcy I had regained within myself while they were home. Even though I hadn't spent as much time with them as I had hoped, having them coming and going from under our roof made me feel more connected to them, more grounded in reality. At least when they were home, I had some clue of where they were and who they were with as opposed to when they were away and I had no idea what they were up to.

Alex drove them back to school on Saturday afternoon and though I really wanted to go along for the ride, I just didn't think I could bear another trip out there. Being that the last trip sent me into a mental tailspin, I figured I'd be better off at home.

With a whole Saturday to myself, I sat down on my bed, surrounding myself with my unfinished boxes, optimistic that I could finish something, anything. I fully expected someone to show up and prod me along, or give me some sort of an idea of where to go with them. But no one showed. I spent the day rifling through papers without typing or writing a single word. I tried closing my eyes and wishing for someone to appear, trying to figure out if there was something I could do to summon one of them. But no luck. It was one of the loneliest days I'd ever spent. Had I scared them away with my efforts to be normal? Were they gone for good?

The buzzing of Holden and Vivian's comings and goings gone, and my characters missing in action, I was left alone with the dreaded task of taking down the holiday decorations. I hated it. It left me feeling cold and empty, like a half-drunk mug of cocoa.

Snow followed. Lots of it. It was one of those bizarre New England winters where it seemed to snow everyday. Roofs caved in from the weight of it. We couldn't even find our mailbox. The snow was piled so high we couldn't see the street from our house. Backing out of the driveway was like taking your life in your hands since you couldn't actually see the street, and anyone coming couldn't see you past the piles of snow.

So, we hibernated, leaving the house only for work and to shovel snow, though I enjoyed quite a few school cancellations. But there was so much to shovel. It wasn't just the driveways and sidewalks. There was so much snow, it needed to be shoveled off the roof, then the roof snow had to be shoveled off the driveway and walk. You could see early-morning delivered newspapers embedded like fossils in different layers of snow that piled up next to the driveway. If you pulled them out you could tell the dates of each massive snowstorm.

The post-holiday emptiness was filled to the ceiling with ice and snow. There was something adventurous about it, yet a little disconcerting that we couldn't see out the front windows. You would think these circumstances would lead me back into writing, where I needed to be. That all those snow days would give me plenty of time to finish something. That it was time to fulfill that promise I made to a very drunken Cody. But somehow, when I sat down to write, I just stared out the window at the mountains of snow.

I tried, really I did. But I felt like I had lost it. Whatever writing ability I once had seemed to be gone now. I was officially afflicted with massive writer's block. I had no idea what I was going to do for Cody. I knew I owed it to him to redeem him in some way. I was definitely feeling the guilt of creating this poor character, a con-man with a heart of gold…or bronze. Some sort of metallic element. Maybe iron…and it rusted. But as far as driving forward any plots for any of these poor people I had been torturing for my entire adult life, I had nothing. The guilt weighed on me like the snow on the roof.

My New Year's Resolutions were the same as they were every year. Do a better job at work and try not to let it get to me, lose that extra ten pounds I'd been carrying around since I quit smoking when I was 22, be a better wife, pay more attention to my sometimes doting husband. This year's bonus resolution was to finish one freaking book. Just one. One freaking story with an ending wasn't too much to ask, was it?

One day, in my resolve to do a better job at work, I was gritting my teeth and actually attempting to talk to the little cherubs in the lunchroom. "Happy New Year," came a whisper from over my shoulder.

I laughed just a little and smiled. Kip was there. Solid. Real. Well, real to me anyway. An unexpected wave of relief washed over me. I ignored him, but only because there were hundreds of people around. I actually wanted to hug him. Instead, I smiled both at him and at the second graders I was talking to, sending them back to their seats to finish their lunches. This was my normal. This was who I was, craziness and all. It felt so good to see him. It felt right.

"Why do you look happy to see me?"

"I actually am happy to see you," I muttered over my shoulder so that only Kip, who had jumped up on the stage and was now sitting criss-cross applesauce on the stage behind me, could hear me.

"Why? Do you want me to keep trying to get you fired?"

"No…" I started to chastise him, "Wait…What do you mean, 'keep trying'?" I asked sharply, forgetting that he wasn't really there.

"Nothing. I didn't do anything."

A thought occurred to me. "Kip? Did you call and complain about me?"

He shrugged and looked away innocently.

"No. That's not possible." I whispered.

"No, it's not." Kip agreed that it couldn't be possible while nodding his head "yes" enthusiastically.

It couldn't be. I couldn't even begin to guess how that would work. These were my demons. They couldn't talk to anyone else. Could they? Or could they? Are there rules of physics with dealing with this kind of thing? I hoped not. Because if there were, then that meant the only person who could've called the principal to complain about me is me and if that were true, I was far crazier than I even thought possible.

Perhaps I should've made a resolution to not completely lose my mind this year. Perhaps it was a little late for that.

****

My mind officially blown, I was driving home in utter silence. Trying to wrap my brain around the idea of me calling to complain about myself.

Even on a regular day when my sanity was intact, it was so loud in school that I couldn't even stand to turn the radio on in the car on the way home. It felt so damn liberating to be alone in the car with just the sound of the engine and the whoosh of the passing trees. I was looking forward to the evening ahead, of a quiet dinner of risotto and a glass of wine with my husband, when my phone rang. The ringtone jostled me out of my daydream. If it was anyone but Alex, I wouldn't have answered it.

"Hey, Belly,"

"Hey," I whispered back.

"You sound quiet. Another rough day at the office?"

"It was fine." I sighed and avoided telling him that I just realized that I'm far crazier than I thought I was. "Just loud."

"Listen, Bell, they called an emergency meeting that I have to be at tonight, so I won't be home for dinner."

Best laid plans. "OK," I whispered, failing miserably at hiding my disappointment.

"Are you ok?"

"I'm fine. I just wanted to have dinner with you."

"I know. I'm sorry. I don't want to work late, you know."

"I know. I just didn't want to be alone tonight," I said, more pathetically than I intended to.

"Speaking of being alone, Belly, have you seen any…I mean you haven't mentioned…Are you still seeing…" Something in his voice was so hopeful. And the visits had slowed so much since they'd started back in September. Just Kip today…and super drunk Cody at the Christmas Party. But they really weren't around like they were in the beginning, when one showed up every time I turned around. Now, I could go for days without seeing anyone. I just didn't see the harm in not telling him. In giving him hope that his wife wasn't completely delusional.

"Nope."

"You haven't seen any then?"

"I haven't."

"Good." He sounded so relieved I knew I had done the right thing. It felt right to give him some peace of mind. "I'll see you when I get home, ok?"

"OK." I said before hanging up and chucking my phone in one of the van's forty-seven cup holders.

I was feeling pretty good about unburdening Alex of my crazy. I was totally sure I had done the right thing for him and for our marriage until Peter showed up in the passenger seat.

"You shouldn't have done that." He shook his head.

Peter in his infinite quirkiness. He was so damn awkward it was almost painful to watch. He rubbed his thumb back and forth against his second and third fingers as if he had a tiny ball in them. He was too compulsive not to call me out on what he thought was wrong, but he was so non-confrontational, it weirded him out and made him fidget.

"I'll handle it, Peter. Thank you." I said, immediately defensive.

"Yes. But…it's just that…you need to be careful of the lies you tell."

"I know that."

"I-I-I guarantee," he stammered, like he always did when he was nervous. "T-t-that your lies will multiply until you're so buried in them you won't be able to remember when you started to lie in the first place. You will wish you never told that first lie."

"Do you?" I asked, trying to divert his attention away from me.

"What?" He stopped rubbing his fingers and stared at me like I just woke him up from a catnap.

"Do you wish you never told that first lie?" I repeated.

"With all my heart," he said sadly. "Why don't you just tell Alex the truth?" He switched his attention back to me.

"Why don't you just tell Monica the truth?" I parried back at him, desperately trying to fight off assertions that I was wrong to hide this from Alex. Though, as I recalled, I made Peter super smart and I was unlikely to beat him in any sort of debate.

"Um. You wrote the story. Why don't I just tell Monica the truth?"

"OK fine." Talking about my failures as a writer seemed to be a far better option than discussing my failures as a wife. "You want to know why you won't tell Monica the truth?"

"Yes." He clenched his fists, steeling himself for the answer.

"Fear," I told him.

"Fear," he agreed in an oddly succinct tone.

"Fear that if you tell her the truth, she won't like you anymore. She won't love you."

"Right." He nodded somberly. "Just like you and Alex."

"Right," I said before quickly correcting myself. "No wait. That doesn't apply to me and Alex."

"Doesn't it?"

"Of course not," I answered matter-of-factly as if he had just asked me the dumbest question ever. "Alex will always love me."

"Yes, but will he always like you?" He asked pointedly.

Damn. "Of course he will."

"If you're so sure, why don't you just tell him the truth?"

"Why don't you just shut up?" I told him and he vanished with a shrug.

****

At home that night, Alex worked so late that I was in bed and he still wasn't home yet. I hated going to bed alone. After sleeping next to someone for twenty years the bed felt off kilter if only one person was in it. That night I was scribbling in my journal. Mostly jotting down ideas for Cody and promptly scratching them out. "Aren't you tired?" came a sudden, whiney voice from the end of my bed.

Bridget was there, yawning, wearing some tacky suit with a ruffled shirt that was probably fashionable in the early '90s. She had on socks and sneakers with her business clothes, commuter wear. Her makeup was worn, giving her eyes a sunken look and her lipstick had faded except for the too-dark liner around the edges. "Yes, but I can't sleep alone." I smiled at her…trying to remember if I was bitchy like Bridget at that age. I probably was. Seems like I would've been. Some sort of leftover teenage angst that grew into something ugly after the freedom of college and entry into the real world. Whatever it was, it wasn't pretty.

"That's not what I mean," she said and took a long, slow, deliberate drag on her cigarette. "I mean, don't you get so tired of pretending to be something you're not?" she asked me with a sigh.

With a flick of her ashes, it occurred to me, this wasn't really bitchy Bridget. This was a rare, vulnerable Bridget, overwhelmed with the sadness of making too many mistakes in her life. The sadness of simply not being happy and not quite knowing how to get out of it. "I'm not even good at it," she whispered sadly.

"Me neither," I said with a sigh that matched hers. And then I knew why I made Bridget a know-it-all bitchy girl. Her fear of failure built those walls, those defenses, insulating her heart from hurt and from Kip. She couldn't take the idea of failing at something, so she took a job that was quite simply, beneath her, so she would be unable to fail.

She took another drag and exhaled.

I waved her smoke away from my face and jotted down: *Bridget doesn't know everything. She doesn't know what she's doing with her life.*

When I looked up, she was gone. I smiled in the silence of the night, alone in bed and suddenly feeling more lucid, productive and inspired than I had in weeks.

But, three visits in one day. Perhaps I shouldn't have given Alex quite so much hope.

CHAPTER 17

EVEN IN HIS EXHAUSTION FROM January's constant snow shoveling, ever-sensitive Alex knew I was struggling with the post-holiday doldrums, as I always did. Though, this year was definitely worse than usual with the holiday doldrums exacerbated by my absent children, hiding my delusions from my husband, and finding a way to help Cody and the rest of my characters. Anyway, Alex came home early one Friday afternoon with the promise of a romantic evening.

On this particular Friday I had had yet another crappy day at work. I started my day ambitiously, settling into writing before going to school. Seeing Bridget in a whole new way that night inspired me. Seeing her changing, changed me and how I felt about her and why she was the way she was.

I was actually making progress on *Bridget & Kip*, so it was pretty defeating when I had to leave for work. I had to physically drag myself away from my laptop, for what? A stupid, crappy job that I hated? It seemed ridiculous.

Even my classroom time was getting frustrating. I was working with Jeremy on the letter 'd' this time. I kept saying it was just like the 'b', which he had finally mastered, only it went the other way. He was resting his head on his arm on the desk as if his little torso was too tiny and tired to hold the rest of him up. "Come on, Jeremy," I coaxed. "Just like the 'b'." He suddenly sat up and looked at me strangely, like he didn't know what I was talking about, and I realized that the little guy had actually fallen asleep right on his table. I tried not to take it personally, but I couldn't help but feel that I had failed, yet again.

A fleeting thought crossed my mind: that Kip's idea of getting me fired was starting to look pretty darn good right about now. But I pushed that thought away, not wanting my subconscious to get any funny ideas.

Anyway, despite Alex's good intentions, romance was the last thing on my mind on that particular Friday afternoon. I just wanted to put my head down and sleep like Jeremy did.

"Come on. I'll cook." He tried to nudge me off the couch.

"Can't we just order a pizza and watch a movie?" My motivation level was too low for talking. I was too tired to work on our relationship.

"No. I want to make you dinner. We've barely seen each other this week." He pulled on my arm, trying to physically remove me from the couch. "Come on, let's go to the store."

"But it's so gross out." I looked out the window at the dreary sleet that was falling on our giant piles of snow, freezing them into giant misshapen ice sculptures. "I don't feel like going out."

"Please, Bella," he whined in an unusually needy way. "Come with me." He kissed my hand. "You can drive and wait in the car and I'll just run in so you won't have to talk to anyone. OK?"

I reluctantly agreed, but only because I couldn't come up with a better reason than "I don't want to."

I went along with him and didn't get out of the car. It was absolutely miserable out. Cold, snowy, sleety. I just wanted to go home and crawl into bed. I didn't feel like talking to Alex or anyone else for that matter. I was working on trying to change my attitude, for Alex's sake, when I realized I wasn't alone.

Daniel sat next to me as I stared out the front windshield. His hair was too long and he was, for the first time, unshaven. He yanked his ear buds out of his ears so they hung from the front of his shirt. I could hear angry, ugly music coming from them.

"You can't just leave us like this, you know," he growled at me, angrily.

"Um. Like what?" I answered, somewhat blindsided by this new, edgy Daniel. This wasn't the boy I created. Or maybe this was the result of not finishing him. Maybe this was what happened when you created something and left it unfinished.

"I left her, alright. I left her and went back to England and now I'm just there. I'm there and I hate her and I hate myself and I can't stand it anymore. Not for one more day." He had finally gotten so tired of watching his mother being abused by her husband that he left her. That was as far as I'd gotten. I'd never figured out how to give them the happy ending they so deserved.

"You need to fix this! Fix us! Finish us!" Daniel yelled at me.

I just stared down at the steering wheel, my eyes filling with tears, my hands shaking. Daniel was so angry. I remembered writing rage into him and was sorry for it now. All the rage of a lifetime of being kept from his mother. And the rage of having to make the decision to leave her in some vain attempt to save her. I couldn't look at him. It hurt too much.

"Look at me," he said softly, but angrily.

I gripped the wheel and shook my head afraid to see the look on his face.

"Look at me!" he screamed again, angrier than I thought he was capable of being.

I had to dig deep to find the nerve to look.

"This may not be real to you, but it's real to us," he pleaded, softening just a little. "It's not a game. It's not a hobby. This is our life, our existence."

"I know it is," I choked out, almost overwhelmed with shame for having hurt these people so badly.

"I can't go back to her. And him. I can't." He shook his head. "She needs to come to me."

He stared at me, tears streaming down his face. I reached out for him with a gloved hand and wiped a tear away from his cheek. He closed his eyes at my touch. He was real. At that moment I could feel his tears soaking through my glove and he was more real than anything. "You need to find her a reason to leave him. Just don't hurt her. I couldn't bear that."

"Daniel, I've tried. I just don't know how." I shook my head. I couldn't bear to hurt her either.

"Find a way. Somehow, please. I'm begging you. I can't take all this anger. All this pain. Please, Mirabelle." It was the first time Daniel called me by name and it burned my heart. "Save me. You're the only one who can."

I stared into his electric blue eyes and almost melted. I loved Daniel. He was a part of me, just like Emily, the perpetual victim, was a part of me. I opened my mouth to tell him so, but the car door opened suddenly.

"Sorry, I took so long." Alex dove into the car from the freezing rain dropping his bags at his feet. "It's miserable out there." He shook off his hair like a wet dog.

I was still in shock from Daniel's visit and just stared at Alex who now sat in Daniel's place in the front seat.

"Bella?"

I blinked my eyes and shook my head. Back to reality, right? Stay with Alex. “Sorry. I guess I was someplace else.” His eyes flinched ever so slightly and I knew I’d been made.

“Alright, who was it?” he asked impatiently.

“What?” I started up the car in an attempt to deflect his question. He leaned over and turned it off, taking the keys. “Alex, what are you doing?”

“Who was it?” he asked again, only this time he sounded really mad. Really mad.

“What?”

“Answer me, Mirabelle. Who was it this time?”

“What do you mean?” I answered his question with a question.

“Bella, don’t play dumb with me. Who were you talking to while I was in the store?”

“No one.” I lied.

“Bella, I’m going to ask you a question and I want you to be completely honest with me. I won’t be mad. I just need to know the truth.” He spoke to me like I was a child who just got caught doing something naughty.

“OK,” I agreed reluctantly, knowing now that Peter was right. I should’ve told Alex the truth in the first place. Why were my characters always right and I was always wrong?

Alex took a deep breath, clearly trying to gather his patience while I prepared to disappoint him yet again.

“Bella, are you or are you not seeing people again?”

I nodded without looking at him. I didn’t want to see the look on his face, that half-disappointed, half-confused look he gets when he doesn’t understand me.

“I knew it,” he shouted, just a little too happy to have caught me in a lie. “Since when?”

"Uh…" I had to think for a minute to remember what lies I had told him. Peter was right. Lying was bad.

"Bella, you said they disappeared after Thanksgiving," Alex pressed. "Were you lying then? Did you lie about our weekend?"

"No. They did disappear, kind of. But then they came back."

"When? When did they come back?"

"I don't know…the Christmas party maybe."

"Maybe?" His frustration with me boiled over like too much pasta when the starchy water spilled over the edges of the pot and messed up the stove.

"Fine. Definitely the Christmas party." I answered tersely. I was not appreciating the third degree from Alex, nor the fact that he was treating me like this was my fault. It wasn't my fault they wouldn't leave me alone.

"And now?" The inquisition continued.

"Now what?" I said, doing my best impression of a hostile witness.

"Now, how often, Mirabelle? How often do you see them?"

"Pretty often, I guess. I don't know. It changes," I cried, tears rolling freely down my cheeks.

"Once a day, often?"

"Sometimes."

"More than that?"

"Sometimes." I repeated sadly.

"Why did you lie to me, Bella?" he asked softly, looking out the windshield at something in the distance that I couldn't see. "Why didn't you tell me they were back?"

I shrugged, ashamed of myself and my insecurities. Too ashamed to tell him that I was afraid he wouldn't like me anymore.

"So, who was it this time?" he sighed and turned back to me.

"You don't want to know, Alex." I looked away. It was easier not to have to see the confusion and sadness in his stupid, beautiful eyes.

"I do. I can't believe it, but I actually do want to know." He said, but he still sounded mad and I didn't really want to tell him.

"It was Daniel." I reluctantly confided anyway.

"Again?" he said with his jaw clenched so tightly I barely saw his lips move.

"Yes, again." I snapped. "Only he was different this time."

"Different how?" he sighed impatiently.

I struggled to choose my next words, feeling the burden of Daniel's anger on my conscience. "He was angry, broken."

"Angry at whom?" Alex never got the who/whom thing wrong. It made me nuts.

"Himself, Emily, Me." I shook my head and stared at the steering wheel again.

"So what'd you tell him?"

"Nothing really. He was so mad, and so sad…" I started to ramble, my emotions catching up with me. "I have to help him, Alex. I need to get him back with his mother."

"How are you going to do that?"

"I don't know," I replied sadly, "but I have to do something to help him. I've never seen him so upset."

Alex shook his head and I knew what he was thinking. And it made me mad.

"I know he's not real, Alex…" I rubbed my hands together and could feel the dampness of Daniel's tears through my gloves. "But he is real to me."

"I didn't say he wasn't." Alex looked far away again, completely disconnected from me.

His complete failure to understand me cut like a knife. This was it. This was the feeling that made me not want to tell him. This was why I lied to him.

"You didn't have to."

****

We came home and Alex cooked dinner and I tried to set aside my encounter with Daniel. But I couldn't. Alex pretended nothing had happened in the car, but it had. I pretended I wasn't mad at him for not understanding me, but I was.

All through dinner I was distracted. Alex kept trying his darndest to make conversation with me but I gave him nothing to work with. I tried, really I did. But all I could think of was Daniel and the feeling of his tears and how I could make those tears go away. I didn't want to talk. I wanted to write. And I certainly didn't want to talk to Alex, who didn't have a clue who I was or what I felt or what I needed right now.

"Fine, Bella," Alex said, frustrated with my inability / refusal to make conversation. "Let's talk about your stupid characters again."

"What?" The once rare display of Alex's temper brought me out of my daydream.

"You know, maybe they just show up when you're supposed to be spending time with me!"

I shrugged. Maybe they did.

"I don't understand you! I am so tired of you pulling me close and then pushing me away! I can't do this anymore!"

"Alex…" I tried to stop his tirade but he cut me off.

"You are not even listening to me. I'm trying to engage you, Bella. I'm begging for your attention and you are a million miles away."

I was feeling pretty ashamed of myself right about now. Alex was absolutely right. I was a million miles away. I couldn't stop thinking about Daniel. I was barely in the same room as Alex, too busy trying to think of a way out for Daniel and Emily.

"I spent the last twenty years of our marriage being second to the children…"

"Now, that's not fair," I defended myself.

"I don't mind that. I didn't. But now that the children are gone, it's time for me to come first. Instead, I'm playing second fiddle to a bunch of your imaginary friends. Do you know how that makes me feel?"

I couldn't answer. I stared at my plate, at the beautiful dinner that Alex had cooked for me that I had completely taken for granted because I was too busy thinking about myself.

"It makes me feel worthless, Bella."

I cringed at his choice of words.

"All I want to do is love you. Why won't you let me?"

That was an excellent question and one I did not have the answer for. "Do you think I'm doing this on purpose?" was all I could muster.

"At this point, I don't know. Every time I try to get close to you, you have some sort of vision or something…whatever."

"I'm sorry. I'm sorry for making you feel worthless, Alex. I hate myself for that, I really do. You are so much of my world, and I know that I take you for granted. But I've been putting myself last for so long…maybe it's not time for you to come first. Maybe it's time for me to come first."

Yes, I knew that was the absolute worst thing I could've said to him at that particular point in time. I know it sounded heartless and cruel. But Alex made me feel ashamed. Ashamed not of something I had done, but of something that I am. And part of me wanted to hurt him for that.

Alex stood up from the table. "Enjoy your dinner," he whispered before he walked out of the dining room and right out the front door.

Well, that went well.

With Alex gone, I tried to channel my guilt into something creative. Sometimes when I argued with Alex, I would have this weird burst of creativity and words just poured out of me. Though, now I just sat feeling guilty for all the times that we fought and I was able to turn it into something productive. How must Alex have felt all those times? I'm clearly the worst wife ever. What kind of wife isn't thrilled when her husband comes home and wants to cook for her and spend an evening with her? A really shitty, self-absorbed one. The whole storming out thing was new for Alex. It was usually me who walked out in a huff.

I was clearly on thin ice with Alex. And not his normal, 'losing patience with me' thin ice. This was real thin ice, where I was afraid I was doing real damage to our marriage. The slope I stood on felt like it was getting more and more slippery and I had to stop it. If only I knew how.

I curled up on the couch under the front picture window, propped my laptop on my lap and popped my ear buds into my ears, but no matter how loud I turned the music, all I could hear was Alex's voice. Over and over again, telling me I made him feel worthless. My heart hurt. It was breaking slowly. It reminded me of when I was a little girl and our neighbor was mowing our lawn. A rock shot out of the lawn mower and hit our sliding glass door. The glass stayed in place, but cracked slowly, all day. New cracks appeared well into the night until you could no longer see outside through all the fissures. It looked like a giant crystal spider web. We couldn't go anywhere near the door because any vibrations and the shards would collapse all over the dining room. That's what my marriage felt like right now. One false move and the whole thing would fall to pieces.

And suddenly, I wasn't alone on the couch. Emily sat opposite me, mirroring me, looking distantly out the picture window at nothing at all. She said nothing. The two of us just sat there for a long time, too wrapped up in our own guilt to acknowledge each other. Frozen in time, in guilt, in sadness.

"Is this how you feel all the time?" I finally whispered to Emily. I guessed she was feeling guilty about letting Daniel go just as I was feeling guilty about letting Alex go.

Emily didn't speak, didn't even look at me. She just nodded silently and stared out the window.

My heart still ached, but now for Emily. I missed Vivian and Holden terribly, but couldn't begin to imagine if my kids hated me the way Daniel hated Emily right now. Or the way Alex hated me right now. Well, maybe I could have, but I didn't want to. The fear of losing my children is what prompted me to write Daniel and Emily's story in the first place.

"I'm sorry. I'm so sorry I did this to you." I said to her

Emily still didn't look at me, but she finally spoke. "I did this to myself."

I reached over and touched Emily's leg and she disappeared right before my eyes.

****

I fell asleep on the couch. I was kind of hoping to be asleep in bed when Alex came home. Then, I wouldn't have to address all the things that were wrong with me. It was probably better for our marriage that I at least looked like I was waiting anxiously for him to return.

When I woke up, he was standing over me, watching me sleep.

"You're back." I whispered.

"Yes." He said with no emotion whatsoever. I had no idea where this conversation was going to go. I couldn't tell if he was still mad or not.

"I'm glad." I said pushing myself up to a sitting position.

He said nothing. Not a good sign. Clearly, the onus was on me to fix this…somehow.

"Are you?" I mustered up the strength to ask him even though I was totally afraid of the answer.

"What?"

"Are you glad you're back?"

"I don't know." He shrugged. Not exactly the answer I was hoping for, but it was better than a "no."

"I am sorry."

"Sorry doesn't make me feel any less lonely, Bella."

Now, it was my turn to shrug. He sat down on the ottoman we used as a coffee table.

"You lied to me. Why?" He asked, no longer sounding angry. This was worse. Now he sounded sad and wounded.

"I didn't lie, Alex. I just didn't tell you."

"You lied, Bella. Don't make it any worse."

"OK fine, I lied," I conceded. "But I didn't do it to hurt you, Alex. I did it to protect you."

"Protect me? From what?"

"From this! From me…from my insanity. Believe it or not, Alex, this isn't fun for me. It's scary as hell and I'm sorry if I don't always do the best job handling it."

He said nothing.

"You know, Alex, I don't enjoy being this crazy," I said sadly. "I would love to go back to being normal."

"You were never normal, Bella." He air quoted 'normal'. "I've always known you were crazy."

"Not crazy like this. You didn't sign on for this insanity. Neither did I. I'm afraid, Alex. I'm afraid of how crazy I am and I'm afraid if I get too crazy for you, you won't like me anymore." There. I said it, Peter. I hope you're happy.

He sighed and I knew he was trying to understand me once again. "It's just that sometimes, it seems like you like it when you see them."

I bit my lip knowing he was right and prepared myself to admit it. "I do. Kind of. Sometimes."

He nodded, but I continued before he had a chance to respond.

"They're interesting to me. They keep my mind off my stupid job. They keep my mind off losing the kids."

"They keep your mind off me."

"I know. You're right. And I'm trying to fix it, Alex. I'm trying to balance it all. But sometimes, I fail."

"Bella, I know you've been going through all this shit with the kids leaving," he stood up. "But what you've totally forgotten is that I'm going through things, too. I miss them, I feel lost and crazy without them, too, and now I feel like I'm losing you. Losing you to someone who's not even real." His voice cracked and though I couldn't see his tears in the darkness, I knew he was crying.

"I know they're not real, Alex." I stood up to join him. "I do. But when they show up, they don't seem like just characters in a book. They really seem real to me."

"You want to know what's real, Bella. I am. I'm real." Alex took my hand and held it over his heart, so I could feel it beating. "And I have real feelings. It hurts me when you ignore me, or choose your imaginary friends over me."

"I'm not choosing..."

He shook his head. "Whether you mean to or not, you are." He took my hand from his heart and kissed my fingertips gently. "I'm real, Bella. Be with me."

He pulled me closer, his eyes wet with tears. I shivered as he leaned in close to me and kissed me so softly, it left me breathless. I kissed him back. He was right, this was far more real than Daniel or Emily or even Cody. Alex pulled away suddenly, looking at me skeptically. He knew that I was thinking of something else.

I reached out to him. I wanted this. I wanted real. I wanted Alex. I put my hand on his face and stroked his cheek. I felt the stubble on his normally clean-shaven chin. I felt the scar on his jaw he got from that rare fight he got into in college defending me, being my hero. I smiled warmly at him then reached around his neck and pulled him to me. He resisted at first, so I knew he was still mad at me. Though, when I pulled just a little harder, he gave in pretty easily, wrapping his arms around me. I stood on my toes as I always did to kiss him and could feel his heart pounding through his shirt again, though, this time I could feel it in my chest and not just in my fingers. As he kissed me back more fervently, I couldn't tell which heartbeat was mine and which was his. The way it should be.

Alex put one hand on my waist and another around my shoulders. He turned me slowly and pressed me up against the wall, pushing his hands against the wall on each side of my face. I felt trapped and I liked it. Completely lost in him, I couldn't have named a character now if I tried. All I wanted was this moment with Alex and the feel of him pressed against me. The two of us locked together where no one, not even my crazies, could get in.

CHAPTER 18

WE WOKE TOGETHER SATURDAY MORNING, cautiously content. Alex seemed to have forgiven me, now I just needed to find a way to be a writer without completely giving myself to my characters or completely losing my husband. It didn't seem entirely fair that I needed to give up my characters, visitors, friends, delusions – whatever I was calling them these days. I loved Alex and I wanted to give him everything he needed. I really did. I wanted him to be happy. But I meant what I said the night before about now being my turn to be first.

Still, I couldn't lose Alex. Alex was my life, my past, and my future. But, I knew now that until I could fix my characters, I'd never be able to fix my marriage. I'd never be able to fix myself.

I still had a promise to keep to Cody. I could keep it. I would keep it. I could help him and Daniel and everyone else. I just had to work even harder to separate it from Alex. Not by lying to him. I'd learned that lesson. But time with Alex had to be just that. Time with Alex. Even at the expense of my characters. They would just have to wait. I'd ignored them before; I'd do it again. That's what Alex told me at the beginning of this mess. "Don't let them control you," he'd said. I could keep them all at arm's length. I could shut them out of my thoughts. I had to. Until Alex left for work. Then I could be all theirs.

I was very successful in keeping my time with Alex separate all weekend. And my friends, for their part, were very cooperative. Both Peter and Kip made cameo appearances in my time with Alex. I was sure Peter was there to make some awkward comments about how right he was about my lying. But neither he nor Kip said a word, as if they finally understood that I needed to keep my two worlds apart.

The trouble was it was so much damn work for me to be normal. It was exhausting, walking on eggshells all weekend. So much so that by Monday morning, I was almost relieved to see Alex go to work. I felt like a tightly wound coil that was going to spring and bounce all over the room.

Alex was barely out the door Monday morning when David appeared in his infinite sadness, except now he was exceptionally drunk in addition to being overwhelmingly sad. His demeanor was more nervous and exaggerated than the last time I saw him. He walked around the room and shook his hands and muttered things to himself.

Grabbing my laptop, I sat down in the living room. I wasn't expecting to work on David that day, but apparently it wasn't up to me.

"How are you David?" I asked him softly.

"How do you think I am?" he barked in return.

"From the looks of you, not very good." I quipped, trying to keep the mood light.

"It's Crane, isn't it? He's the Mercy Killer."

"Who?" My memory failed me for a moment.

"Crane. He's the killer, right?"

Then, I remembered. David was referring to a tertiary character I had thrown into Mercy to give David someone to argue with. But he wasn't the killer. He was a bit of an ass, but not the killer, not the Mercy Killer, anyway.

"Can't be." I shook my head. "What's his motive?"

"He's a psychopath." David guzzled from his bottle. What was with my characters being such drunkards?

"Even a psychopath needs a motive, David. Maybe an irrational motive, but a motive all the same."

"It's him! I just know it's him." He said softly, shaking his head.

"Just because you don't like him doesn't make him a serial killer."

David raised his voice and gestured wildly. "It's his fault Foster's dead!" He paced the floor like a caged animal. His holster was empty, which meant two things: he'd already been suspended and I was a little bit safer. "He's hiding something, I know it!" he continued to rant.

"David, I need you to listen to me. I can help you." I approached him cautiously, just wanting to settle him down a bit.

"I've been a cop for twenty years," he rambled. "Do you think I don't know a killer when I see one? Do you think you know better than I do?" He had me there. Everything I knew about police work I learned from TV and movies. All the same, David was spiraling out of control and I need to get a grip on him.

"I think that you're upset and not seeing things quite so clearly right now," I said calmly, trying to rein him in.

"I'm the only one who *is* seeing things clearly!" He screamed and stumbled backward just a bit. "Why isn't anyone listening to me?" He collapsed onto the couch and started to cry.

What a mess I'd made of him. Then again, that was the point. He needed to hit rock bottom. He needed to be so miserable that he would call Goliath at the suicide hotline. I decided to give him a little push just to advance his story a little bit. This was where I got stuck though. It was hard to push someone into contemplating suicide. But, taking a deep breath, I tried.

"David, no one's listening to you because you're not making any sense. You're completely wasted and you're acting crazy." I gritted my teeth and pushed again. "No wonder you got suspended."

He sobbed some more.

I didn't feel good about this, hurting David's feelings. It was like kicking a wounded dog. But I knew if I could push him just far enough to call Goliath, then Goliath would come to him. And then I could write an ending.

David continued crying on my couch as I opened my laptop and opened the file labeled "Mercy." I was relieved it opened. I couldn't even venture a guess what version of Microsoft Word this was typed in. I read a few pages, refreshing my memory before I got to the last thing I had written:

David slouched on the couch with a half bottle of vodka in his lap. He was still wearing the same crumpled suit from his date with Sarah. He was very drunk and having difficulty holding his head up. The television was the only light in the room. David laughed half-heartedly at The Three Stooges and drank from the bottle before sighing in boredom. He changed the channel.

The news was on. The anchor spoke, "The latest victim of the Mercy Killer is still in critical condition tonight after being shot in the head with her late husband's gun. The serial killer left his usual signature on the wall, 'MERCY' written in the victim's blood, and left her for dead. The victim, 26-year-

old Rebecca Foster, is the widow of Officer Jeffrey Foster who was shot and killed earlier this week in the line of duty. Doctors say the victim is in a persistent vegetative state and believe it is unlikely she will survive off a respirator."

The news sobered David slightly. Foster's wife. Shit. "When will it end?" he asked himself. "I just want it to end," he sobbed out loud to no one. He took one more slug from the bottle before capping it and tossing it on the couch. He made an attempt to stand up, but his level of inebriation was more than he anticipated and he couldn't quite steady himself. "The hell with it," he muttered before lying back down on the couch to sleep it off.

In another room, in another house, another man sat on his couch in front of the same news story. He was drunk, too. The room was pitch-black except for the glow of the television. The man threw a phone book at the TV with such precise aim, the TV shut off. He sat in total darkness.

Finally, as David sobbed on the other end of my couch, I knew what to do. I wrote. I made David call that suicide hotline one last time. And though he was still drunk and exhausted and crying incessantly, he finally figured it out.

He stopped bawling suddenly and sat up straight on the couch. "It's not Crane."

"No. It's not," I told him.

"It's Goliath," he whispered.

I nodded silently.

"I should've known," he breathed.

"Maybe." I sighed.

"He's coming, isn't he?" he asked, already knowing the answer.

Now here's where I got just a little bit scared. I finally knew what was going to happen to the David and Goliath in my head. But what was going to happen to the David that was sitting on my couch? I didn't want to bear actual physical witness to their confrontation, which I fully expected to be bloody and violent.

"You're playing with fire, you know?" I heard from a familiar, husky voice over my shoulder. But when I turned to face him, he looked like a whole new Cody. Last time I'd seen him he was crying on my bed at the Christmas party. Now, he looked at ease, settled, in control. His tuxedo was gone, as was his highball glass. "Are you sure you know what you're doing?" he asked.

I smiled, more than a little relieved to see him and to see him with his act together, no less. I hadn't even started trying to fix him yet and here he was acting all normal. "Do I look like I have any idea what I'm doing?" I asked him.

He raised one eyebrow with a smirk and shook his head. "No. You don't look like you have any idea what you're doing. But you're writing, and that's good. Granted you're writing some mediocre story about some second-rate cop –" he teased.

"Hey, watch it, pal!" David snapped.

I grabbed my temples. Two of my totally unrelated characters were talking to each other and it made my brain hurt.

"I'm just here to make sure no one gets hurt, buddy, relax. I need her." Cody explained to David.

"I'm not going to get hurt," I asserted, then immediately questioned myself, "am I?" Why I was looking to Cody for guidance, I couldn't tell you. But at this point, he seemed like the sane one. Somehow, since the last time I'd seen him, something had changed in him. He was still him, still a little slick, and definitely edgy, but now he seemed a little softer around the edges, a little kinder, a little less angry.

"Hey, that's why I'm here. To keep you safe." I was charmed by his desire to protect me. Confused by his transformation, but charmed nonetheless.

David approached Cody until they stood toe to toe. "Why don't you just take off, punk? This is my story."

"Yeah, well, if your story ends badly, it ends all of our stories, pal. I'm staying right here." Cody held his ground even though David had a good four inches and thirty pounds on him.

"Your story is going to end badly anyway…" David snarled.

"Is that right?" Cody growled back.

"Enough!" I yelled at the two of them. "Stop your pissing match and let me write!"

"Sorry," they muttered in submission and in unison.

"Cody, you can stay." I told him. "But you HAVE to stay quiet."

He nodded, smirked victoriously at David, and sat down on the steps behind me.

Back to work. David knew who the Mercy Killer was. Now, he had to stop him. He paced around the room while Cody sat silently behind me on the stairs. I bought the Cure's "Like Cockatoos" on iTunes and set about finally finishing the first book I ever wrote. I listened to that song over and over again when I started this damn book in college; the only thing missing now was the constant stream of smoke from incense and cigarettes.

David didn't physically act out the scenes as I wrote them like I thought he might. Instead, he responded with nods and eye rolls as if he were reading the words over my shoulder, but he wasn't actually looking. It was like he just knew what was happening. He crinkled his brow in frustration and shook his head when his captain told him the Mercy Killer had already confessed – and it wasn't Goliath. David bit his lip as I wrote about how he tried to convince his captain that he just talked to the Mercy Killer and that he was coming over to kill him right now. He sniffed back his tears when the captain didn't believe his theory about the suicide hotline.

After his captain left the scene, David sat down quietly in the white chair and stared off intently, waiting for Goliath to show. His drunkenness still with him, he nodded off on paper and in my living room.

I hesitated for a moment before having Goliath make his grand entrance, mostly because I was afraid I was inviting a serial killer into my living room. An imaginary serial killer. But he was still a serial killer. My heart was pounding and my hands started to sweat. This new level of crazy was terrifying to me, not because it was a new level of crazy but because it felt more like a new level of reality. It all seemed to make perfect sense. And, it felt pretty darn good to actually be getting to the end of something.

"I'm still here." Cody reassured me. And I had to laugh because it seemed to me like Cody was working on his own redemption instead of me writing it for him. I glanced over my shoulder to get a visual on him, to make sure he was close enough to help me if I needed it. David muttered something in his sleep. I wanted to wake him up and tell him it was time, to tell him that Goliath was coming for him. But he was asleep on my screen. It seemed like he had to be asleep here and now.

I took a deep breath and swallowed hard as I wrote of Goliath standing outside the house on the sidewalk. I didn't look to see if he was really there. I was too afraid to. I pounded away, typing every creepy detail of the scene I could think of, delaying Goliath's actually arrival. When I finally wrote of Goliath knocking on the front door, David sat up startled, but shook his head and went back to sleep. I couldn't blame him for going back to sleep. What kind of serial killer knocks? One with impeccable manners or maybe a vampire, but I was definitely not writing a vampire story.

Again, I wrote of Goliath knocking. David sat up again and this time he stayed awake, his eyes intent on the door right over my shoulder, right in front of Cody. David stood up ever so slowly and I started to wish David's holster wasn't empty after all. My typing slowed as I prepared myself for what might happen next.

"Go ahead, Bella," Cody urged me on. And I listened.

David watched the front door intently as an elbow broke through the door and he saw a white, frail hand push through a pane of glass, skin scraping along the shards and blood soaking the white sleeve that reached through to unlock the door.

My palms were sweating so much they kept slipping off the edge of the keyboard. The Cure blasting through my ear buds was not loud enough to cover the sound of my pounding heartbeat. I was afraid to blink, as if closing my eyes would make Goliath appear. Suddenly, I felt a hand on my shoulder, but I didn't jump, I didn't scream. He wasn't here for me, right? "Keep writing," I told myself silently. I looked at David standing in front of the white chair. But he didn't look afraid. He just looked confused.

I was too afraid to look at the hand on my shoulder, too sure it would be white and dripping with blood. I wondered: would the blood stain my clothes?

David slumped back down in the white chair and rolled his eyes. I continued typing.

"Hello, David," Goliath said. "Tsk. Tsk. You are not looking well." He approached David slowly. David just stood there facing him, paralyzed, almost hypnotized by his voice.

I was just wondering why David was just sitting there while Goliath was in the house, and why that hand was still on my shoulder, and where the hell was Cody, when someone pulled my ear bud out of my ear. "Bella?" I jumped, not so much out of fear, but because the interruption in my music was jarring to my senses. Almost painful.

"Are you alright?" asked a very concerned looking Alex who was now standing over me next to the couch in the living room.

"What are you doing here?" I asked, almost annoyed with him as if he'd just woken me from a dream, a dream he had no business being in.

"I live here," he laughed at me. I hated when he laughed at me. Like I was so silly all he could do was laugh.

I was caught red-handed in between my two worlds. David was gone. He vanished the moment I realized Alex was here and not Goliath. When I looked over my shoulder to the stairs, Cody was still sitting there. Though, now instead of being on guard he was shaking his head and rolling his eyes, looking entirely too pissed off.

"I mean what are you doing home so early?"

"It's 6:00, Bella. It's dark out."

"It is?" I sat up to look out the front window. When in the hell did it get dark out? It had been dark out for me since I opened my laptop, though I had no idea what time that was either. "I guess I lost track of time." I said, still disoriented and trying to process the time I'd somehow just lost.

"What are you writing?" he looked over my shoulder.

I shrugged and closed my laptop, prompting Cody to call out, "No wonder you never finish anything with Mr. Boring interrupting all the time."

It was a struggle, but I managed to ignore Cody's comment. "Just working on something old," I said, stretching my arms over my head. I was so close to finishing, but I had to shift gears back to Alex.

"You were looking pretty intense. Do you want to keep working?"

Yes, desperately, was what I wanted to say. But I had promised myself that when Alex was here I would be intent on Alex. (Next, I promised myself that I'd stop making so many promises to myself.)

While I wondered if Alex had promised himself to let me work when I needed to, I knew that continuing with David wouldn't work. Not with Alex here. "No. I'm at a good stopping point," I lied.

"Ha!" was Cody's response to that. "Oh yeah, just as the serial killer breaks in the front door, that's a great place to stop." I flinched at the sound of his voice. Alex looked at me funny for a moment, but I could almost see him decide not to ask me. I put my laptop on the coffee table, stretched again and tried to get up. My legs were so stiff I could barely move. I groaned as I tried to stand.

Alex laughed again as he helped me to my feet. "How long were you sitting there?"

"I honestly have no idea."

"Did you go to work?"

Shit. I forgot to go to work again. What was wrong with me? "Yeah," I lied again and made a mental note to be sure to erase the scores of messages from people looking for me that were bound to be on the voicemail. "So, I guess I've only been there a couple of hours." I lied again and looked around for Peter.

"Pretty intense though, huh?"

"You can say that again, genius," Cody laughed at Alex.

I ignored him and nodded. "Yeah, intense, but good."

"Good." Alex nodded back in approval. God, if he only knew what had been going on in his living room before he came home. "I'm going to get changed. Wanna have a glass of wine before dinner?" He stroked my cheek. And I know, he was kind and affectionate and supportive. But all I wanted was for him to leave so I could finish what I started. I nodded and smiled anyway.

I watched him bound up the stairs, right past Cody who stood up and pressed himself against the wall to let Alex past. I folded my arms in front of my chest and waited for Cody to say something snarky. "I'll be back." He smiled and winked before disappearing.

My heart felt really weird when I realized that I wanted Cody to stay and Alex to leave. It felt heavy and wiggly at the same time. It didn't feel good. It didn't feel right. I put my face into my palms and exhaled deeply, hoping to somehow blow all of my craziness right out my mouth.

CHAPTER 19

I SPENT THE REMAINDER OF THE evening devoting myself to my husband, trying to drink just enough that I would forget that nagging thing in the back of my head telling me there was something else I should be doing. This was what I should be doing. Working on my marriage. Losing Alex was the thing that scared me more than anything. More than being crazy. More than being a failure. More than never accomplishing anything. Being alone was far scarier than anything I could dream up to put in a book.

Alex was relishing the attention I was showering on him. And I certainly didn't mind his attention either. I felt good and safe and stable if just ever-so-slightly distracted. I managed to almost forget about the serial killer I had spent the afternoon with. I was in complete control of my delusions and had simply pushed them aside for the sake of my marriage.

But when I went upstairs to change into my pajamas, things began to unravel. For good.

Alex was downstairs doing the dishes when I entered our bedroom, completely forgetting the pitfalls of my being alone. Maybe I had had a little bit too much to wine.

He was standing facing the window when I walked in, his white robe stained at the sleeve from punching through the glass in the front door.

"Well, there you are my dear." Father Cummings turned to face me. He had told David to call him Goliath when he called the suicide hotline, as some sort of quirky attempt at anonymity between the two of them. "I've been waiting for you," he said in such a way that a chill shot up my spine.

I scanned the room in a panic, looking for an ally of some kind: Cody, David or even Alex would be helpful right about now. But there was no one. It was just me and Goliath. If I had any brains at all, I would've turned and walked right out, right out of the room, right back down the stairs to Alex. He was my only ally, my only weapon. But stupid me always had to engage my characters.

"I understand you've been having some…shall we say…difficulties lately," he said softly with just a hint of a brogue.

I knew where Goliath was going with this. His whole M.O. was to kill people who were about to commit the unforgivable sin of suicide and thereby saving them from eternal damnation. "I'm perfectly fine, thank you. Find yourself another victim."

That's right. I was even stupid enough to play tough guy with my imaginary serial killer, once again forgetting exactly how vivid my overactive imagination could be.

"Oh, dear. You don't really think you're going to be a victim, Mirabelle, do you? I'm going to save you, remember?"

"Don't give me that crap," I said angrily. "I made you. I know who you are, what you are."

He shrugged and ignored my comment, "Mirabelle, dear. Are you really fine?"

Dammit, Cody. Where are you when I need you? I thought to myself. I needed him to tell me I was fine. I needed him to protect me. Goliath was making my skin crawl.

"You're seeing things," he continued. "Though that's an understatement, isn't it, my dear? You're hallucinating."

I hated that word. It made me feel crazy. I tried to will myself to walk away from him and his vitriol, but my feet were stuck to the floor. His voice was so bloody hypnotic.

"You have no career. Your children are gone," Goliath reminded me. "And poor, sweet Alex would be so much better off without you, don't you think?" he said, and my breath started to catch in my throat. "He'll find someone who'll pay attention to him and his needs instead of being wrapped up in themselves the way you are."

I shook my head. "Shut up," I whispered, sticking my fingers in my ears.

"It's ok to be selfish, Mirabelle. That's how you are. It's how you've always been. A little selfish and a little lazy. But you can give him a gift now. Give Alex the gift of freedom. Freedom from being chained to you. Freedom to find happiness with someone who will give him what he needs. A grown-up."

"He is happy with me," I insisted, trying to push my doubts away. Goliath hit all the right buttons and all my insecurities about my marriage, my life, rose right to the surface and made me question everything I thought I was sure of.

"Is he? Are you sure?"

Was I sure? He said he was. He said it all the time. But did he seem happy? Sometimes. But then again sometimes, like last week, he didn't seem to be so happy with me.

"Mirabelle, wouldn't it be better to let him go instead of dragging him down into your madness with you?"

I hated that word, too. Madness. I got another chill as Goliath took a slow step toward me.

"Don't come near me!" I barked. I meant for it to be loud enough that Alex would hear me, but it only came out as a barely audible whisper, like when you have one of those dreams where you scream and scream but no sound comes out.

"There's no need to be afraid, Mirabelle. I'm only here to help you." He took another tiny step toward me, his hands open to me like he was going to hug me, the blood on his hand from the front door still wet.

Shaking my head again. "It's not going to happen. I'm going to end you," I told him fiercely.

He smiled, "That's funny. I was thinking the same thing about you." And with those words, he charged me like a bull, knocking me backward. I barely saw him coming.

Goliath jumped on top of me, pinning down my arms with his knees and damn that hurt. He was crazy-strong for an old guy. He looked so frail but was somehow extremely powerful. "*Shhh.* Don't struggle, Mirabelle, dear. You'll be at peace so very soon." He pulled a straight razor out of his bloody sleeve and picked up my wrist firmly.

I fought him. With everything I had I kicked and wrestled and tried to get him off me but he was too strong. I felt the cold steel of the blade on my skin and finally managed an audible scream before everything went dark.

****

"Bella! It's me! Bella, stop!" I thrashed around on the bedroom floor still fighting Goliath with everything I had. But now it was Alex who was straddling me and trying to get a grip on my shoulders, trying to get a grip on me since I clearly couldn't get a grip on myself.

"No!" I screamed. Still fighting, the sensation of Goliath on top of me still there.

"Bella!" He tightened his grip until my arms were burning. The pain bringing me back to reality. I stopped thrashing long enough to look at him. "It's me. Belly, it's me," he whispered, his voice quivering.

The sound of his voice. The smell of his skin. I stopped fighting.

Alex pulled me up to sitting and I collapsed into him, bawling.

"I'm here, Belly, I'm here." He stroked the back of my head.

I inhaled and soaked him up. His strength recharged me, grounded me. "I'm ok. I'm fine." I checked my wrists and though they hurt, there were no marks, cuts, slashes, or blood. I couldn't believe it.

"What the hell just happened?" He pulled away from me, still holding my shoulders but now glaring deeply into my eyes.

"He tried to kill me." I said softly, not entirely believing it myself. I looked away from Alex. I couldn't stand the look on his face. That incredulous look that told me he thought, no, he knew, that I was certifiably insane.

"Who, Bella? Who tried to kill you?" He said softly, cradling my face in his hands and making me look at him.

"Goliath. He was here." I looked around for something, proof, a sign, something that said I wasn't crazy.

"Goliath?" Alex knew well the characters from my first attempt at writing a novel. "Bella, it can't be. It just can't be. Look around. There is no one here." He pulled my chin back toward him, forcing me to meet his gaze again. "Just me." He smiled at me hopefully as if his mere presence could cure me of whatever was making me crazy.

"You don't believe me." I looked down. "Do you think I'm making this up?"

"No." He waited for a moment before continuing. Probably trying to come up with the right words that wouldn't send me into a tailspin. The joke was on him because those words didn't exist. "I…I…I believe you believe you saw something, but…"

I got myself to my feet, knowing I needed to finish Goliath right freaking now. "But, what?"

"But it just can't be, Bella. It just can't." Alex shook his head, stood up and tried to hold me.

"He wanted to kill me. He was real." I pushed away from him and walked over to the window where Goliath had been before. I stared outside, knowing full well that he was not out there, but in my head.

"He's not real, Bella. How could he try to kill you?" Alex tried to rationalize.

"I don't know, Alex. But I can feel them now. When they touch me, I feel them." I was done explaining, done trying to save him from my craziness. It was too late for that. Right now, I had something I needed to do. "I have to stop him."

"Bella?" I didn't answer him. I was far too busy calculating what I was going to do to Goliath. He'd messed with someone for the last time.

"I need to be alone." I said suddenly without looking at him.

"Hell, no, Bella. I'm not leaving you alone."

"I need to finish him. It's the only way he'll leave me alone."

"He doesn't exist, Bella! He doesn't have to follow whatever rules you're making up as you go along."

"I'm not making it up," I said. "This is real to me."

"I don't understand."

"I'm not asking you to understand, Alex. We're way past understanding. I'm asking you to leave me alone so I can do what I need to do."

I could feel him staring at my back, making that face he made when he was trying to restrain himself from saying something he would regret later.

"Fine, Mirabelle. Have it your way," he said coldly and walked out silently.

I waited until he was gone before turning away from the window. I picked up my laptop, closed the drapes, and turned out the lights, the bluish glow of my screen providing the only light in the room. I typed and typed and typed. Not stopping, not checking the time. Not thinking about Alex or what I had just done to my marriage. Not thinking of anything but Goliath and ending him. Tears streamed down my face for Alex, for David, for me, and even for Goliath.

It was harder than I thought to kill Goliath. I hadn't originally expected to kill him. I figured I'd send him off to prison forever, but once the final conflict with David started, it seemed that there was no way for it to go anyplace else.

There was no way for anything but death to be the end for Goliath. Not to mention, after the attempt he made on my life, and the things he said about Alex, I really wanted him dead. (And yes, I'm aware the things he said about Alex came right out of my own sub-conscious. Out of my very own insecurities and fears.) I just hoped that I was right: that finishing and killing Goliath meant that he couldn't visit me ever again.

David regained his footing on the back of the couch and released his neck from the noose Father Cummings had fashioned for him. He climbed down and walked carefully to where the priest lay face down. David approached tentatively and rolled him over.

David appeared in the corner of my bedroom, kneeling down with a heavy sigh.

Goliath was still alive. His eyes open, but his face looking peaceful. No longer menacing as the killer who just tried to hang David. "Well, thank you, David," he whispered. "You saved me. You helped me fall on my own sword." And with those words, the light left his eyes.

David brushed his hands down Goliath's face, closing his eyes. He couldn't help but feel badly for the guy who just tried to kill him. Maybe Sarah was right, maybe it was time to hang it up.

At the thought of her, David grinned. As if on cue, Sarah burst through the door, her gun drawn.

David smiled at her weakly and brushed the sweat off his brow with the back of his hand. "You're late."

I hit Control + S and it was all over. I couldn't help but feel a little badly for Goliath. His intentions were mostly good, really. All he wanted was to save people from the unforgivable sin of suicide. He was just overly enthusiastic about it. How far was his crazy from my crazy?

David, for his part, got to his feet, favoring his left leg that had been slashed in the fight with Goliath. He breathed in deeply, like a weight had been lifted off his chest, and disappeared.

I sat on my bed hugging my knees, feeling both the relief and pain of Goliath's loss and David's success. I cried for awhile, allowing all the emotions of both David and Goliath to overwhelm me. David's depression lifted from me, but didn't quite turn into happiness – more like a resigned acceptance that life wasn't always all that great. Goliath was dead and though he was a dangerous man, David wasn't entirely happy that he was gone, and I wasn't sure I was either.

Suddenly, it dawned on me. I just finished a book.

I thought I'd feel happy and elated when I finally finished one. I thought it would feel like the pinnacle of something. But instead, the powerful emotions of my characters stuck with me and I couldn't quite shake them long enough to enjoy the small victory of finally finishing a book.

And I couldn't enjoy finishing when I knew I had just brought a tidal wave of devastation to my marriage. Any joy I felt at finishing this book was marred by the hangover of guilt at what I'd done to Alex.

I found him downstairs, asleep on the couch, and was filled with relief that he was still there. After our last argument, I thought that maybe he had left me. Left me truly alone. After all, that was what I asked him to do. But he didn't. Alex stayed with me, weathering my storm. I watched him sleeping on the couch for a long while. He looked different. Normally he slept like a baby, but watching him now, he looked worried. And sad. Goliath was right. Alex deserved better. Alex deserved someone who would take care of him. All the pain I caused him, it tortured me knowing what I was doing to him. Yet, somehow, I couldn't stop.

Alex opened his eyes suddenly with a start. He looked at me, standing there, crying, helpless and he jumped to his feet, grabbing my hands.

"Bella, what's wrong, baby?"

The look of concern in his eyes almost crippled me. I thought he'd be angry with me, but he just looked scared, terrified. I shook my head, unable to articulate how sorry I was. How awful I felt to be hurting him like this.

"Talk to me, Bella. It's me. Talk to me." He held my face in his hands. "What is it? What happened?"

How was it possible that he was still even speaking to me? And what could I say to make him understand? He wouldn't understand, he couldn't understand. I pulled his hands off my face and held them to my heart before turning away. "Don't you see, Alex? I feel what they feel. All these characters. They're all part of me. They are me."

I turned away, afraid to look at him. Afraid he wouldn't understand. Afraid he'd give me that eye roll that he sometimes gave me when I was being all too melodramatic. But instead I felt him slip his arms around my waist from behind. I exhaled deeply and leaned back into him, resting my head on his chest so I could feel his heart beating through the back of my head. My shoulders, pinned to my ears for so long, slid down. We swayed for a moment until my legs would no longer support me, the exhaustion of putting all my mental energy, all of myself, into something finally caught up with me. Alex, who must have felt my weariness, kissed the top of my head and gently slid down to the floor in front of the couch with me in his arms.

I have no idea how long we sat there entwined on the floor. Maybe minutes, maybe hours. I felt an occasional head stroke and a kiss on the back of my neck here and there, but I had no concept of time. I was too spent and exhausted to keep track of time. All I knew was that here, with Alex, in his arms, I was safe. My demons couldn't get to me in here.

"Bella, honey," Alex finally spoke. "I think maybe things have gotten to be a little too much for you."

I heard him, but it took me a minute to respond. "I can handle it," I lied into the space in front of me.

"Can you?" He squeezed his arms around me and whispered in my ear. "Because you kind of just fell apart on me for a bit there."

"I'm fine. Just over emotional." I shook my head, pulling away from him ever so slightly.

"That was not just over emotional, Mirabelle." He spoke sternly, seriously.

"You know how I get when I write."

"I do know how you get…and that wasn't it. You're hallucinating. I'm worried that you're going to hurt yourself."

I couldn't argue with that. But I still hated that word.

"Maybe you need to get some help with this. You could see the doctor Maya saw for her anxiety problems."

Now, it was my turn to roll my eyes. "I don't have anxiety problems."

"I know that. But a doctor could probably help you. Don't you think?"

I didn't answer him and instead chewed on my bottom lip.

"For me, Belly. Do you think maybe you could just do it for me?"

I nodded. Of course, I could. Alex was right. I knew that. I really was going crazy and I needed to stop it before it destroyed not only me, but everyone else around me.

I forgot to tell Alex that I had finished a book. And he didn't ask.

****

I couldn't sleep that night, too haunted by the feeling of Goliath sitting on top of me. How had I let my craziness get that far? The escalation of my insanity had fully hit home. I went from seeing people who weren't there, to talking to them, to touching their tears and feeling their kisses, to being assaulted by them. All the while being grounded in reality enough to know that none of them were actually there. Then why did they seem more real to me than anything else in my life?

I actually knew the answer to that one. I made them more real because my real life was just not very interesting. And now that the kids were gone I had the time to notice. My real life had literally bored me into insanity.

I cuddled closer to Alex trying to will myself to sleep, trying to hold myself to him to keep my demons away. Why wasn't having a simple life with a wonderful husband and two beautiful children enough for me? Why was I so desperate for more that I fabricated an entire other existence?

On the plus side, I finished a book. I wrote a book. It took me twenty-three years, but I wrote a book. Could I call myself a writer now, please? Of course, if writing that book cost me my sanity or my marriage, or both, was it really worth it? Maybe some things are better left unfinished.

Suddenly, I heard a crash downstairs. Alex didn't flinch, not that he ever stirred while he was sleeping, but I knew that I just thought myself right into another delusion. I could've ignored it. I should've ignored it. I could've just stayed there and hid under the covers until it went away. But I'd come this far and my curiosity always got the best of me. I'd opened

Pandora's Box and, as scary as it was, part of me couldn't wait to see what was inside.

As I descended the stairs, I heard laughter. For a moment, I thought Vivian and Holden were in the kitchen. My heart sank only a bit when I heard Bridget say, "*Shhh*. Shut up, Kip," followed by more laughter, drunken laughter.

"Alright, what's so funny?" I asked them as I entered the kitchen which reeked of the skunky, smoky smell of pot.

"Hey!" they both cheered and put their arms out to hug me, like I was a long-lost friend and they couldn't wait for me to join the party. Their sloppy embrace enveloped me.

I broke away quickly while Bridget and Kip continued to hang on each other. "So, what are you two crazy kids up to?" I asked them.

Kip got a very serious look on his face, though it looked like he was trying not to laugh. "Listen, Bella. We just wanted to talk to you about this whole doctor thing." He put the word 'doctor' in air quotes.

"What about it?"

"Well, what exactly is the goal here?" He stroked his goatee.

"What do you mean?"

"Well, is the goal here to get rid of us?"

Standing face to face with them and the idea of getting rid of them, I got a little sad, and a little scared. "Not exactly."

"Isn't it?" Bridget chimed in with a giggle as she plopped down in a chair at the kitchen table. She hiccupped and broke into hysterics, almost falling off her chair.

Why were my hallucinations so often drunk?

"No," I said firmly. "I don't want to get rid of you." I told them, because I didn't. I didn't want to get rid of them. I liked them. I didn't like Goliath trying to kill me, but that was all over now.

"Then what is the point? What are you hoping to achieve by going?" Kip's face had grown sober.

I shrugged. "I just don't want anyone to get hurt. I don't want to hurt myself and I don't want to hurt Alex."

"But we're not here to hurt you," Bridget said from the table, tucking her hair behind her ears and looking a little less drunk.

"We're here to help you," Kip added. "You know that. You know us." Bridget nodded and looked at Kip adoringly.

I nodded, too. "Look, I know you guys aren't here to hurt me, but this whole thing has gotten a little out of control. I just don't think I can manage it anymore. It's gone too far."

"You know you'd feel better if you wrote more," Kip said with a smirk.

"And there he goes," Bridget stood up. "C'mon, you." She stood up, hooked her arm through his and pulled him away. "Let's get out of here."

Kip went willingly, but paused, giving me a backward glance before disappearing.

CHAPTER 20

ALEX WAS ABLE TO GET me some sort of "emergency" appointment with Maya's doctor for late the next day. He stayed home with me all day, thinking, I'm sure, that if he didn't leave my side, then no one could show up and try to kill me. Or I couldn't try to kill myself, whatever. Looking at it from his perspective, I couldn't blame him. What must I have looked like writhing around and screaming on the floor, pinned down by a figment of my imagination? I was mortified he had seen me that way. It made me not want to look him in his lovely eyes. Consequently, I spent much of the day trying to avoid him, where he spent his time trying to be with me.

Our tug-of-war of avoidance and attachment continued all day so that by the time the afternoon came, I was feeling much less interested in this 'doctor thing,' as Kip called it. The trauma of Goliath's attack had faded considerably, like a bad dream that seems so vivid when you first wake up but by the end of the day you can barely remember what scared you so much in the first place. Anyway, talking to a doctor about it suddenly seemed less urgent.

I was only going to the doctor for Alex, anyway. Goliath was gone. I was quite sure he was gone and wouldn't be coming back. I killed him. I wasn't in danger anymore. I could handle all the others. I know Daniel was really angry last time I saw him, but I didn't write any violence into him. Peter wouldn't hurt a fly, Monica *couldn't* hurt a fly. Kip and Bridget weren't interested in flies. The only wild card was Cody and he didn't seem so scary anymore. In fact, somewhere along the way, Cody went from being the character I hated to see, to the character I couldn't wait to talk to. I wondered if he changed or if I did.

"Are you sure you don't want me to come with you?" Alex asked, following me to my car. Making sure I was alone for as little time as possible.

"I have to do this on my own, Alex. I have to be the one to make it happen." I told him, with the emphasis on the "I."

He reluctantly accepted. I suspect he thought there was a pretty good chance I wouldn't go at all and he wasn't entirely wrong. There was probably a solid 20% chance that I was going to get in the car and go hide somewhere for an hour. I had every intention of going to, and talking to this doctor, to try and get some control over what was happening to me. But I was pretty unstable and feeling fairly impulsive right then and if Kip showed up, I was pretty sure he could easily talk me out of going.

"Bella?" Alex called after me.

"What?" I turned back to him impatiently, suddenly desperate to get out of the house. Desperate to be alone.

"I love you," he said sort of sheepishly, and it was so damn charming I remembered why I was going to the doctor in the first place.

"I love you, too." I said back as I got into my van. "Don't worry."

"I *am* worried."

"Well, don't be. I'm going to be fine," I said, not because I was sure I would be, but because Alex looked so damn terrified, I wanted to make him feel better. In reality, I had no idea whether I was going to be ok or not.

As I backed out of the driveway, I turned to look left and right and when I went to look left again, Cody appeared in the passenger seat, looking like he had been there all along. He still had no tuxedo and no glass.

I knew he would come.

"Tell me you're not going through with this?" he said. "You can't do this."

"I can and I want to do this," I said through my fake smile as I waved to Alex who was now standing eagerly in the driveway.

"I don't believe you." Cody waved to Alex, too, who, of course, couldn't see him.

"I do." I insisted. "I can't live like this, talking to myself all the time."

"Talking to yourself? What am I, chopped liver?" Cody threw his hands up and pretended to be hurt.

"You know what I mean." I rolled my eyes and tried not to laugh.

"I know. But some doctor's not going to be able to help you with that, with us." He shook his head at me.

"Maybe he can." I shrugged.

"Nope. Won't happen."

"What do you know, Cody? You could probably use a doctor yourself," I muttered at him.

"Ha, you would know."

"God, you're exasperating." And he was. But honestly, I was glad for his company on my trip to the doctor. Other than that, I'd be sitting here thinking myself dizzy.

"Thank you." Cody answered, pretty damn pleased with himself.

I looked him over for a second, remembering that creepy tuxedo guy that used to hang around. "What happened to you?" I asked.

"What do you mean?" He stared out the window, avoiding me as if we were on a really long car trip together and he didn't feel like talking to me anymore.

"You know."

"No, I don't. If I knew, I wouldn't ask. What are you talking about?" He fixed his hair in the side-view mirror.

"You know, the clothes, the drink, or lack thereof... you're different." It really wasn't that long ago that he was a sobbing puddle passed out on my bed.

"Oh that. Yeah, I don't know." He shrugged and traced the outline of the window with his index finger.

"You don't know?"

"Nope. But I bet you do." He smirked his crooked grin at me. "Maybe I changed because you wanted me to change. You *needed* me to change."

Why were the figments of my imagination so much more intuitive than I was? "You know, you are the one that's making me crazy," I told Cody. "It's all you."

"Thanks, babe. That's probably the nicest thing anyone's said about me in a long time." He sighed and smiled sadly at the same time.

We drove the rest of the way there in silence. So much silence that I wondered why Cody was there in the first place. What was his purpose if he wasn't going to be bitching at me about something? When I got out of the car in the parking garage of the doctor's office, he got out, too. "Hey," he jogged around to my side of the car, stopped me and took both of my hands, "Listen, uh. Good luck in there," he stammered. There was a sense of insecurity about him that I hadn't noticed before, or maybe he didn't have before. He seemed like he had something more to say, but didn't want to say it.

"Thanks." I said. I started to turn away but Cody held onto my hands.

"You know, I think maybe I should come with you."

"No way." I jerked my hands out of his grasp and backed away.

"Bella, your brain is far too valuable to me to let someone pick around in there unsupervised."

"No, Cody."

"Come on. It'll be fun. Maybe I could learn something about myself," he pleaded.

"You're not coming," I told him and I meant it.

"You just try and stop me." He smiled that creepy, crooked smile I remembered from the gas station. Though, now it seemed more charming than creepy.

"I will." I meant that, too. I would try and stop him. I would push every thought of him out of my brain until he was so far from my thoughts, he couldn't interfere. I had to keep him out of this appointment. For Alex.

****

I was expecting a balding, late-middle aged, poorly dressed, male doctor in an office with a brown leather chaise. I'm not sure why. It's just the picture I always got in my head when I thought "psychiatrist." What I got instead was an impeccably dressed, younger-than-me, pretty female doctor in a room painted sea-glass green with overstuffed Pottery Barn furniture. It looked more like a cottage on the Cape than a doctor's office.

"Mirabelle." She stood up and offered her hand as I entered her office. "I'm Dr. Brennan."

“Nice to meet you,” I said and obliged her with a handshake, even though I really didn’t think it was nice to meet her at all.

“Have a seat.” She gestured to a fluffy neutral chair opposite her fluffy neutral chair that faced halfway toward mine and halfway away. As if she was only half-interested in hearing what I had to say. I closed my eyes and tried to shake off the negativity, remembering Alex and why I was here.

“So, what brings you here today?” She asked, typing her notes into her iPad.

“Didn’t my husband tell you?” I asked, slouching into the furniture. It was comfortable…too comfortable.

“He did, but I want you to tell me.” She said, finally looking up from her notes. She was awfully pretty. My face must have turned the color of the sea-glass walls. I suddenly couldn’t stand the thought of Alex talking to this beautiful woman about me in what I’m sure made me sound, at the very least, pathetic and the very most, completely insane.

Alex. I’m here for Alex. I thought, as I steeled myself to explain what I’d been going through. “Well, I’ve been seeing things.”

“Seeing things?” She looked at me over the rim of her $500 eyeglasses.

“Yeah. Well not things exactly. People.” Ugh, I thought telling this to Alex was tough. Telling it to a stranger was unbearable. My palms started to sweat so much I felt the need to put my hands in my lap to keep from staining her pretty furniture.

The doctor nodded and tapped something on her tablet. I was sure it was less about me seeing people and more about the way I said it.

"So, you see people that aren't really there?"

Strike one. I nodded.

"And do you talk to them?

Strike two. "I do."

"Can you touch them or feel them?" she asked me without looking up, like she was checking things off a list.

Strike three, you're out. "Yes."

She let me sit there in agonizing silence for what seemed like an eternity.

"I'm not as crazy as I sound," I said, unable to stand the silence any longer.

"I don't care for the word 'crazy'." She smiled in a way that was probably supposed to be warm, but to me it felt manipulative. Though, maybe in my next session I could talk to her about my paranoia. Not that I was planning on having a next session.

"I bet you don't," I snarked back at her.

She didn't react. Not a blink. Not a sigh. No reaction at all. "So, when did this all start?" she continued, ignoring my attitude.

I took a deep breath and tried to remember when this all began.

"It was me, wasn't it?" Cody said, appearing over the shoulder of Dr. Brennan.

Dammit, Cody, you just couldn't stay away, could you? I said. Not out loud, of course. Though now that I saw what I was up against, I was glad he was there. I needed someone in my corner. Again.

"It was right after we dropped the kids at college."

She nodded knowingly, like in that one sentence she had me all figured out.

"Tell me about it," she pried.

I shrugged. "We stopped for gas and I saw this guy in a tuxedo getting coffee."

Cody smiled and winked at me, at the memory of our first meeting. He was so pleased with himself.

"And who was it that you saw?"

I hesitated.

"Was it someone you recognized?"

"No." I thought back to that moment that seemed so long ago. "Not at first. But he definitely seemed familiar. And he was at a gas station off the highway and didn't seem to have a car, and he was wearing a tuxedo in the morning. So I noticed him, but didn't think he was anything more than strange." I suddenly babbled on nervously.

"So you recognize him now?"

I nodded. "He's a character from a book I was writing...a long time ago." I couldn't actually remember when I started writing about Cody. Across the room, he uncrossed his arms long enough to wave at me with a smirk.

"And the next time you saw him?" She didn't look up from her notes as I tried, successfully, to stifle a giggle.

"The next time was someone else."

"And who was that?" She kept typing. Maybe she should write a book. She probably already had. Damn over-achieving doctors.

"Another character – from another book."

"And what happened?"

"He spoke to me."

"And did you answer him?"

"Of course I did." I answered her like she was the crazy one.

Cody peered over Dr. Brennan's shoulder to see what she was writing. "She thinks you're traumatized by the loss of your children. No shit, Sherlock." He said to the doctor who couldn't hear him.

I bit my lip to keep from laughing.

"Have you noticed any particular pattern to their appearance?" she continued her interrogation. "What do you mean? Like do they only show up on Tuesdays after a full moon?"

"Like do they appear when you're stressed or afraid or happy?"

"They usually just show up when I'm alone."

"Usually." Cody laughed.

"Usually?" the doctor asked.

"Yes, usually. But not always." She raised her eyes to me and I knew I had said too much. Though I was glad for the diversion. I didn't want to tell her that I've known for some time that my characters definitely related to a certain emotion. I didn't want her to know that.

"Is there someone here with us now?" She sat up, clearly intrigued.

"No," I lied and the look on her face told me she knew I wasn't being honest.

I was frustrating her. I wasn't doing it on purpose, really. Maybe I was. I just wasn't getting the feeling from her that she was going to be terribly understanding about my feelings. She was an ice princess. A young ice princess with no life experience. How was I supposed to tell her what I was really going through? How could she possibly understand what it's like to look back on your life and feel like the best was behind you? How could she even look back on her life? She was so young; her whole damn life was still in front of her.

"Mirabelle," she leaned forward, "I can't help you if you don't talk to me. Your husband called me because he's concerned about your safety. I don't need to tell you how worried he is about you. He's afraid that you're going to hurt yourself."

Damn. She played the husband card. I had promised Alex I would get help but I wasn't trying very hard. I looked to Cody for support but he just shrugged, knowing he had no more power here, and vanished.

"Ok. You're right." I nodded. "There was someone here, but he just left."

She looked at me skeptically, trying to gauge my truthfulness.

"I swear. He just left. He doesn't like to talk about Alex." I tried to look as honest as possible. "Listen, I'm sorry I'm not more forthcoming. I have a hard time taking things seriously sometimes. It's a defense mechanism."

She smiled at my self-diagnosis. "Mirabelle, I'd say if you ever felt physically threatened by these 'people,' then that's something to take very seriously."

"That's why I'm here."

"But every single thing about you tells me that you're not fully vested in this. Your body language, your jokes, even your tone of voice says that you don't want to be here."

"You're right, I don't," I confessed. "I don't want to tell you what I'm going through because I just don't feel crazy."

She sighed at my repeated usage of the word 'crazy.' "Why don't you tell me what happened yesterday? Why did Alex call me?"

I told her the story of Goliath, how I had been writing his arrival all afternoon, and how he knocked me down and tried to cut my wrists, and just how vivid and real it all seemed.

"It sounds pretty serious."

"But, that's just one of them. Most of them aren't like that. Most of them are pretty friendly and fairly interesting."

"How many are there?"

I counted on my fingers, surprised that I had never taken the time to count them before: *David, Goliath, Daniel, Emily, Monica, Peter, Cody, Kip,* and *Bridget.* "Nine." Nine? Was it that many?

"And none of the others have ever threatened you?"

I thought about Cody and his past threats, which I was always mostly sure were empty. Though, the glass throwing was pretty threatening. And there was the last time I saw Daniel; he was fairly menacing. Still, I answered. "No."

"And why do you think Goliath tried to hurt you?"

"Because he was the bad guy," I said to her like she was stupid.

"Mirabelle, that attitude's not helpful," she scolded.

"Sorry." *No, I'm not.* "Goliath won't be back, though. He's gone for good."

"Gone?"

"I wrote him away."

She looked at me incredulously.

"I killed him. I mean, in the story, I killed him."

Dr. Brennan lifted her chin at me and then tucked it down again, disapprovingly.

"What do you think they want? These characters."

"I know what they want. Most of them just want to get finished. If I finish their stories, they'll stop…" I trailed off a bit, realizing I was talking too much again.

"Really?"

"I think so."

She typed some more stuff on her iPad.

"So, what do you think is wrong with me?" I asked in a vain attempt to divert her doubt.

"What do you think is wrong with you?"

"Nothing."

"Nothing?"

I nodded.

The doctor took her glasses off and leaned forward. "Mirabelle, I think these things you are seeing are a physical manifestation of the loss you feel from sending your kids off to college. It's not unusual for a mother to feel exceptional loss at this time."

I rolled my eyes.

"You don't agree?"

"I don't deny that I was terribly depressed when my kids left. I miss them tremendously. But can't this all just be a sign from my psyche that I need to write?"

"You're over-simplifying."

"Maybe you're under-simplifying."

She looked at me quizzically.

"You're making it too complicated," I clarified. *Stupid-head.*

"Mirabelle, you are dealing with very serious issues here. You can't just write this problem away."

"You don't think my writing will help?"

"Not if it fuels your hallucinations."

"So what do you suggest I do, Doctor?"

****

I climbed back into my car, throwing the stupid bottle of pills the stupid doctor gave me to "settle down my brain" in the center console. Closing my eyes, I covered my face with my hands and leaned forward onto the steering wheel.

"What'd I miss?" Cody said, right on cue.

I leaned back in the driver's seat, put my head back and stared at the ceiling before reaching into the console and handing him the bottle of pills.

"What are these supposed to do?" he asked, looking at the label.

"Guess." I answered without looking at him.

"Oh. Get rid of us, huh?" He laughed just a little bit and was quiet for a moment before asking, "So, uh, what are you going to do?" For the first time, Cody sounded nervous. He had lost more than a bit of that arrogant swagger he had when I first saw him.

"I don't know, Cody. I can't risk another scene like last night with Goliath."

"No, I guess you can't…" he said sadly.

"But I finished a book last night. It took me twenty freaking years, but I finally finished one."

"And how did that make you feel?"

I sighed. "Well, at first I felt drained and exhausted and then really just awful, sad, and scared. Alex and I had had a huge fight and it took so much out of me to kill Goliath –"

"You killed him?" Cody interrupted.

"I had to," I insisted.

Cody smirked. "I didn't know you had it in you."

"It was kind of a kill-or-be-killed scenario, he left me no choice." Cody nodded knowingly, and I considered that maybe he had killed someone in a similar scene.

"OK, so after all that, how did you feel?"

"Fucking great. I felt like I won the lottery. I accomplished something. I wrote a fucking book."

"And now you want more?" he asked, I think. It may have sounded a little bit more like a statement than a question.

"I want to write more," I agreed.

"Then write more."

"It's not that simple, Cody."

"Of course it is. It's time for you to do what you want, what you *need* to do."

I nodded a little.

"What's stopping you? Is it Alex?"

I shrugged. "I promised him I'd get help."

"And you did. You went to the doctor. She was very helpful. But you can't let him hold you back, Bella."

"It's not about him holding me back. This is not healthy. I'm not healthy. Even you can see that."

"Your writing will make this better. It will make *you* better."

"You just want me to finish you, to fix you?"

"Really, Bella?" Cody looked at me with a tenderness I had not seen from him before. "Do you really think any of this has ever been about me?"

He was right, of course. How could it be about him? He didn't exist. This was about me. About me succeeding or failing, just trying to achieve something for the love of god. This was about all the dreams I happily put on the shelf in favor of so many other things, none of which I regret, by the way. But now it was time for me clean out the closets, both in my bedroom and in my brain.

CHAPTER 21

I DROVE HOME ALONE, BUT I couldn't seem to get all the way there. Instead, I found myself parked around the corner, trying to figure out what I was going to tell Alex about the doctor, about my writing, about us.

The doctor was sure her magic pills would make everything better. I knew they wouldn't. I knew now the only way to make anything better, to make me better was to finish.

Alex was all too eager when I got home, greeting me at the door like a lonely puppy. "How did it go? What'd the doctor say?" Peppering me with a million questions before I even crossed the threshold.

"Can I get in the door first?" I snapped, annoyed with his impatience, and desperate for a moment to collect my thoughts.

"Sorry." He backed away quietly, wounded. "So?" he asked timidly after I had closed the door behind me.

Taking a deep breath, trying to sound matter-of-fact, I said, "She said I have some sort of empty-nest syndrome that is manifesting itself in hallucinations. She says I miss the children and am searching for something else to care for. She gave me these." I tossed the bottle at him.

He caught the bottle and turned it in his hand to read the label, his eagerness melting into concern. The look on his face told me that even he wasn't sure this was such a great idea.

"I can't do it, Alex," I told him. "I know I said I would get some help, but I'm sorry. I can't take them," I said, pushing past him.

"Bella," he followed me, grabbed my hand from behind and pulled me back to him. "I know you're scared, honey, but if this is what the doctor said, maybe it will help. Maybe you will feel better. Maybe your hallucinations will go away." He pushed thc hair out of my face and I wished he was right.

"I'm afraid that if I take them, then I will go away," I told him, shaking my head.

"You won't," he reassured me, holding my shoulders tightly.

"But part of me will."

"I won't let it." He took my face in his hands. I couldn't look at him. As strong as his words were, his eyes were filled with fear. He was afraid for me, afraid of me. I so wanted to make things right for him. But I just couldn't. I turned away from him yet again.

"Alex, what if I don't want them to go away?" I asked with my back to him.

"What do you mean?"

"What if I like them, my hallucinations?" I still hated that word, but the reality was that's what they were. "What if I need them to stay?"

I didn't have to turn back to see the expression on his face. "Need them? Why would you need them?" he asked, just a hint of panic in his voice.

I took a deep breath in preparation to make my case.

"Mirabelle, what are you getting at?"

Turning back to Alex, I took his hands and pulled him to the couch; he resisted, skeptically, but came along. I sat down criss-cross applesauce, he sat with his feet on the floor, arms crossed. "Alex, these things that I've been seeing, they're part of me…part of what I feel. Every one of these characters exists because of something I feel or have felt at one time or another, or something that happened to me or something I wanted to happen. Sending them away is just hiding my feelings. That's what is making me crazy, Alex. I need to deal with these things. There is no magic pill that's going to fix me."

His brow furrowed, he thought for what seemed like forever, before he said, "So you don't want to take the pills? OK, Bella, what do you want to do then?"

"I need to finish them, Alex. All of them," I said firmly.

He didn't even try to conceal his disgust. "Oh, is that what *they* told you?" The way he said 'they' made me hate him.

"Not in so many words, but…"

"You know what?" He cut me off, holding his hands up. "Stop. I don't care what they told you…because they don't exist. You know who exists? Me. And you. Take the pills, Bella. I'm begging you. Please, before this gets any worse. Before something terrible happens."

"Nothing bad is going to happen, and it's not going to get worse."

"You thought 'whoever it was' was going to kill you last night!" Alex's voice rose with his temper as he stood up from the couch.

"Goliath. His name's Goliath."

"I don't care what the hell his name is! You were rolling around on the floor screaming, fighting someone that wasn't even there. Do you know what that was like for me? To walk in and see you like that? Do you know how terrified I was? Do you even care?"

"Of course I care." I reached out to touch his face, but he recoiled.

"It's too dangerous, Bella. You're not just talking to yourself in the bathroom anymore. You're going to get hurt."

"Goliath was the only one who was dangerous and I took care of him last night. He's done. He won't be back. None of the others are dangerous. Cody could be a little bit, but he would never hurt me…" I started to ramble.

"Stop it!" he yelled. "*You* are the one who is dangerous Bella! *You* are the one who tried to hurt you last night, don't you see that?"

I stood in defiant silence.

"Listen to me, Bella." Alex clenched his fists, trying to talk some sense into me. "They don't exist. None of them do! Not Goliath, not Kip, not Daniel, not Emily. None of them! Everything you think they say is just YOU!"

Ouch. "My brain knows that, Alex. It does," I said softly.

He stared at me for a moment. A very painful moment. "I can't do this. I can't watch you go crazy." He started to walk out of the room.

"I'm not crazy! I'm just…" I called after him. I wasn't crazy.

He stormed back into the room, which was way worse than watching him storm out. "What, Bella? You're just what?" He continued before I even had the chance to answer him, "And don't give me that overactive imagination crap, Belly. You're having arguments with people who aren't there! They hurt you. I can't just sit here and watch you go insane…or worse."

"Don't call me insane, Alex," I snapped at him, feeling truly insulted by his words. "I feel more sane now than I ever have in my life."

"Great. That's great. It must be me then. I must be the crazy one."

"No. Alex, listen. I just need some time to finish them. If I finish them, they'll go away. I know how crazy this all sounds. I know. But I have to finish them. Please don't be angry with me."

"Angry? This isn't angry, Mirabelle. This is scared. I'm scared of what you're capable of at this point."

"When I finish them, they will go away, I know they will," I pleaded with him.

It was Alex's turn to turn away. He ran his hands through his hair. "How many are there?"

"Nine."

"Nine?!" He turned back to me.

"But only seven are left! I took care of David and Goliath last night. And it's really just four stories with seven characters left."

He was silent for a moment. "I don't know what to do, Bella." He shook his head so sadly I felt my heart crack. "Why are you making this so hard? Why can't you just take the damn pills and we can get back to normal?"

"Normal? Dammit, Alex, I'm not normal! As normal as I try to be, it's not enough. Do you know how hard it is for me with you being so damn perfect all the time. So damn in control of everything! I watch you and wonder what it must be like. To be so in control of your emotions, your life, all the damn time. And when I'm not in control, when I'm not normal, I feel like I'm just a giant disappointment to you."

"No, Bella, that's not true." He tried to hold me, but I resisted him. "You're never…"

"It's true that that's how I feel. I feel like I can't live up to what you want me to be, or need me to be, or expect me to be."

"You are everything I need you to be." I knew he believed he meant it, but my heart didn't believe it.

"You may feel that way about me, Alex. But I don't feel that way about myself." Alex sat down on the couch and put his face in his hands. He took a deep breath, reeling in his emotions. I knelt down in front of him taking my own deep breath. "I need to finish them."

"OK," he nodded. "I get it," though I'm not sure he did. "What do you need from me? What can I do?"

I sat up straight, trying to steel my heart, preparing to hurt him worse than I ever had before. "I need to finish them, Alex. But I don't think I can do it with you here."

It took him a minute to figure out what I was saying. "What? Wait, you want me to leave? You want me to leave you here – alone – with them."

"No, I don't *want* you to leave," I spoke quietly, as if my volume would diminish the impact of my words. "But I think I *need* you to leave."

He shook his head. "I won't. I won't leave you alone in this mess."

"You can't help me with this, Alex. I have to get *myself* out of it. I'm sorry."

"Sorry? All this time I've been trying to help you and now you're saying you don't want my help at all. You'd rather I just leave you alone?" He got up and walked away.

"Please don't be angry."

"Oh, now you don't want me to be angry? You're the one who's been telling me that I'm *supposed* to be angry with you!" In a flash, his anger sparked as he grabbed a vase off the shelf and threw it at the fireplace.

I bit my lip and looked down in shame, sitting back on my heels. Now that I'd gone and made him really angry, I didn't want him to be angry. He was scary when he was angry, when he had no control. I'd never seen him like this and I hated what I had done. I wanted to take it all back. I didn't want him to leave me. I wanted him to stay and hold me and tell me everything was going to be ok, just like he always did. When I fall, he picks me up. It's what we do. It's what we've always done.

"You know what, Bella? Thank you for helping me get in touch with my emotions. This feels fucking great. I hope you're happy now you've made us both fucking crazy." He stormed out of the room, into the garage. I let him go this time, but I didn't hear his car start or peel away so I knew he hadn't gone far. I could just imagine him in the garage, running his hands through his too-long hair. Shaking his head at the insanity of me.

I followed him into the garage.

"I don't know how to do this. I don't know how to help you," he said as soon as I opened the door. He was standing right there, like he was on his way back in to talk to me.

"Alex," I began slowly and took his hand. "I used to be able to see my future. I could see myself sitting at a table in a bookstore, signing copies of my latest bestseller. I could see my name on the spine of my books in the library. But somewhere along the line, I stopped being able to see it. Everything else got in the way and now when I look forward, I just can't see it anymore and it terrifies me.

"You have your success at work. I need something for me. I need to finish them. I need to finish me," I said softly, hoping that these were the magic words that would make him understand. And forgive.

He wandered away, looking around the garage. Looking anywhere but at me. "Is it forever?" he asked suddenly, without turning back to me.

"What?"

"Do you want me to leave forever?"

"No. God no, Alex. I just need to be alone to finish them. I need to totally give myself to them and I can't do that with you here, without worrying that you're going to walk in on me talking to them or fighting with them. Without having to transition to being some kind of normalish kind of wife for you at the end of the day."

"You know, I don't need you to be normal."

"Yes, you do. At least sometimes, you do. You need it. You deserve that much. But right now, I need to totally give myself to them so I can totally give myself to you when I'm done."

He sat down on the hood of his car, which in itself was a strange gesture for him. I could practically see the wheels turning in his head. I was praying that he'd say yes, while hoping he'd say no.

"How long?" he finally asked, still not looking at me.

"I don't know. I don't really know how long it will take me."

"Ballpark it for me," he commanded, like he was in a business meeting.

"If I'm doing nothing but writing all day? At best, it will take me a few weeks." I hoped.

"And at worst?"

"A few months."

He ran his hands through his hair again while shaking his head. I think he even pulled a few pieces out. I had to be the worst wife on the planet. Here I was, making this poor man literally yank the hair out of his head.

"OK, Bella, I'm going to go," he said as he got off the car with a little hop. "But I'm going to say something to you first."

He stood facing me and took each of my hands. "You know that I'm a man of few words, but I will not leave without you knowing exactly what I think about you."

This was going to be painful. I steeled myself for the worst.

"You already know I love you. But what I've never told you, probably because I thought you already knew, is how proud I am of you. You have accomplished more than you know. You've raised two beautiful, hard-working, amazing children. You gave them everything they ever needed, including the wings they needed to fly out of this crazy birdhouse. That is no small accomplishment, Bella. That is not something you should just ignore. There are lots of mothers out there, but there are none like you.

"And I know you're not normal. God, I never wanted normal, Belly. I only ever wanted you.

"So, I'm going to go, Bella, and let you do whatever it is you think you need to do. But I want you to know, no, I *need* you to know that you are my success. Everything I am today, everything I've ever achieved, everything I've ever done, is because I've had you at home waiting for me every night. So, if I need to wait for you this time, it's the least I can do."

It took me a moment to realize I was holding my breath. "Alex," was all I could muster before I fell into him. How could I possibly let him go? I held onto him like crazy glue. I couldn't seem to unstick myself from the front of his shirt.

"Still want me to go?" he smirked, as he peeled me off of him.

I shook my head and whispered, "Yes."

He looked down, resigned to the answer.

"I'll work as fast as I can." I promised, and I meant it.

"Promise me you'll be ok," he pleaded with me.

"I'll be ok. Don't worry."

"I am definitely going to worry. I love you, Mirabelle."

"And I love you." I kissed him softly on the lips, standing on my tip toes, holding onto his shirt so I wouldn't lose my balance.

"You'll call me if you need me…if you need anything. Anything. I'll be here."

"I know," I said as the tears started to pour out of my eyes. Really pouring.

"You know, Bella," Alex said with a sigh, looking off in the distance. The sun was setting and the sky was lit with only purples and pinks visible through the rectangular windows in the garage. "This would be a great time for a really melodramatic, ride-off-into-the-sunset kind of exit, but I have to pack."

CHAPTER 22

MY FIRST NIGHT ALONE WITHOUT Alex was pure torture. Every time I closed my eyes, all I could see was the look on his face as he told me exactly what he thought of me. Damn him for waiting twenty years to dump that beautiful speech on me. I couldn't help thinking that I had just made the biggest mistake of my entire life. I resisted the urge to text him all night though I'm quite sure he was awake all night, feeling the same thing I was. At least I had the task of making something out of myself to keep myself busy. Poor Alex just got kicked out of his house until his crazy wife could get her shit together.

I got out of bed in the morning after having slept none. Zero sleep at all. Too filled with guilt, fear, sadness and excitement. Before beginning my life as a writer, I had to call work. "Yeah, hi, it's Mirabelle."

"Mirabelle, are you feeling better? Or are you not coming in AGAIN today?" the principal's assistant asked me bitterly. I couldn't blame her for being irritated with me. I had been beyond flaky lately.

"I'm feeling better, but I'm not coming in today."

"What is it this time, Mirabelle?" she said with an exasperated sigh.

"Excuse me?"

"Your excuse, what is it this time?"

"Oh, actually, I'm resigning."

"What? When?"

"I'm done. I quit. Effective right now." Those words almost, almost took the sting out of missing Alex.

"You can't just quit. You have to give us some notice."

"Actually, I don't. It would be courteous of me to do so, but I don't have to."

"So, you're not coming in today?" she asked, still sounding confused though I thought I was being pretty darn clear. I don't know why she was so surprised. I'd been threatening to quit since the first day I started. Maybe she was just surprised that after all this time, I'd finally found the guts to actually do it.

"I'm never coming in again. I quit," I said, to make sure she understood. "OK?"

"Uh, ok, Mirabelle. Good luck."

That felt good. I was free. No more yelling, barking, clapping. No more hating on kids, who were really just being kids. Relief flushed over me as the weight of that stupid job was lifted from my shoulders.

There was nothing quite like quitting a job you hated with every fiber of your being to get the creative juices flowing. Time to write. My only question was who to start with. I went up to the closet and opened the door, ready to face down all my little demons in their perfectly coordinated boxes.

Cody, I told myself. I had to start with Cody. I made a promise to him. I owed it to him. He'd changed, or something changed him, and it was up to me to make it stick. I pulled his box off the closet shelf, expecting him to show up and give me some direction.

"You really did it!?" Kip appeared on my unmade bed instead. I should've guessed Kip would show up the minute I quit my job. I suppose it made the most sense to start with Bridget and Kip. Their story was next chronologically after

David and Goliath, in the order I started them, anyway. Plus, the sentiment of quitting your job and finally doing what you want to be doing was a recurring theme throughout Bridget and Kip's story.

"Did what?" I played coy with him, hoping to use whatever dialogue he gave me here at the end of his story.

"You quit."

"I did. I quit." God, it felt good to say it out loud. Even if it was out loud to nobody.

"So, what finally did it?"

Hmmm. Good question. What did it? Perhaps it was the fact that I was completely insane. Did that do it? Or was it just the prospect of a better life. A life where I accomplished something if not daily, then maybe weekly. Heck, I'd settle for monthly at this point. Even yearly would be a start. A life where something I did mattered to someone, somewhere.

The idea that maybe somebody would read something that I wrote sometime and it would move them ever so slightly, made me positively giddy in a way that no job I ever had before did. Except maybe motherhood. I always got a thrill out of watching my kids be good people. Making our little corner of the world a better place. And maybe that's all I wanted. Just to make the world a better place. Put something positive out there and maybe in some small way, make the world better.

"So, what was it?" Kip's voice interrupted my internal rambles.

"Huh?" I had completely forgotten the question.

"What was the straw that broke the proverbial camel's back?"

I smiled at my always witty, imaginary friend. "I just realized I could do better."

He smiled back. "Now, haven't I been telling you that for years? You really should listen to me more. I'm a wealth of knowledge." He sat down on my bed.

"You? The bartender?"

"It's all about the life experience, baby. Behind that bar, I've learned things you can't find in those fancy books you're always reading."

"Whatever, Kip," I said, mimicking a favorite quote of Bridget's when suddenly Kip got a real far away look in his eyes. "Kip?" I called. When he didn't answer, I followed his gaze across the room to a very sad Bridget looking out my bedroom window, smoking a cigarette. Ah, my twenties, and the early nineties, when smoking didn't carry quite the social stigma it does today. (I'm sure my kids would be mortified to learn that I was a bona fide social smoker at their age.)

Turning back to the closet, I reached up to the shelf and pulled down the *Bridget & Kip* box. I almost dropped it, but I managed to catch it before it fell and laid it gently on the bed next to Kip. This was it. Time to put Kip and Bridget to bed. I grabbed my laptop from my dresser and sat down next to him on the bed, opening my computer and their file.

Kip just continued to stare at Bridget as if he were frozen in time, but still breathing, almost like he was stuck. Bridget, too, was completely still, just staring out the window, her burning cigarette ignored. "Do you want to talk to her?" I asked.

He shook his head ever so slightly, as if he could barely move, and closed his eyes slowly. I exhaled slowly. "I guess I'm on my own here." I said out loud, quietly, to no one in particular. Well, I guess I was saying it to myself because, technically, neither one of them was actually there.

I opened the box slowly, fearing an explosion of failures under the lid. So much time and energy went into what was in there. Yet I had nothing to show for it except a box filled with notebooks, scraps and the usual from my novel graveyard. I picked up a few snippets, trying to get an idea, looking for the end, but it just didn't seem to be in the box.

I had stopped writing just after Bridget figured out what Kip had been doing. The alarm clock, the shoe stealing, the customer complaints – it had been Kip all along.

I reread:

The light bulb turned on in her head. "It was you," she whispered.

Kip looked proud for just a moment, but was suddenly filled with shame when he saw how devastated she looked. She looked like someone who'd just lost her best friend.

"The alarm clock? The shoes?" The pieces were all falling into place in Bridget's head. "How?" she choked out.

"I had a key made," he confessed.

"And you've been sneaking into my apartment in the middle of the night?"

"You always were such a sound sleeper..." he said with the tiniest of smirks, suddenly filled with the memory of sneaking into her room when they were kids and struggling to wake her up without alerting her parents.

"How could you do this, Kip?"

"I wanted to help you," he answered, kicking at the floor.

"Help me?" Bridget's voice finally rose above a whisper and Kip forced himself to lift his eyes to see the pain on her face. "Maybe you could've tried being supportive of me at the

end of a hard day, doing a job I did not particularly like, or maybe you could have made some small attempt to understand that sometimes you do what you have to do instead of what you want to do? Maybe you could have been there for me, Kip. That's what friends do. Not lie and steal and manipulate." She was full-on yelling now.

Kip was suddenly terrified. It all seemed like such a good idea at the time. He'd never meant for it to go so far. He'd never really thought about how far it would go, he just wanted Bridget to be happy. "Bridget, I just –" he tried to explain.

But she wouldn't let him finish. "You just what, Kip? What kind of stupid explanation could you possibly give me to excuse this kind of bullshit?" She was angry now, angrier than he'd ever seen her. He'd seen her pissed off...but never angry. And never at him. Not like this.

"I'm sorry," was all he could whisper.

"Sorry?" She sneered at him. "You're sorry?"

"I am."

"Would you be sorry to know that I got fired today?

"Fired?" He whispered, wondering how in the hell that had happened.

"Yes. Are you sorry now?"

"Yes." He nodded ever so slightly.

Bridget stared at him for a minute and saw right through him. "Liar." She said through gritted teeth as she picked up his alarm clock from the bedside table and hurled it at him.

He ducked just in time. "Ok! No! I'm not sorry. But Bridget..."

"Stop, Kip. Stop talking. Stop everything."

"Bridget, please..."

"I'm done, Kip. It's over."

"Over? What's over?" He couldn't understand what she could've possibly meant by that. "Bridget, please listen to me," he pleaded.

"Why should I listen to you? So you can lie to me some more? For twelve years, I've listened to you. You and your stupid plans. Your stupid plays. Your asinine ideas. And what has it gotten me...nothing but having a stupid, immature, asshole making my life hell. I'm done, Kip. I'm done with you."

She turned on her heel and marched out the front door with Kip following.

"Please don't leave, Bridget. Let me fix this."

She stopped and looked at him. "No, Kip," she choked on his name. "You can't fix this. You can't. Don't call me, don't visit me, don't talk to me."

She stared him down as his eyes filled with tears. "Ever."

It took him a moment to realize she meant forever. "No, Bridget, please," he begged. "I only did it because I –"

"Goodbye, Kip." She cut him off, making sure he couldn't say what she'd known all along, only suddenly she just didn't care.

So, Bridget walks out on Kip and never sees him again? She goes on to have a fabulous career in finance, marries someone she works with and moves to the suburbs?

I looked at Bridget looking out the window into the distance, looking for something she just couldn't seem to see. Kip's gaze was fixed on her. But she couldn't seem to bring herself to look at him.

It didn't seem right, not having them together. It didn't feel right. Perhaps that's why I stopped writing them years ago.

Deep down, I knew that Kip could never let Bridget go. He just couldn't. Their history was too rich. Their ties were too strong. And deep down, I knew she couldn't let him go either. But did she know it?

When it came right down to it, I just didn't have the heart to keep these two crazy kids apart. So as cliché as it was to keep them together, I just couldn't help myself.

As I started to type, I felt the life flow back into Kip. He moved. Just a bit and very slowly, but he moved. Bridget even managed to extinguish her cigarette.

I wrote all day, into the night, and past the dawn again. They stayed silent, patiently, waiting for the end, for all the answers. Bridget didn't really get fired. She only told Kip that to see how he would react. She had actually quit her job, finally reaching the place where she knew she wasn't meant to be there, she knew she could do better. In my heart, I could feel Kip rejoice, not because he was glad it wasn't his fault. Not because he won some silly war between them, but because in his heart, he honestly knew that this was the best thing for Bridget. In his heart, he truly believed that she was the most talented writer that ever lived and she should spend all day, everyday, writing. All he really wanted was for her to believe it, too.

Bridget stood alone on the beach with her cigarette, the smoke blowing violently away from her in the bitter wind. No one went to the beach in February in Chicago. Unless you wanted to be utterly and completely alone. And she deserved to be alone after the way she had treated Kip. Why was she always so very cruel to him? So hard on him? Of course, he shouldn't have done what he did – but in his own twisted way, he really was trying to help her. And he was right about that stupid job anyway. Which was why she had gone to his apartment in the first place. To tell him that. To tell him he was right.

Glancing over at Kip whose eyes were wide with panic, still unsure of where I was going with this, I said. "Are you ok?"

He nodded ever so slightly, barely moving, never taking his eyes off Bridget, and looking more than a little apprehensive. He didn't entirely trust me with his ending. Why should he? He spent the last twenty years in a box.

I gave him a wink to reassure him and went back to work. He didn't buy it. He still looked terrified, like he was about to lose his best friend.

Bridget shivered by the window.

"I knew you'd be here." She heard his voice in the wind and was sure she imagined it. "Bridget," he called again and this time she turned around, her hair tangling wildly around her, and there he was, his hands jammed into the pockets of his thrift store pea coat. Leave it to Kip to come to what was likely the coldest and windiest place in the universe without any gloves.

Kip clenched his hands into fists.

"How did you know?" she asked him loudly enough that he could hear her voice over the crashing waves and stormy wind and know that she was still mad, but softly enough that he knew she was sorry.

"I dunno. I just knew," he said with a shrug and a head tilt.

"Why do you know so damn much about me?"

Kip shrugged just a little. He might have shrugged more, but his shoulders felt like they were frozen to his ears.

"Why?" she demanded.

"Why what?"

"Why do you know so much about me... more than I know about myself? You know what I'm going to do before I even decide to do it. Why do you let me belittle you and your life and yet you allow me to get angry when you do the same thing to me? Why? And why, for the love of god, why do you put up with me, Kip?" she babbled tearfully, finally dropping that tough exterior she held up in front of her face all the time. Finally willing to show Kip some sort of emotion other than irritability.

He stepped closer to her. Just for warmth, she told herself.

"I think you know the answer to that." He answered quietly, pretty sure that his heart had stopped.

Bridget smiled. Not a huge, laughy smile. A closed-mouth, relaxed smile. Almost a Mona Lisa smile, but a little less uptight. She was prettier when she smiled.

He loved her. She'd always known that.

"I didn't get fired," she told him.

"You didn't?" Relief washed over him like the waves of Lake Michigan.

"I quit," she said.

"You didn't have to do that for me."

"Well, I didn't do it for you. I did it for me."

They stood toe to toe, neither one willing to make that first move. The move that would change everything and nothing about their relationship.

"I'm sorry," she said, not loudly enough into the howling wind.

"What?"

"I'm sorry. About before. About everything I said. It's not true, Kip. None of it's true."

"I know that. Besides, I deserved it."

"No you didn't. Maybe a little...but your intentions were good. Your methods...But you were right about me, about everything."

"I know that, too." He smirked.

"You know so much about me that it scares me sometimes."

"And then you push me away. It's what you do."

Bridget nodded, ashamed.

"The thing is Bridget...And I've never told you this before because I knew it would scare you. But you must already know. Bridget, I love you. I've always loved you. I can't remember a time when I didn't love you." When she didn't respond, he lifted her chin. "Did you hear what I said?"

She looked into his eyes and nodded, finally, finally letting his love flow over her though she didn't know if she wanted to laugh or cry. "I did. I'm just gathering up the courage to say it back."

He shook his head at her. "How about this for courage?" He leaned in slowly, giving her a chance to back away, then softly put his lips to hers. He pulled away after a moment, trying to gage her reaction and she responded by wrapping her arms around his neck, eagerly kissing him back.

The kiss seemed to free them both from a spell. Bridget turned away from the window, "Kip?" she said, her face stained with her tears.

Kip got up off the bed to meet Bridget at the window. "Bridget," he whispered.

She took his hands, "Your hands are freezing." She held them tight in her hands, warming them up.

I kept typing.

"I love you," she whispered directly into his ear so he'd be sure to hear her.

"I know," he whispered back.

"You think you know everything about me, don't you?"

"I think," he mulled his answer. "I think we should go home before I lose my hands to frostbite."

"Good idea, we might need those hands for something." She giggled.

They kissed passionately in front of my window, then slipped into an embrace so tight I thought they'd never let go. An embrace filled with years of unrequited emotion. Years of refusing to admit to each other what they both already knew themselves. An embrace filled with the hope of a future they never really expected to have. Bridget buried herself in Kip's chest. "Thank you," he mouthed to me over her head.

I smiled back, feeling pretty pleased with myself for giving Bridget everything she never knew she wanted.

I gave them a little wave and they vanished.

So, Kip and Bridget were finished and out of my life forever. They had been living in my brain since college and now they were gone. I'm not going to it was bittersweet for me. I lost a part of myself in sending them away.

But I gained something, too. I gained self-satisfaction. I gained self-respect. And I re-gained some of the dignity I lost during so many hours in the cafeteria. I felt like I could finally say I was a writer. With two actual finished books under my belt, it seemed less weird to say that now than before. The only thing missing now was sharing it with Alex.

To: Alex
From: Mirabelle
Re: Bridget & Kip
Attachments: Bridgetandkip.doc
Alex,
One down, three more to go. Let me know what you think.
I miss you. I love you. Thank you for doing this for me.
Bella

My fingers stopped short of hitting send. Don't ask me why, but for some reason I had never really let Alex read anything I wrote. We'd talk about whatever I was working on, but I never could bring myself to actually give him pages to read. I'm sure it has something to do with some deep-seated insecurities. I knew I couldn't take it if Alex didn't like something I wrote. Plus, as rational as he was, sometimes he had trouble with his suspension of disbelief.

But, how could I ever succeed if I couldn't let the person I trusted most in the world read my writing? Alex used to ask me all the time if he could read things, but I never felt ready and eventually he just stopped asking. So, it was a big deal for me to share my work with him. But, really, it was the least I could do after kicking him out of the house.

Gathering my courage and forcing it into my index finger, I hit send. His response came almost immediately.

To: Mirabelle
From: Alex
Re: Re: Bridget & Kip
Belly,

That was fast! This will fill my long, lonely nights ;-) I'm looking forward to reading it…and I'll be sure to tell you exactly what I think of it…

I'm glad you're making progress. Get back to work.

Alex

I was relieved that he seemed to be in good spirits. I emailed him right back, missing him, craving his attention.

To: Alex
From: Mirabelle
Re: Re: Re: Bridget & Kip
Darling,
Please be kind…remember, I'm over-sensitive.
Bella

To: Mirabelle
From: Alex
Re: Re: Re: Re: Bridget & Kip

I'll try. But I'm still kinda pissed that you kicked me out of the house. ;)

Now, stop messing around with your emails and go write something, so I can come home

and we can discuss your books over dinner and a proper glass of wine.

A

I fell asleep smiling, starting to feel, beginning to believe that things really were going to be ok.

CHAPTER 23

WHEN I WOKE, IT WAS morning, though I couldn't tell you what day it was. I might have been sleeping for days, for all I knew. I woke with a start, starving and anxious to get back to work, anxious to bring Alex home.

After a breakfast of peanut butter on toast (Clearly, food shopping was not my highest priority.) I curled up on the couch with my laptop, ready to work. But who this time? Whose story would I end next? I opened Cody's file again and tried typing something, anything, hoping the words would just come to me like they sometimes did. But no words magically appeared. I dug around in some of the boxes, all of which had been removed from the top shelf of the closet and now lay open in various locations throughout the house. Nothing in them inspired me.

I wished Cody would show up and help me. He hadn't come to me since the doctor's office and honestly, I missed him. Probably more than I should have. I sucked down another Coca-Cola waiting for inspiration to strike, wondering what would happen if Alex could actually see Cody. Would they argue? Would they be buddies? Two people so completely different, from two completely different realities. Then I had an idea. And the words did magically appear.

Monica and Peter were making dinner in the kitchen. They laughed and drank wine and bumped into each other accidentally on purpose. Neither one could ever remember feeling as happy or as comfortable as they did right at that moment. They were so at ease, in fact, neither one heard the key in the front door.

I could hear things clanging around in my kitchen. The sounds of cooking, the smell of bubbling butter. I could hear the sound of a whisk on the bottom of a pan. I didn't need to get up to see who was making all the racket.

Peter sautéed the mushrooms while Monica stirred the sauce constantly. No one heard the duffel bag drop in the front hall. The music was too loud for them to hear the footsteps approaching the kitchen. Their laughter drowned out the noise of someone walking through the apartment calling, "Hello?"

When he finally appeared in the doorway, Monica jumped, practically into Peter's arms. Peter wasn't startled, like Monica. He placed his spatula down gently on the counter in silent resignation as if he knew all along this moment would come. He just hoped it wouldn't. Or it wouldn't be so soon.

"Hey, buddy," the figure in the doorway said. "You made me dinner! You shouldn't have." He joked.

Peter said nothing.

"Peter," Monica whispered, clutching Peter's arm. "Who is this?"

Peter rubbed his thumb against the tip of his index finger, back and forth and back and forth, wearing away his skin.

"Peter?" the other guy said. "He's not Peter."

Monica looked at this man: tall, rugged, athletic. He was tan and strong-looking. He looked windswept, like he'd just climbed a mountain. And before he said another word, she knew.

"I am," said the guy in the doorway. "Tell her, buddy. Tell her I live here."

But Peter said nothing. He peeled Monica's fingers off his sleeve and very calmly walked out. Bumping into 'Real Peter' on the way out. Not on purpose, he just wasn't coordinated enough to avoid him.

"Peter?" she called after him, but he didn't stop, as if he didn't hear his name. Or because that wasn't his name at all.

Fake Peter walked right past me in the living room and right out the front door. I heard the stove click off and the sound of a chair sliding on the floor. I didn't look but I knew Monica was sitting at my kitchen table with her head in her hands.

She spent days looking for him. But he wasn't in the apartment anymore. He didn't go to work. He didn't answer his phone. He vanished off the face of the earth. Real Peter explained to her that he had been traveling around the world for the better part of a year. He'd met Fake Peter, whose real name escaped him, through a friend. Real Peter was looking for someone to watch his apartment and Fake Peter needed a home.

Real Peter was a mountain climber, an adventurer, a world traveler. He'd been everywhere and done everything. He was everything Monica had been looking for when she met Fake Peter. And he was a pompous twit. She hated him. He was a boring drag. Everything was "When I was in Tibet I met a monk who could do the moonwalk...or I met this guy in Tahiti who had bongos and we stayed up all night jamming..." He was annoying as hell. A pretentious douche. Everything he said was an anecdote, and none of it seemed real. She only visited him hoping to find Fake Peter. Her Peter.

She missed him. She missed his warmth and sense of humor. She missed the way he viewed the world at a funny angle. She missed his tics and his overwhelming fear of sticky things.

She realized that it wasn't where Fake Peter had been (or not been) that made her fall in love with him. It was just him. He was funny and strange and he made her laugh. He made her see things that were never there before. He could garden like a magician. His landscapes took her places she couldn't travel to. She wanted to spend the rest of her life with him.

But she couldn't find him anywhere to tell him so.

Until finally one day, about three weeks after she'd last seen him, he reappeared. She was in the elevator, making the dreaded trip to Real Peter's apartment to see if he'd heard from him. When the elevator doors opened, there he was.

"You're here!" she nearly shouted, so excited to see him.

I heard the kitchen table shift as if someone pushed their chair away from the table to stand, followed by the roll of wheels like on a suitcase bumping over the threshold of the kitchen.

"I...I...was just getting my stuff back from...Peter," he stammered and stuttered as if it hurt to say his name. "Aren't you getting out?"

"No," she scoffed. "I was only up here looking for you."

"You found me." He said emotionlessly as he stepped into the elevator, pulling a suitcase behind him.

"I know, I found you," she giggled. "I've been looking everywhere for you."

"Why? Do you want to tell me how much you hate me now that you know who I really am?"

"No…I needed to tell you…You see the thing is…I love you. I don't care that you lied, I don't care that you're not some world traveler, I don't care. I just love you."

"But you want me to take you on some grand adventure…and I can't give you that."

"Peter…" she said and he cringed.

"My name's not Peter. It's Max."

"Max." She smiled. "I like that much better than Peter."

He rolled his eyes.

"Max," she said as she pushed the button to stop the elevator between floors. "I know I had this crazy idea in my head of what I thought I wanted. I thought I needed someone adventurous because I wanted an escape from my boring life. But since I met you, my life isn't boring anymore. I have never, ever been bored with you, not for one second ever."

Max just watched the numbers in the elevator not ticking down because the elevator wasn't moving, until she grabbed his shoulders and turned him to face her.

I wanted to get up and take a look at what was going on in my kitchen, to see their faces as they professed their love for each other, but I wasn't sure it was any of my business. It felt like a little too much of an intrusion.

"Don't you see?" she insisted. "You are *my adventure. You* are *what I've been searching for all along."*

Max shook his head. "You barely know me. You only know what I've been pretending to be."

"I don't know what you're really like. And I don't know where you've been..."

"Nowhere. I haven't been anywhere. I don't even like to travel," he insisted sullenly.

She smiled. She couldn't help it. He was so damn cute when he was obstinate. "I know your heart, Max. I know how kind and bright you are. I know that you made flowers grow where nothing ever grew before. I know you're a little shy. I know that you can't help but make some sort of little sculpture out of a paper clip if there's one sitting on the table in front of you."

"It's a nervous habit," he whined and started rubbing his index finger on his thumb.

"I know that. And I love it because I love you."

He shook his head again, closing his eyes, unable to look at her. Physically unable to believe that what she was saying was true.

"Max?" She took his face in her hands and tried to force him to look at her. He opened his eyes but still looked away. "Max?" He was getting used to her saying his name. His real name. "I think deep down inside, I knew all along that you'd never climbed Machu Picchu."

He scratched his head and finally looked into her eyes. "And you fell in love with me anyway?"

"I did."

"Well, I love you, too," he said as awkwardly as she expected. "...but I guess you already knew that."

"I did...but it's really nice to hear."

"I shouldn't have...I shouldn't have lied to you," he stammered.

"No, you shouldn't have. I'll forgive you if you promise never to do it again."

"I promise," he said and then suddenly, remembering where he was, "Hey, can we go? I hate elevators."

"Sure." She smiled at him, released the elevator and then held his hands in hers to keep him from fidgeting.

"Monica?"

"Max?"

"Are you going to kick me out for illegally subletting an apartment in the building you own?"

"No... but I may kick out Real Peter for illegally subletting an apartment in the building I own."

"Oh. OK." Max said, his brow furrowed like it always did when he wasn't sure if she was kidding. "Are there any apartments available in that building you own?" he asked matter-of-factly.

"You know, I think there might be one opening up soon."

These two were so wrapped up in each other, they didn't even look at me before walking out the front door, pulling his rolling suitcase behind them. Sitting up on the couch, I stretched my back, shrugging my shoulders, ticking off another box on my to-do list. I couldn't say I was thrilled with the end of Max & Monica. Another happy ending, another cliché. All these happy endings were making me sick to my stomach. And making me miss my husband. I wanted my own happy ending.

With a sigh and a heavy heart, I emailed Alex.

To: Alex
From: Bella
Re: Next

It's not my best, but it's finished. Does every one have to be brilliant?

Love, Me

To: Bella
From: Alex
Re: re: Next

I'm sure it's brilliant. You're just getting so used to being a writer, you're getting jaded.

Who's left?

A

To: Alex
From: Bella
Re: re: re: Next

Just *The Woodpecker* and the dreaded Cody.

To: Bella
From: Alex
Re: re: re: re: Next

Pick one and hurry. You are so close ;)

To: Alex
From: Bella
Re: re: re: re: re: Next

So close, yet so far…

To: Bella

From: Alex

Re: Hurry

Would you please, stop emailing me and write. I want to come home.

Love, A

Ugh. He was absolutely killing me with kindness. No wonder I couldn't write anything but happy endings.

CHAPTER 24

IT HAD BEEN ALMOST THREE weeks without Alex, when I started to put the pieces of Daniel and Emily's puzzle in place. At least I think it had been about three weeks. Honestly, I wasn't exactly sure how long it had been. For the first time in my life, my days lacked all structure. No mealtimes, bedtimes, worktimes. Just me and my stories. I waffled between feeling monstrously productive and completely lost. After Alex left, I expected that I'd see my little friends all the time. I figured I'd never be really alone; that they'd be waiting for me in every corner, wanting to help me, to fix me. But for some inexplicable reason, now that I was more alone than ever, they wouldn't show. Leaving me abandoned, and frustrated, and afraid. Reminding me that I had no control over anything.

I didn't write much after finishing Monica and Peter, or Max or whatever the hell his name was. I took some time for me to breathe, to rejoice in my current successes, to give myself a little pat on the back, but mostly to miss my husband. I embraced the loneliness of being away from Alex and held it in a quiet, little place in my heart, knowing that loneliness was going to help me with Daniel and Emily.

I had left them on opposite sides of the Atlantic Ocean, Daniel and Emily. Both angry with each other and with themselves, both sad and lonely and unable to function in their current existence. I didn't even bother with the box this time. There were no answers in that damn box that I had put on the shelf a few months ago. All the answers were in me; I just had to pull them out. I knew Emily would have to chase after Daniel. She was his mother. She had to go to him. But I couldn't think of anything that would break the spell that Thomas had over her. How could she leave him? Why would she leave him? How far would he have to push her?

I took my spot on the couch by the front window and tortured Daniel and Emily with their conflicted emotions for just a little bit longer before the answer finally came to me. Daniel showed up and slumped angrily in the white chair, ear buds jammed firmly into his ears, his face looking like he'd rather be anywhere but here, and Emily appeared curled up in a ball at my feet on the other end of the couch. Neither seemed to be able to see the other, like they weren't actually in the same room.

He shook his head, "I'm sorry. For all the awful things I said to you that night, I shouldn't have hurt you like that." His voice began to crack, as he choked on his tears. "I was wrong to do that to you."

In my living room, Daniel pulled out his ear buds and began to weep openly, loudly. Waking from her stupor, Emily got up quickly and went to her son. She knelt down at his feet and took his hands until he collapsed on his knees and into her shoulder. Emily stroked his hair with a quiet strength she had not demonstrated before, finally acting like his mother. Taking care of him, like she should have been doing all along instead of forcing him into a position where he had to take care of her.

"No, Daniel, honey, you were right." Emily insisted, putting her hand on Daniel's back. "I don't love Thomas. I was

dependent on him, I needed him and I was afraid of him. But I don't love him. God, it feels so good to say that!" she laughed and raised her voice just a touch, "I don't love him!" she shouted to the ceiling in an uncharacteristically silly voice. "And you showed me that. You showed me what it means to really love someone. Even when that means making a really tough decision."

"I'm so sorry I left you. I left you alone with him. I walked out on you – just like everyone else." He let his tears go. His guilt and frustration leaked out of him in big salty drops. "I just didn't know what to do. I hated watching him with you... the way he treated you. I just couldn't stand it..."

"Oh, Daniel, I know. It's okay." She held him tighter now as he bawled into her shoulder. "I'm the one who should be sorry. All you tried to do was help me. I never should have put you through any of that. None of this is your fault," she lifted his chin and cupped his face in her hands. "Do you hear me? This was all my doing, my choices. And I am so sorry that I chose wrong."

"Will you stay here, then?" He looked down, as if he were afraid of her answer. "With me?" he added hopefully.

She smiled. "Oh, Daniel...I would absolutely love to stay here with you." Emily wiped a tear from her son's cheek with her thumb.

They stood up together, wiped each other's tears away and held hands to face me as if their ordeal was over. But their reunion wouldn't be complete without a scene where Emily finally stands up to that jackass, Thomas. I had to give her the opportunity to tell him off. It was time for her grow a spine and tell him exactly what she thought of him. If I was going to save myself in all this, I needed to save Emily, too.

As I started to type, I wondered if Thomas would show up in my living room. I hoped he wouldn't. He was just a one dimensional, ridiculous villain. An under-written caricature of an abusive husband. My connection to him, or lack thereof, may have prevented me from finishing *The damn Woodpecker* to begin with.

"Do you want to know what I feel?" Emily asked bitterly.

"Sure, why not?" Thomas leaned forward, as if he was actually interested in what she was feeling.

"I feel happy. Happy because I'm free of you." She smiled, and resisted looking at Daniel who was positioned about twenty feet behind Thomas. "Happy because all that time you told me I wasn't worth anything...it turns out you're the one who was worthless.

"What was it like keeping a secret like that, Thomas?" she continued. "What was it like to look me in the eye everyday knowing you had the power to give me the only thing I ever wanted? And, then to keep it from me."

Thomas just looked at her, seemingly unimpressed with her stand. Emily wondered if her words had any effect on him or if he really was so callous, so cold, that being faced with his sins, he truly didn't care.

"But, I know now. I know exactly how low you are. I know that you're not capable of loving anyone, not your wife, not your children."

Thomas flinched at the word 'children' and Emily knew she had hurt him. "I suppose your beloved Daniel taught you that," he remarked snidely.

"Believe it or not, I came to that conclusion on my own. All Daniel did was remind me what it felt like to be loved. Being

married to you, I had quite forgotten," she said with a bit of an accent herself.

No Thomas appeared. All that remained in my living room was a very happy Daniel and an elated Emily. Her happiness made her almost unrecognizable.

So finally, a happily-ever-after for Daniel and Emily. I know, I know. Another happy ending. Was it real enough? I always wanted my stories to be real, or at the very least "real-ish," but sometimes things do work out the way you plan or the way you hope. Sometimes, everything does get tied up into a nice little bow; sometimes people do ride off into the sunset and enjoy the rest of their lives together. So, despite my aversions to happily-ever-afters, I found myself now wanting to give my characters that. After all, hadn't I put them all through enough?

Emily smiled and laughed. And though the sun was hidden behind the London clouds, she was warm all over. She felt the warmth of loving her son and of finally feeling worthy of his love. She felt the joy of finally standing on her own two feet, of, for once in her life, making the right choice. She felt the peace of knowing that she had been looking for more than just Daniel her whole life, she had been looking for herself and, through some miracle, she found her.

Emily gazed happily up at the dull, grey London sky like she was on a tropical island with the sun shining on her face. Her mind was filled with nothing but pure contentment, no overwhelming worries, no stifling pain, no crippling sorrow. She felt her heart swelling with joy, the joy of new friendships, a new job, a new life. A new home.

Daniel and Emily sat together on the piano bench in my living room smiling contentedly. They looked at each other and giggled as if they were sharing an inside joke that I was no longer privy to. When they looked back to me, still smiling, they disappeared.

Finishing Daniel and Emily was actually far easier than I expected it to be. Made me wonder why I didn't just finish them in the first place. Maybe I was getting good at this.

To: Alex
From: Bella
Re: Another one bites the dust…
Attachments: *The Woodpecker*
Alex, here's the second to last.
Love, me

His response came instantly again.

To: Bella
From: Alex
Re: *The Woodpecker*
Dear Mirabelle,

You're writing too fast! I haven't finished the last one yet. What does that say about me if I can't even read as fast as you're writing?

On that note, hurry up. I miss you and want to come home.

Love, your slow-reading, but extremely patient husband,
Alex

To: Alex

From: Bella

Re: *The Woodpecker*

To my darling, sweet, caring, patient, but slow-reading husband,

You'll have plenty of time to catch up on reading…I've saved my hardest for last.

I have no idea what to do for Cody. So, it may take me awhile…

Sorry…as always.

I love you.

Belly

P.S.-Perhaps your slow reading is just a direct reflection of your never-ending patience.

To: Mirabelle

From: Alex

Re: <3

Belly,

You can do this. Cody may be your hardest, but that's only because he means the most to you. You'll find the answer for him, just like you found the answers for all the others. His ending is already running around in your crazy brain along with a thousand other brilliant ideas. You just have to catch it.

If worse comes to worse, ask Cody what to do. I'm sure he'll have an idea. ;-)

I love you.

A

CHAPTER 25

I REREAD ALEX'S LAST EMAIL WITH a sigh, hating myself again for kicking him out of the house. For as much success as I was having with my writing, I couldn't help but wonder what kind of a toll all this was taking on our marriage. It couldn't be good. I could practically picture us in therapy years from now, Alex explaining how I asked him to leave so I could focus on my non-existent career or my imaginary friends, or whatever you wanted to call them. Between my self-loathing and the resentment Alex was bound to have toward me, the pieces weren't going to be easy to put back into place.

I missed him. I loved him, but this time apart had been so good for me. What did that say about me? About us? And what was going to happen when he came back? Could we just pick up where we left off, or at least where we left off before I went off the deep end?

I couldn't shake the idea that I had done damage to our marriage that I was not going to be able to undo. I spent the next few days obsessing over what I had done to Alex and how I could possibly make it up to him. Maybe actually selling one of my now completed masterpieces would help…it couldn't hurt. I tried to regain focus on my writing, but all I could think about was Alex and all the wonderful things about him that I just sent away.

"Would you get over it already?" Cody said one day as I sat on the couch in the family room with my feet propped up on the coffee table, laptop on my knees, the screen blank in front of me. "You're wasting too much time and energy on Alex."

I smiled at him, but said nothing. He sat on the couch next to me, dressed in jeans and a tight fitting green Henley. His tuxedo days were apparently gone for good.

"Despite my disparaging comments, you actually look happy to see me," he noted when I didn't respond.

"I actually am happy to see you."

He sat up straight, taken aback. "Really? And why is that?"

"Because you are the one person who might actually be able to distract me from hating myself for what I've done." I sighed.

"Come on. You did what you needed to do. You're looking out for number one."

"That's your routine. Not mine." I shook my head and put my hands on the keyboard like I was actually going to type something.

"There's a place for that routine in everyone. It's not just me."

"It just feels wrong. I mean, what's the point of succeeding at anything, if I don't have Alex?" I pushed my hair out of my eyes, but it fell right back across my forehead.

"But you're doing so well. You're accomplishing everything you wanted to accomplish."

"I'm just not sure the end justifies the means."

"But you're not at the end…yet." He smiled that handsome, crooked smile.

"That's what I'm afraid of. What am I going to do next? What happens at my end?"

"You're over thinking…as usual." He shook his head and suppressed a yawn. Clearly, my crisis of conscience was boring him.

"No, Cody. What you don't understand is that there are consequences for this kind of thing. People do get hurt."

"Eh, who needs people?" He said with a shrug.

"I do," I insisted. "And you do, too, even though you refuse to admit it."

"Do I? Or have you given me no reason to need anyone… ever?"

I walked right into that one. "Crap, I hate when all your character flaws are my fault."

"Aren't they?" He raised one cocky eyebrow at me.

"Of course they are, but I still hate it."

Cody looked at me sideways, sat back and raised his arms over his head, clasping his hands in a stretch.

"I know, I know, I need to fix you."

"'fraid so, babe. Maybe give me some of them people skills you keep talking about."

"But why? You said yourself, you don't want them. That's what's so hard about fixing you."

"You need to give me a reason. Give me a reason to want them. Show me why it would be good for me to have something, someone to live for."

I furrowed my brows, staring at my blank screen.

"Go on." He gestured at my hands sitting on the keys just waiting for the words from my brain. "Do it for me," he said with a wink.

I stared at my screen and closed my eyes for a moment, as if the answers were printed on the insides of my eyelids. And in a way, they were. I had a sudden vision of Cody, back in his tuxedo, and smiling. Not that creepy, arrogant smile, but a soft, gentle, genuine smile.

Suddenly, my phone rang and with that, he was gone – from my eyelids and my family room.

My caller ID said it was Vivi. I'd barely heard from her since Christmas. I figured she needed money.

"Mom? Are you ok?" she demanded, sounding panicked.

"Vivi, hi!" I tried to sound excited, but something in her voice told me this wasn't a social call.

"What's going on?" Crap, I definitely should have called the children to explain why Mom and Dad weren't living together anymore.

"What do you mean?" Deny, deny, deny.

"Holden called Dad to ask for money for something and…"

"And…"

"Daddy said you guys were separated." Vivi started to cry.

Then, I started to cry, quietly so not to alert Vivi. "Separated? He said that?"

"That's what Holden said!" OK, it was third party information. He must've misunderstood.

"Viv, calm down."

"Well, are you…sss-separated?" She bawled.

"I don't think separated is the right word. Are you sure your father said separated?"

"Yes, Mom! Dad said you were separated! Are you getting divorced?"

Divorced? What the hell just happened? This was awfully melodramatic for the normally calm, cool and collected, Vivian. "Vivi, no. Listen to me; I should've called you guys to talk about this, but it is true that your father and I are not currently living together."

"Separated."

"We are currently living separately, yes." I answered her, feeling like I was under cross-examination. "But we're not separated, separated." Were we?

"We're gone for a few months and you guys can't hold your marriage together?"

"No, Vivian. It's not like that…" Right?

"What happened? Why did Daddy leave you?" She persisted through tears.

"Vivi, he didn't leave me. I asked him to go…temporarily." Ouch. My heart ached when I said it out loud. It made me wonder how people who actually got divorced managed to tell their children.

"Temporarily? Then, when's he coming back?"

"Soon."

"Why? Why, Mom? Why did you ask him to leave?"

How was I to explain this one? How do you tell your barely adult daughter that you asked her father to leave you so you could spend some time writing and talking to yourself? "It's complicated, Vivian. I can't really get into it now, but…"

"Mom…"

"But," I continued, "I promise you, it has nothing to do with how I feel about your father or how he feels about me. He will be back home before you're back for Spring Break." Did I just give myself a deadline?

"Oh, uh, that's why Holden needed money from Dad… we wanted to go to a friend's place in L.A. for Spring Break."

"Of course you do." I shook my head. It figured.

"But, that was before we heard about you and Daddy," she covered quickly.

"Don't worry about me and Daddy. We're fine." I think.

"So we can go to L.A.?" Ah, the resiliency of teenagers. She certainly recovered quickly from her parents impending divorce.

"Can we talk about this later, Vivi?"

"Sure, Mom…and Mom?"

"What is it, honey?" I asked, losing patience with her and wanting to get off the phone before I completely lost it.

"If you need to talk to someone…I'm here for you. I mean, I don't know much, but people tell me I'm a pretty good listener."

"Thanks," I replied, choking back tears, overwhelmed with a wave of pride for my daughter who suddenly seemed less like a teenager and more like an adult. "Bye, Vivian. I love you."

"I love you, too, Mommy."

Sigh. She called me Mommy.

My pride for Vivian faded quickly when I remembered why she called in the first place. Why would Alex tell the kids we were separated? Why would he use that word? *Separated.* It had such negative connotations. Like two halves of a whole were broken apart. It sounded like the last stop on the train before divorce. I'd just heard from him yesterday, didn't I? And wasn't he warm and supportive? He was. But despite his encouragement, he must be losing patience with me. I was losing him.

To: Alex

From: Bella

Re: Kids

Alex,

Vivi called. She said Holden said you said we were separated.

☹

To: Bella
From: Alex
Re: re: Kids
I did.

To: Alex
From: Bella
Re: re: re: Kids
That's the word you're using? *Separated*?

To: Bella
From: Alex
Re: re: re: re: Kids
Don't overreact. It's just a word. Besides, aren't we?
Alex

I hate when he tells me not to overreact.

To: Alex
From: Bella
Re: re: re: re: re: Kids
But I thought we were ok…I hate that word. It sounds so permanent.

To: Bella
From: Alex
Re: re: re: re: re: re: Kids
Bella, we are ok. But I'm not happy about all of this. You know that. And I'm not going to pretend that I am. If you don't like the way I told them, you should have told them yourself.

I'm trying here, Bella. You know I'm trying. But I'm tired and I miss my home. I miss my wife and I miss our life together. I'm sorry if I didn't choose the perfect word

to describe our current "situation." You're the writer. What would you call it?

I wasn't sure if that last question was rhetorical or not. But I figured I'd better answer it anyway.

To: Alex

From: Bella

Re: re: re: re: re: re: re: Kids

What would I call it? I don't know. Not currently living together? That's what I told Vivi. *Separated* sounds like we don't love each other anymore. And I love you with all my heart.

CHAPTER 26

HE DIDN'T RESPOND. I WAITED for what seemed like an eternity but he didn't respond. Alex was running out of patience and I was running out of time. I had to finish and quickly.

Cody.

I exhaled deeply, knowing there was no easy fix for Cody. Knowing that I still had enormous amounts of work to do to make him whole. Knowing he needed people. People to bounce off of, to learn from, to love and to hate. But everyone I thought of to add to Cody's life just seemed too cliché: long-lost father, child, sister, mother, girlfriend – all too obvious. I couldn't force him into a relationship with some long-estranged family member. That was just too easy.

Cody needed something more, something different, something special. Something no one had ever thought of before. Something he'd never expect. Alex was right when he said that Cody was the hardest because he meant the most to me. He did mean the most to me, but he was only so close to my heart because I was so very afraid of him. Not afraid of him, really, but he was everything I was afraid of becoming: lost and lonely. And then hostile and mean and angry. I was well on my way to the lost and lonely part; the hostile part couldn't be that far behind, could it?

For all my successes over the past few weeks, only my failures sat with me now. My inability to finish Cody and the damage I'd surely done to my marriage weighed on me. Heavily.

Crawling into bed and under the covers, my laptop taking Alex's place on the other side, I waited for Cody to come back and help me, give me some brilliant idea, give me something more to go on. But he didn't show. Finally, I dozed off, but not really into sleep. Just one of those sleeps where you're on the edge of sleep and though you're dreaming, you're totally aware that you're sleeping.

My dreams were filled with characters…everyone but Cody. Daniel, Emily, David, Goliath all there. But they were all silent. Even some characters I had written that never fleshed themselves out into real people appeared. Silhouettes of ideas half-formed in my crazy brain.

Every time I came close to falling into a real deep sleep, I woke with a start before dozing off again. Finally, knowing real sleep was eluding me tonight, I opened my laptop and tried to plug some of those half-formed characters into Cody's life. But none of them fit. Honestly, the only person I'd ever been able to make Cody have a meaningful dialogue with was me.

And it hit me like a brick. Dammit, just as he'd been telling me all along, I realized, *I* was Cody's answer. It wasn't the dark parts of us that made us the same. It was our fears. It was my fear that created Cody. Fear of losing someone, something important to me. Cody and I felt the same, it was the way we reacted to our fears that made us different.

My biggest fear, always, was that I had such a charmed life, and somewhere along the way, I would have to pay for it with some sort of tragedy. Having never actually experienced great loss, sometimes, I felt the sky was falling and it was going to land squarely on me or on someone I loved. Having escaped being touched by tragedy my whole life, some sort of karmic payback felt inevitable.

Sometimes, when something even a little bit bad happened, I almost felt relieved. Like I was paying some small portion of a very large credit card bill. It was like the minimum balance on my life. When his teachers told us Holden had dyslexia, I felt like ok, this is bad, but not so bad that I can't handle it. I can deal with this…just please don't take my children from me.

Now that I think about it: Having never had to experience real loss, real pain, maybe, just maybe, I overreacted a bit to my kids going to college. Creating a loss where there wasn't one.

Part of me was so very much like Cody in my fears of losing and loss. He was a monster I created out of my own fears and insecurities. And I had needed to save him to save myself.

By the glow of my laptop, I began to sketch Cody out on paper, brainstorming phrases describing Cody's loneliness, some of which was really mine. I scrawled broken sentences about how he longed to have a friend he could connect with, but he'd lost so much, he just didn't know how to let anyone else in long enough. So he sat behind his walls, alone and sometimes mean and often selfish. But only because he really didn't know any better.

I went back to my original manuscript and tried to give Cody a loss and a pain that would at least excuse his behavior, if not make you feel just a little bit sorry for him (even though he definitely did not want your pity). I took his parents from him at a young age to give him a reason for being such a cold-hearted jerk. I made him grow up alone. And whenever he made a friend, I took him or her away until he no longer let anyone in, or drove them away before they could get too close. Until finally he was the completed angry man that had come to visit me so often these past few months. A man who was capable of just about any kind of deceit. A man who couldn't, or wouldn't, help a soul if there wasn't something in it for him.

How could I give a guy like that redemption? Who could possibly come into his life and change it? Change him? But, Cody *had* changed since that first day I'd met him in the gas station. He was softer and kinder and dare I say it, a little less selfish. He was drinking less, if at all, and was definitely less arrogant. Come to think of it, the last few times I'd see him he'd been a lot more concerned with me than himself.

I was so on the verge of a revelation and getting all the pieces of Cody in all the right places, when I heard a noise downstairs. Annoyed by the interruption, but expecting it would be Cody, I bounced out of bed, pointed my feet into my slippers, threw on a sweater over my pj's which consisted of Alex's old T-shirt and my ratty sweats, and flew down the stairs.

When I got to the front door, right at the bottom of the stairs, someone or something was outside and trying to get in. The knob was twisting. Seemed odd…Cody never came to the door, he just popped in wherever the hell he pleased. Could he even open doors? I thought for a moment that maybe it was Alex, which made me happy and sad at the same time. But Alex wouldn't come to the front door. He would come through the garage like he always did. Could it be the kids? Didn't seem like they'd pop in, and they'd have no way of getting here.

After running through all the possibilities in my head, it finally occurred to me that someone might actually be breaking into the house for real, not just someone breaking into my imaginary world. A real live criminal may be trying to get into the house.

I thought about calling the police, but what if it was one of my hallucinations? What would I tell them then? Just as I had made up my mind to make the call, that I was better safe than sorry, the door suddenly popped ajar and slowly creaked open. And I, once again paralyzed with fear, just stood there.

In the darkness, I saw the shadowy figure of a man, sticking his head into my home. *He's not really there,* I told myself. He couldn't be. I stepped back silently, hiding around the corner in the kitchen.

"Come out, come out, wherever you are," a voice with an ever-so-slight British accent called through the darkness. Relief flooded over me. It wasn't some crazed psycho come to kill me. Well, it was, but it wasn't a real one. It was Thomas, Emily's now-estranged husband who was really more of a sociopath than a psychopath, which was somehow comforting. I knew I had tied her story up a little too tightly, but I also knew Thomas wouldn't give up on her so easily.

"Come on, now. I won't bite. Where are you?" I knew full well he was capable of biting, among other things. He crept around the corner, searching for me and I tiptoed away from him into the family room, all the while chanting to myself: *He's not real. He's not real. He's not real. He's not real. He's not real. He's not real. He's not real. He's not real. He's not real.* As if that would make him disappear.

"I'm going to find you, so you may as well come out now." His fancy Italian leather wingtips tapped along on my hardwood floors as he searched each room for me. Calmly. Methodically. "I just want to talk to you, darling. Don't be afraid." I got a chill as the memory of Goliath danced down my spine. Why did all my wicked characters tell me not to be afraid? And why was he calling me darling? Creepy.

"OK, love, hide if you like. I'll do all the talking." I was now cowering in the corner of the family room, behind a big chair. Pathetic, I know. I used to think I was a pretty brave person, but when faced with "real" adversity, I hid behind a chair.

"So," he called out looking around, unsure of my location. "You apparently felt it necessary to take away not only my loving wife but also my adoring children." His footsteps grew closer. "I'm wondering if you gave the ending enough thought. Perhaps you were a bit hasty in your writing. You were in such a hurry just to finish and get your husband back. I just want my children back. Surely you can understand that." When I didn't answer him, he said, "I hope you're planning a sequel, as you know full well I will never let Emily keep those children." His voice grew distant as he continued his search for me in the next room.

"She's not keeping them; she returned them to their mother." I snapped at him, revealing my location.

He wheeled around at the sound of my voice. Stupid of me to reveal myself, I know. But as I was hiding behind that chair I realized that he wasn't going to go away and by avoiding him, I was just prolonging the agony. He wasn't going to leave and no one was coming to save me. I had to confront him.

"The point is," he said succinctly, "I want my children back and you're going to give them to me."

The nerve of this jackass. I hated him and immediately began calculating his demise in my head.

"No, I won't, Thomas." I stood up to face him.

"Oh, there you are, my dear," he said, looking me over. "What are you doing back there? You're not hiding from little old me, are you? You silly girl. Now, come on out of there and get your computer so you can get me my children back." He reached out his hand to help me out of my hiding place.

I ignored his hand and climbed out from behind the chair myself. "I'm not giving you your children back."

"Now, you of all people know what those children mean to me. You wrote that into me." Did I?

"I know that any affection you have for them is conditional. I know you only want them back because Emily took them. I know she did to you exactly what was done to her, and I know you deserved it."

Thomas stared at me, his mouth agape, and for a brief moment I thought I had won. But before I knew it, Thomas lunged for me and grabbed my wrist. Damn he was fast.

"Let go," I demanded, as I tried to squirm away.

"I'll let go when you agree to give my children back to me."

"No. The book is finished! I can't change it now."

"I think you can," he jerked me close and whispered creepily in my ear. "I want them back because they are mine." He pulled a gun out of his jacket. "And you're going to give them to me."

Crap. Where the hell did he get that? I never gave him a gun. Maybe an imaginary gun wouldn't hurt me. I remembered the cold steel of Goliath's blade and thought, *then again, maybe it would.* I couldn't take that chance. Alex would never forgive me or himself for that matter. "OK, Thomas. Calm down," I told him, trying to buy some time. "Let me get my computer and I'll see if I can fix this."

"Wonderful. I'll come with you," he chirped and smiled – not a warm smile, but a creepy *'I've got you right where I want you'* smile.

"Fantastic." I rolled my eyes at him.

So, Thomas followed me up the stairs, holding my wrist the whole way. "You know, if you break my wrist, I won't be able to type." I snapped at him as we struggled awkwardly back down the stairs.

"You'll manage." He twisted just a bit, just like he had done to Emily in Chapter 1. Jerk. I should've had Emily kill him when I had the chance. It would have done wonders for her character to have put a bullet in this guy.

I pulled Thomas along with me back to the living room couch where I'd finished Daniel and Emily last week. I sat myself down, propped my feet up on the coffee table, and got to work. Thomas, finally letting go of my wrist, placed himself right damn next to me, poking me in the ribs with his imaginary gun, which hurt an awful lot for something that didn't exist. I wondered if Daniel and Emily would return to the piano bench when I started typing. I hoped they wouldn't. I didn't think I would be able to stand the look of devastation on Emily's face or the look of disappointment on Daniel's.

"Get going," Thomas barked with an extra poke at my ribs.

"Give me a minute," I growled at him. "I have to figure out how I'm going to do it first."

"I'm not a patient man, darling."

"I'm aware of that. But you're going to have to wait until I come up with an idea that doesn't involve anybody getting hurt."

"I don't care if anyone gets hurt. Just type, 'Emily happily gave the children back to Thomas. The End.'" He smirked.

"Well, I do care if someone gets hurt. You're going to have to wait."

Bastard. I had to kill him. If I did it quickly enough, I might be able to off him before he realized what I was doing. But with him looking over my shoulder, I was pretty sure I couldn't type fast enough to beat the bullet from his gun at point-blank range in my side. I was trying to think of a sentence that started with him getting kids and ended with him dying. How fast could I type, "and he dropped dead," and would that even work? It didn't when I tried to kill Cody. Then again, I didn't want Cody dead nearly as much as I wanted Thomas dead.

"You know, if you kill me, you'll never get the kids back." I said, still stalling.

"I'm not going to kill you," he scoffed. "I'm well aware that if you die, I go with you, my dear."

"Good. Then you can put the gun away." I shifted ever so slightly away from him.

"Silly girl. You misunderstood me. If you don't do what I tell you, I won't kill you. But I will shoot you. Just to hurt you. Do you know how much it hurts to get shot?" He put his arm around my shoulders and pulled me back to him.

I felt my chest tighten. Did I really make this bastard that twisted? I thought Cody was nasty. This guy made Cody look like Mary Poppins.

"I'll just shoot you in the leg," he squeezed my thigh, "or maybe the hand," he said, stroking the back of my hand, when I didn't answer his question. "And don't think for a moment that I won't."

"You're really not making it easy for me to give the children back to you, you know."

"Just remember, they're my children. Not yours." He dug his fingers into my arm and poked me harder in the ribs with the gun.

"Ow. Knock it off. I'm trying to work here."

I couldn't give him the kids. Lord knows what kind of miserable existence they'd have with this jerk as their father, especially without Emily as his punching bag. But maybe I could give him the kids now and then kill him in some sort of accident after he and his imaginary gun were gone. Or Emily could kill him and end her career as a perpetual victim. It was long overdo for Emily to assert herself over this jackass. Not a bad idea.

My plan in place, I started to type. Emily had had a change of heart, feeling that even wretched Thomas deserved a shot at redemption.

"Who was that?" Daniel asked as Emily hung up the phone. By the way she jumped at the sound of his voice, he knew she was hiding something.

"Uh, Daniel...I didn't know you were home," she stammered.

"It was Thomas, wasn't it?" he accused.

"Thomas? What makes you say that?" she asked, without looking at him, putting a kettle on for tea.

He stood in front of her and forced her to look at him. "Because your voice is different when you talk to him."

"That's ridiculous." Emily tried to turn away from him, but he took her hand and pulled her back around, softly, so that she wouldn't look away.

"Is it?" He glared at her with his damn piercing eyes that were so like his father's. She couldn't lie to him.

"Alright, fine. It was Thomas," she relented.

"I knew he wouldn't leave us alone." He ran his hand through his already-tousled hair.

"He wants to see the children." She looked away from him again. She couldn't stand to look at him when they were talking about Thomas.

"Of course he does. Wait...you're not going to let him, are you?" he asked incredulously.

"He misses them," Emily whined in that defeated voice she had whenever she needed to justify something.

"Too bad." Daniel shrugged. "He should've thought of that before."

"It's not right keeping him from them, Daniel," she pleaded. "We're doing to him what he did to us."

"Yeah, except for the little fact that you're not a sociopath."

"He's not a sociopath...he's just an asshole," Emily laughed just a little, like she always did when she was nervous.

"Vanessa will never agree to this." He shook his head.

"I'll talk to her. It's just a visit..."

"Not just a visit!" Thomas growled over my shoulder and squeezed my arm hard.

"OW!" I yelled. "Give me a minute! I have to start somewhere." I barked. "It won't work if I don't put it in context." I shook my head in exasperation. "Now, stop interrupting me so I can think."

"No good can come of this, Mum."

"I know that, Daniel. I do," Emily said sadly.

"Then why are you doing it?"

Emily didn't have an answer for this. She had no logical reason. She didn't know why Thomas still had such a strong hold over her. She couldn't explain it. She knew this was a bad idea, but Thomas had been hounding her – and she was, quite simply, crumbling under the constant pressure from him.

And they were keeping him apart from his children, just like she and Daniel had been kept apart all those years. That didn't seem right.

There was good in Thomas, wasn't there? Somewhere?

Thomas chuckled next to me, but I didn't pay any attention to him. I was too busy looking at Vanessa's underdeveloped shadow now lurking in the corner of my living room, head in her hands, shoulders hunched forward, like she was carrying some unbearable sadness on her back. I knew instantly that I was responsible. I wanted to hold her, to tell her to be patient, to tell her I have a plan. I wanted to tell her I would never send Harry and Sophie back to their father. That I was going to end this once and for all, the way I should've ended it in the first place.

My computer cast the only light in the room on my face as I kept typing and hating myself for it. Thomas was beginning to smirk victoriously when, in the glare of my computer, I saw a shadow move behind us. Now what? I paused for a moment.

"Keep going," Thomas whispered, not noticing anyone else in the room. His voice made me shudder. I should've just taken the damn pills. Then I could be safe with Alex and not pursuing this stupid ridiculous dream of mine. I was selfish and stupid to give up my husband for a fantasy. What was I thinking, listening to Kip and Cody and all the other stupid characters that screwed up my life after they were done screwing up their own?

Suddenly, from behind us came the sound of glass exploding. Thomas and I both turned quickly to look but there was no one there. I could see the broken fragments of something reflecting the moonlight like diamonds all over the floor. I frantically thought back to every character I'd ever written, trying to decide if the figure moving in the shadows was friend or foe. Was there anybody else out there, no matter how trivial, who would have a problem with how I ended, or didn't end, things for them?

Thomas grabbed my arm and jerked me to my feet. "Get up. Let's go."

"Who's there?" he called into the darkness still poking that gun in my side. "Daniel, is that you? You little bastard. Don't make me do something you'll regret. You know I will." But there was no answer from Daniel or anyone else.

Thomas dragged me away from the light of my laptop and we stepped into the darkness together, feeling the crunch of broken glass under our feet, my slippers and his loafers. He eased his grip on me ever so slightly, clearly unnerved by the stranger in the darkness, when from somewhere, I have no idea where, a body came flying between us, taking Thomas to the ground and pounding on him.

I stood stunned and confused for a moment as the two figures wrestled on the ground. "Finish him!" came a voice from the person who wasn't Thomas. It took me just a millisecond to realize it was Cody, and I knew what he wanted me to do. He straddled Thomas and was punching him furiously, taking out a lifetime of his own pain on him. Thomas managed to free himself and flip Cody off to the side, clocking him in the head with the butt of his gun. Cody shook his head, dazed, but still conscious.

My fingers shaking, I rushed back to my computer to kill off Thomas once and for all, while trying to ignore the battle going on on my living room floor. Vanessa was still sobbing in the corner, but her shadow started to become clear, her edges defined. She became a person right before my eyes, her long blonde hair cascading over her shoulders as she raised her hands, clasped together out in front of her as if she had a gun and was aiming for Thomas who, for now, seemed to be getting the upper-hand on Cody.

Vanessa was done with Thomas. Done with being hurt. Done with him hurting her children. Hurting Emily. Hurting Daniel. Hurting everyone and anyone who got in his way.

She fired and didn't regret it for a moment.

I heard her shot echo across the room, so loud it sounded like a firing squad. Thomas fell off of Cody and vanished as I wrote of his last breath.

Thomas choked and coughed and sputtered and writhed on the floor pathetically enough that Vanessa almost ran to his side. But she didn't. She watched him slip away from across the room. She watched him die alone, the way he deserved to die. Alone.

Vanessa closed her eyes and exhaled in relief. She dropped the gun from her hands, though it disappeared before it hit the floor, and she vanished.

"That was close," I said out loud to Cody as I turned on the living room lights. My back was to him and the lights came on softly as I waited for him to make some snarky comment. But all he did was cough and make a sound I can best describe as a sputter. I wheeled around on the heel of my slipper and my heart sank. Literally, everything that was holding my heart in place let go at one time and it fell into my stomach, splashing acid back into my throat.

Cody was still on the ground, lying there dressed once again in his tuxedo, Thomas' gun still smoking in his hand, blood seeping through his white shirt. Blood that I thought was Thomas' until Cody let out a groan.

No. No. No. No. I did not write that. Vanessa shot Thomas. That's what I wrote. I didn't write anything about Thomas shooting Cody. This couldn't happen. Could it?

Shaking off my shock I ran to his side, cradling his head in my lap. "Cody?"

His eyes fluttered open. "Hey there, baby." He reached out for my face but didn't seem to have the strength to reach me. Grabbing his outstretched hand, I held it tightly.

"Don't you die on me, Cody. Not now."

"Now's as good a time as any, sweetheart," he quipped weakly.

"No, it's not. This isn't your ending." I sobbed. "I didn't write it yet."

"I think we both knew this was how I needed to end," he sputtered.

"No," I cried, real tears pouring out of my eyes in big, heavy drops. Tears for losing both my friend and my purpose. "I was going to fix you. I wanted to fix you."

"You just did, baby." He exhaled sharply, his breath catching in his throat and I held him just a little tighter. I didn't feel ready to let him go. "Consider me saved," he whispered.

"No, you saved me, I didn't save you."

"You're welcome. Whatever. I told you this wasn't about me." Cody coughed again and still managed a little smirk.

"Yeah, and I told you, you weren't such a bad guy."

"No, you didn't," he winced. "But thanks, anyway."

"This doesn't feel right."

"Don't." He coughed again and I knew it was over. "Just go get that goofy husband of yours and get your happily-ever-after. And enjoy it for chrissakes. I'd hate to have saved you for nothing." He tried to smile again, but it looked more like a grimace.

"I'll miss you, Cody."

"You'd damn well better, baby. You damn well better." He closed his eyes like he was going to sleep and took his last breath. I held him for a moment until he vanished from my arms.

I sat there on the floor of my empty living room. No dead bodies, no bloodstains. Just me, a broken glass and my tears, grieving for the friend I lost who never really existed in the first place. Pink light flooded my living room with the rising sun, catching the shattered remains of Cody's glass and casting rainbows all over my floor. I picked up a piece and held it tightly, holding on to the one little piece of him that I had left.

Taking one last look at the crystal in my hand, I grabbed my computer and started Cody back at the beginning.

He always knew he wouldn't be allowed to keep her. She was too good and everything good in his short life was taken from him. Still, he always hoped this day would never come. The day of his little sister's funeral.

He was sixteen that night. When his uncle told him that Julianne was dead, he ran. He ran from the house. He wanted to run until it didn't hurt anymore. He ran down the street where he and Juli had lived with his uncle since their parents died. He ran into town and down Main Street, cars passing him on both sides, the brake lights dizzying him on one side, the headlights blinding him on the other. He was fast. Though he was always small for his age, he was strong and quick. He ran like he would never stop until finally, his grief caught him from behind and yanked him to his knees right there on the double yellow line. He knelt on that double line crying for the pain to stop but unable to throw himself into the path of the cars passing him on either side. It hurt so badly, far more than when his parents died when he was ten, far more than the beatings he took from his uncle.

Even before his parents died, Cooper was never a happy kid, never a smiley baby. He always had a little bit of a chip on his shoulder. The only thing that ever made him happy was Julianne. These two kids had a pretty crappy life, but where Cooper responded with anger and resentment, Julianne responded with grace and caring. She evened Cooper out, settled him down, made him almost happy.

The day of Julianne's funeral, Cooper died, too. She was the only thing that ever meant anything to him. With her gone, all the rage, all the anger that he had spent his life trying to hide from her, came to the surface and made his blood boil.

He changed his name. She would never say it again, so he never wanted to hear it again. With Julianne gone, Cooper died and Cody was born. Cody had no family, no friends, no past, nothing but the desire to take from other people whatever they had that he wanted.

He was clever about it, at least. The stealing. He started sitting in on college classes. Other kids just assumed he was enrolled there. He befriended them. Learned from them. Talked their talk and walked their walk. And then stole from them. He was so good at it, that most of the time they didn't even know that they'd had anything stolen from them. Most of his victims were so rich, they didn't even miss what he'd stolen. He wouldn't steal from someone who wasn't rich. Well, he might, but it wouldn't be as much fun for him. He thoroughly enjoyed taking things from people that had more than they knew. But none of it brought back what he had truly lost.

Still, he made a pretty good living for ten years, crossing the country going from college to college. He kept his nose pretty clean, and wasn't especially violent. But he didn't shy away from a fight. A good fight always helped him release all that pent-up anger. As his late twenties approached, he knew his face was showing his age and it was time for a new con, time to up his game. He bought himself a tuxedo and moved to Vegas.

I finished Cody's story right then and there, no delays, no procrastinating. After a few years in Vegas, he met Vanessa, a single mother of a set of lively twins. He was grifting and thieving and she was a cocktail waitress at one of the clubs he frequented. They hated each other at first. She recognized the con man in him immediately. And he knew she had his number.

But Vanessa reminded Cody of the softness and grace that Julianne always had. And then they were friends for awhile. Before they could really fall in love, he saved her from her Thomas, and Thomas killed him for it. Just like in real-life. Well, my real-life anyway. He saved her just like he saved me. I always knew he had it in him. OK, I didn't always know he had it in him. But definitely toward the end there, I knew.

This time when I killed Cody, I didn't have him killed by someone who hated him, who wanted to punish him for all the bad things he had done. I killed him doing something honorable, helping someone, saving someone, redeeming himself.

Vanessa cradled Cody's head in her lap, the red stain growing on his crisp, white tuxedo shirt. "Don't you die on me, Cody," she sobbed. Her tears dripped onto his face and he actually managed to smile.

"Now's as good a time as any, sweetheart," he quipped weakly.

"No..." she barely mustered through her tears.

"It's better this way..."

"No it's not better! It's not better this way, dammit, Cody! You can't leave me!" she cried over him.

"Please don't cry. Don't cry for me," Cody reached for Vanessa's face but couldn't quite reach her. "Be happy. I want you to be happy." He whispered. So softly, she had to lean closer to him to hear. As she did, she kissed him softly. He smiled. Not his usual cocky, smirky grin. But he smiled a soft and peaceful smile as he exhaled his last breath and was gone. No more anger, no more pain, no more running.

The End.

Cody was finished. I looked around my empty house. The silence in my brain was almost deafening, but in a good way. I could actually hear myself think. My friends were gone. All of them. And I wouldn't mourn their loss. It was like sending my kids off to college, though this time I was ready. It was time for my characters to go. They had been with me for far too long.

With my brain now quiet, I could finally think about me – my future as a writer and what I'd just been through. I was sort of feeling accomplished, yet not sure if anything I'd just finished was even remotely suitable for publication. So, had I really accomplished anything? Then I was thinking about how to go about actually getting published. I was thinking about Alex and rebuilding my marriage. And I was thinking that I still had one more character to finish. Me.

CHAPTER 27

I DIDN'T EMAIL ALEX RIGHT AWAY when I was done with Cody. I needed to be alone, really alone for a night. And I needed to figure out how exactly I was going to tell him that I didn't want him to come home just yet.

I mean, I wanted him home. Of course, I did. I just had one more story rattling around in my now officially crazy brain, and I needed to be alone to write it. Something told me Alex was not going to be happy about this development. I was crazy not stupid.

So, I waited until the clouds of dust in my brain had settled and until I had a good solid outline, a real outline with a real (almost) ending, for my next story before emailing Alex that I had finished Cody. I procrastinated because I knew I was about to do damage that was not going to be fixable. All I could hope was that I could finish the next one quickly and bring Alex home to me.

To: Alex
From: Mirabelle
Re: (No Subject)
Attachments: Cody
Alex,
Call me when you're done reading.
B

Short and sweet. Maybe it would buy me some time. Maybe he'd forget that this was the last story and that he was supposed to come home now. Maybe by the time Alex finished reading everything I had written so far, I would have this last project finished.

The phone rang right away, of course.

My first instinct was to not answer it…how bad would that be?

After deciding that it would be pretty bad, I answered it. "I am so proud of you," came Alex's voice through the phone, before I even had the chance to say hello. His voice was like ice cream. It made me feel good and guilty at the same time. I couldn't speak. "Bella? Are you there?"

"I'm here," I whispered.

"God, it is so good to hear your voice," he said excitedly. "You finished!"

"I finished," I tried to say firmly, but I couldn't make my voice come out any louder than a whisper.

"Bella?"

"Yes?"

"Why don't you sound happy?"

Because I don't like the idea of ripping out your heart and stomping all over it. Again.

"Bella?" he said again. Though, now his voice was getting whispery, too.

"There's one more," I said quickly and quietly and then braced for the backlash.

It took him a moment to process what I had just said. "One more? How can there be one more?" He didn't wait for me to answer his questions. "You said five stories, Mirabelle. You finished five stories. It's been six goddamn weeks."

That last part was news to me. I had no idea how long it had been. I hadn't been counting. "I know, but…"

"But what, Belly?" he asked, his irritation growing stronger, getting closer to anger than exasperation.

"There's just one more thing I need to finish."

He sighed. "What is it?"

"I can't explain it." I probably could have, but it wasn't easy to put into words without sounding stupid. What was I going to say? *I need to write about me.* Ugh. Stupid, pretentious and egocentric.

"You can't explain it? Nice, Belly. You know, maybe by the time you let me come home, I won't want to."

"Please don't be angry with me, Alex." Why was I always saying that?

"Angry? Why would I be angry? Just because my wife of twenty years would rather talk to her imaginary friends than be with me? Why would that make me angry? Why…."

"They're gone, Alex!" I cut him off. "There are no more imaginary friends."

His tone softened ever so slightly. "They're gone?"

"Yes."

"All of them?"

"All of them. Every last one," I said, and tried to sound happy about it.

Alex exhaled in relief. "It worked?"

"It worked," I agreed.

His irritation with me took hold again. "So why can't I come home then?" he asked impatiently. "Don't you want me to come home?" he questioned.

"Of course, I want you to come home. Of course, I do. But…"

"But what?"

"There's another story I have to finish," I said quickly, hoping if I said it fast it would hurt him less.

He digested this for a moment. "But you said they were gone," he whispered.

"They are. This is different."

"Different how, Bella? Who is it this time?"

"Me. This time it's me."

"You?"

"I'm sorry, Alex. There's one more story I need to finish… for me."

"Fine. Whatever, Bella. Whatever you say." His resignation hurt more than his anger and impatience.

"Alex, please, try to understand."

"I don't want to understand, Bella. I'm done understanding. Right now, I just want to come home."

And with that he was gone. Vanished, just like one of my characters.

So, that went well. I knew it wouldn't. How could it? Alex had been gone for almost six weeks, but I needed more time because there was one story that was still unfinished: my story, our story. I knew I was being selfish, but if I brought Alex home before I was done, I knew I'd resent him. I'd resent him and then I'd go crazy all over again. I had to hope and pray that when I was done he would understand. With me stronger and accomplished, our relationship could be stronger. Should be stronger. *Would* be stronger. But, I couldn't give myself fully to our marriage when I was still such a mess inside.

CHAPTER 28

WITH A DEEP SIGH AND a heavy heart I started to recount my journey. All the crazy things that brought me to this point right here. This point where I have not exactly become successful, but have achieved something by actually finishing something I'd started.

I began the story with dropping the kids at school and wrote my way through the past eight months. Seeing Cody at the gas station. That first conversation with Kip in my bedroom. All my job struggles. The fight with Goliath and my appointment with the shrink. I wrote of fighting with Thomas and my heartbreak at losing Cody. And I wrote of Alex. Of course, Alex.

The words poured out easily. So easily that my fingers could barely keep up with my brain. I wrote for four days straight. Nodding off occasionally, but mostly existing on a diet of Coke, Triscuits and Polly-O-Cheese Sticks.

It wasn't hard to write. The words came easily, more easily than any of my other stories. This just may have been the story I was born to write. Despite the potential damage to my marriage, I felt like this was what I was supposed to be doing everyday. I almost felt like, dare I say it, a real live writer and it felt amazing. It felt to me like the world had stopped spinning. And it had, at least my world had. The rest of the world was still doing what it always did, while I was stuck and happy to be. Unable to move on until I got this story out of my system and down on paper. I'd never written a story in first person before. It was massively liberating not to be hiding my own flaws behind a façade of characters.

So here we are. This is as far as I've gotten in our story. The story of a mother who invested her whole life in her children only to find she wasn't left with a life of her own. The story of a wife who had to lose her husband and face her darkest fears to find out what really mattered to her.

When it was finished, I attached the first few pages to an email, right about up to where I first saw Cody in the gas station, and immediately forwarded them to Alex, keeping my fingers crossed that he wasn't too sick of my antics to read them.

To: Alex
From: Mirabelle
Re:
Attachment: Unfinished.doc
Please read this. I'll be there soon.
Love, me

As soon as I hit send, I wished I had added a smiley face, or a winky face. Some sort of virtual plea for forgiveness.

Prying myself off the couch where I'd been stuck for days, I took a brief moment to stretch my atrophied muscles, then hopped in the shower to wash the stench of the last few days off me. I scrubbed quickly, dried myself off, threw on a pretty, comfortable dress, and tied my wet hair back away from my face. No time for primping, I had a marriage to save.

I printed the rest of what I had written so far. All 47,255 words in my first draft.

Grabbing the paper off the printer, I dashed out to my van, my eyes squinting in the sunlight since I hadn't been outside the house in so long. I drove the ten minutes to Alex's office, all the while praying he'd be willing to see me, hoping I could give myself the happy ending I had been working so hard for.

I ran through the parking lot to the doors, which was moronic because I hadn't so much as jogged in years and I was wearing stupid shoes for running. My forty-five-year-old knees creaked and buckled with every step.

Through the glass doors in the front I could see Alex smiling and shaking hands with someone and I froze. He was doing that "Sure, you're my client, but we're buddies" thing, slapping the guy on the shoulder. Damn, I had almost forgotten how handsome he was. He was unshaven now, growing the beard that I always made him shave. It looked good on him and it made me just a little sad and a little bit scared. He looked so different, I couldn't help but wonder what else had changed.

As I watched him through the glass, my heart stopped beating. I had never been so terrified in my life as I was right then. Terrified that I had pushed Alex too far away, so far away that I couldn't pull him back. Terrified that I had destroyed the only thing in my life that was real over some pipe dream fantasy. Alex patted his client on the back again and I ducked behind a shrub just as his client opened the front door. Not ready to face what was likely to be the biggest rejection of my life, my biggest failure to date.

Still afraid to move, I could see Alex return to his office. I willed myself forward, but I was too afraid of his possible denial. Fear nailed my stupid shoes to the ground. Suddenly, I was 19 again and back in college and I'd come crawling back to him, begging for forgiveness, after starting some stupid, over-dramatic argument. He took me back then, maybe he'd take me back now…

I forced myself forward and managed to make it out from behind the shrub, when Alex came out of his office and back into the lobby, looking breathless and shaken. He must have read my email because he looked as afraid as I felt. I willed myself into his sightline, pushing myself forward ever so slightly, just enough that I could catch his eye. He saw me and took a sudden, quick step forward, but then must've remembered how angry he was with me and stopped himself. It was on me to go to him, as it should be. I was the jerk here.

Stepping forward through the glass doors, I approached him cautiously. When I got close, it was hard not to throw my arms around him, I wanted to kiss him and touch his stubbly face. I would've settled for holding his hand, but he looked so darn mad at me. Instead, I handed him my latest manuscript silently, awkwardly, which he looked at wordlessly for a moment before flipping through the pages.

"It's about you?" he finally whispered with an edge of judgment in his voice.

"It's about us," I said with a nod.

He looked at me disapprovingly.

"It's loosely based on us," I relented.

"How loosely?" he demanded.

"The names have been changed to protect the innocent."

"Which one of us is the innocent?"

"You…and I need your help."

"My help? Why?" He stroked his new beard nervously.

"With all my other stories, I had help from my characters for the end. Since this is about us…"

"Damn it, Bella. I don't want to play games," he rolled his eyes, losing patience with me again. I knew he wouldn't let the moment play out. "How does it end?" he demanded.

I couldn't help but smile at him. "It doesn't."

He flipped through the pages again, this time pausing to read a few lines. "Is that what we are? Unfinished?" he asked, looking at the title page and wrinkling his eyebrows.

I nodded and smiled in response. Alex just looked confused. "That's not a bad thing," I said.

"It's not?" he asked, still clearly confused. "What does it mean?"

"It means our story is just beginning. It means we still have a whole lifetime to live together. It means that every change we go through is just one more step on the journey of our lives together. And it means I don't want our story to end... ever."

He looked back down at the manuscript. "You wrote this in four days?"

"I know this sounds incredibly corny, Alex, but we've been writing this for twenty-two years. It just took me four days to get it down on paper."

Alex looked down at me, looking completely angry and frustrated for a moment before brushing away the stray hair that never stayed pulled back and hung in front of my eyes.

"Bella..." he breathed and shook his head just a little, tiny bit.

I wanted to tell him how sorry I was. That I knew I had hurt him time and time again in the name of my own creative fulfillment. It sounded so silly when I thought about it like that. But before I had a chance to tell him everything that was in my heart, he grabbed me and kissed me softly on the mouth.

Like he was kissing me for the first time, his stubble tickling my face. A tiny part of me was afraid he was going to vanish when he was done. But when we separated, his cashmere eyes stared into mine and I was glad he could see my soul. I wanted to share it with him, I wanted to share everything with him. I wanted to be old with him. I wanted to be that wrinkled old woman in a lime-green sundress showing way more skin than I should be at my age, with him walking proudly by my side in the supermarket.

"I'm so damn mad at you…" he said, "But I'm so damn happy to see you, I almost don't care."

I reached up and put my hand on his beard, noticing a little more salt and less pepper than there used to be.

"I know. I'll shave." He rolled his eyes.

I shook my head. "Keep it. It looks good on you."

"Really?"

"Alex, honey. I don't care if you shave your head bald and pierce your nose, just come home."

EPILOGUE

I'D LIKE TO SAY THAT all six books that I finished were published and sold millions and millions of copies and now we're fabulously rich and reluctantly famous, but that would be a lie. After completing the Herculean task of editing and revising six novels, I can proudly say that I self-published *The Woodpecker*, made a little money and got a lot of positive reviews on Amazon.com. I'm still working on *Unfinished*, which should be my masterpiece when I'm ever done editing it. It is literally, my life's work. It's so close to my heart that everyday, I find something new to add or change. It changes when I do, and sometimes changes me, almost as if it has a life of its own.

Since I quit my job and finished my novels, I've also written some short articles for our local newspaper and even managed to get something published in a national magazine. So, I am actually, finally, making a living writing. No fame or fortune, but it beats the hell out of working in the cafeteria.

As for Alex and I, it took time and lots and lots of patience (mostly on his end), but we have somehow managed to put the pieces of our marriage back into place. Some of the pieces are in a different place than they were before. But it's working.

I have finally managed to marry my creative self to my real-world life, instead of blurring that line between my imagination and the world around me. And I've finally learned to embrace my artistry instead of treating it like an affliction.

For his part, Alex managed to earn himself a promotion for all those extra hours he put in during our "separation." Seems the boss was pretty impressed with his new-found dedication, when really he was just burying himself in his work to deal with the crumbling of our marriage. Anyway, he has to travel a bit more and put in a few more hours, and we have to go to more of those ghastly dinners. But Alex seems to be enjoying it. And after what I put him through, I'm happy to do what I can. Dreaded dinners and all.

Holden and Vivian are doing well in school and are thrilled that Mom and Dad have managed to end their "separation." We don't see them or hear from them as much as we'd like. But we've raised two pretty awesomely, terrific kids and we're proud of them everyday, even the days we don't get to see them.

My characters never returned to visit me again after their stories were done. Yet, I still see them when I'm out and about at the gym or the mall or the supermarket. They don't recognize me or acknowledge me in any way. I've come up with two possible reasons for this. One is that these characters I envisioned are actually real people who have lived around here for as long as I have and perhaps my brain merged their physical characteristics with people I've written about. The second possibility is that I am just straight up crazy and these "people" are part of my brain and always will be. They will always exist in my world. I've seen almost all of them: Monica, Peter, David, Daniel, Emily, Kip, Bridget. I've even seen Vanessa. But not Goliath. Not Thomas. And not Cody. They're gone for good.

I can't deny I miss them. I miss talking to them. I miss watching them. I miss them showing up in unexpected places. I miss learning about myself from them. But I'm glad I was able to give most of them a happy ending. Most of them. I'm sorry for the way things ended with Cody. I miss him most of all. Sometimes I think maybe I could bring him back. Maybe I could do a prequel to his story. Or maybe he could be reincarnated.

Then again, maybe it's about time for me to come up with some new friends.

THE END

CPSIA information can be obtained
at www.ICGtesting.com
Printed in the USA
BVOW08s0546080917
494271BV00001B/40/P